THE C

Jeremy Sheldon was _____ still lives, working as _____ and a DJ. He studied at the University of East Anglia where he was awarded an MA in creative writing.

For more information, please try the following:

www.jezzaroona.com

www.escapecommittee.net

Jeremy Sheldon

THE COMFORT ZONE

V

VINTAGE

Published by Vintage 2003

2 4 6 8 10 9 7 5 3 1

First published in Great Britain in 2002 by
Jonathan Cape Ltd

Vintage
Random House, 20 Vauxhall Bridge Road,
London SW1V 2SA

Random House Australia (Pty) Limited
20 Alfred Street, Milsons Point, Sydney
New South Wales 2061, Australia

Random House New Zealand Limited
18 Poland Road, Glenfield, Auckland 10, New Zealand

Random House (Pty) Limited
Endulini, 5A Jubilee Road, Parktown 2193, South Africa

The Random House Group Limited Reg. No. 954009
www.randomhouse.co.uk

Grateful acknowledgement is made to the following for pemission to reprint previously published material: 'Star Dust' Words by Mitchell Parish and Music by Hoagy Carmichael © 1929, EMI Mills Music Inc, USA. Reproduced by permission of Lawrence Wright Music Co Ltd, London WC2H 0QY

The Long Goodbye by Raymond Chandler (Penguin Books, 1959) © 1953 by Raymond Chandler. Reproduced by permission of Penguin Books Ltd

A CIP catalogue record for this book
is available from the British Library

ISBN 0 099 43696 5

Papers used by Random House are natural, recyclable products made from wood grown in sustainable forests. The manufacturing processes conform to the environmental regulations of the country of origin

Printed and bound in Great Britain by
Cox & Wyman Limited, Reading, Berkshire

To Richard and Cissy Sheldon for their irreducible faith

Contents

LET'S GET OUTTA HERE

When I was a child, I spake as
a child, I understood as a child,
I thought as a child: but when I
became a man, I put away my
childish things.

Corinthians 13, xi

1

There are two types of people in this world. There are those who lay around on the floor as children and imagined what it would have been like if we all lived upside-down. And plainly there are those who didn't. Either you were the sort of person who imagined a scenario where everyone had huge lights coming out of the floor of their living-rooms – or you weren't. Take me, for example. As a child, I spent many an afternoon lying on the carpet in the paths of dusty sunbeams, imagining everyone having floor-level windows and staircase-shaped ceilings. But my wife, on the other hand (my *ex*-wife, actually) didn't. Never had. Never thought she might. End of story.

•

Not much else in life is like that. For instance: some people like football. They *love* it, are absolutely *crazy* for it. They go starry-eyed over memories of ruddy-faced men with perms and sideburns, can tell you the winners of the League Cup in 1962 and 1985 (Norwich City, both years) and drink their tea out of a 'lucky Bobby Moore mug' every Saturday morning during the season.

Then there are those who hate The Beautiful Game. They loathe it, won't let you talk about it at the dinner table and pretty soon you end up reading your weekly copy of *A Game of Two Halves* while you smoke 'your' fags in 'their' garden. My ex-wife was – and, to the best of my knowledge, still is – exactly that kind of person. To be fair, she grew up having a couple of fanatical Port Vale fans as parents (a vale of serious tears by anyone's standards) and it should have come as no surprise that she spent the next six years and three months doing anything she could to sabotage my viewing of *Match of the Day* and other sporting highlights. Tickets to abysmal plays, her mother, her birthday or an anniversary every so often. Candlelit dinners ('we always eat in front of the telly, I thought it would make a nice change . . .'), tropical underwear, cans of whipped cream and going into labour. These were all some of the diversionary tactics employed over that long and arduous campaign. She even tried going into labour a second time, one midweek evening a few years after her previous attempt, and I can still summon up the memory of the satisfied look that glittered in her eyes as she breathed deeply and told me that *it was time* through increasingly clenched teeth. Luckily the gods knew the truth on that occasion, saw what she was up to and rained off all the cup-ties that night. Furthermore, I'd learnt my lesson by then and had acquired a pocket-radio for hospital waiting-rooms, car journeys to dying aunts, school reunions (hers) and other eventualities. She hated it, of course, but that was fine by me. I just kept it out of harm's way in a box in the greenhouse and checked its batteries every Saturday afternoon between three and five o' clock.

Of course there are also all the other type of people as well: people who 'don't mind' football, people who 'catch the odd game after the news', who watch the Cup Final with their family each May the same way they sit down to the Queen's Speech every December. And there are people who simply couldn't care either way. The world is not, by any frantic tugging on the apron-strings of the imagination, simply divided into those who know where they were the night Gazza cried and those who cry when you try to put his framed picture up in the lounge. Football, unlike staring at the ceiling with a puzzled look on your face, is something that one can be neutral towards.

2

It was armed with these awarenesses and my pocket-radio (I'd 'won' it by saving the coupons from all the alfresco cigarettes I'd smoked during the first three years of my marriage) that I recently travelled to California to catch up with friends and relatives and to enjoy a little post-divorce R & R. Once there, I was to stay with my cousin Stephanie at her bungalow in Belmont a few miles south of San Francisco. According to my mother (who'd stayed there the previous summer), it sat high up on a hill amongst groves of eucalyptus trees. According to my mother, it was a paradise under unbroken skies. According to my mother, it was a sun-drenched utopia where crazy deer were known to crap into your swimming pool and jump out at your car at STOP signs.

And of course there was TV. Let me tell you now: *never* miss Tina Friggers' talkshow on KCUF, 10 a.m. Pacific time. I also recommend the luscious Maria (star of the eponymously titled *Maria!*) who lost me early on in each episode with her volcanic Spanish but quickly won my heart with her tartan trouser-suits and her passionate discussions on *Jovenes Alcoholicos* and *Allegados a los Famosos*.

You see, I spent my first mornings in California sitting by the pool, watching cable, trying out fruit-juice combinations and eating bags of *chips* until lunchtime before retreating inside to eat watermelon in front of MTV for the rest of the day. And by the Friday of the first week of my stay, things had escalated. I was up to six bags of chilli-flavoured Yam Slices with my talkshows and would spend the entire afternoon contemplating Life, the tailoring on Maria's white blouses and the possibilities of Stephanie's ceiling over several microbrews. Of course, if you

5

haven't guessed already, this was one of my most recent reveries with regards the whole inverted-floor conundrum ... *except that something different happened this time!* There I was, lying on the polished floorboards, drunkenly spilling beer and cigarette ash all over my t-shirt and imagining how I would get socks out of an imaginary chest of drawers that I'd stuck into the corner of the ceiling, when I suddenly remembered another childhood musing that I'd never mentioned to anyone in my life.

Top Cat.

Do you remember? He lived in an alleyway on the wrong side of town, had a gang and a great signature tune, harassed a poor police officer named Dibble and generally lived it up. After a few verses of *Top Cat ... ta tant ta ta ta ... the most incredible leader of the pack*, I tried to remember the names of the rest of TC's gang other than Choo Choo, Brain and the regrettable Benny – couldn't – but ended up being reminded of another thing that used to puzzle me. You see, during the credits at the very end of every episode, TC used to hang up his snazzy purple waistcoat and hat, put on his polka-dot pyjamas, pop in his ear plugs, put up his television aerial for some late-night NFL action and climb wearily into his garbage-can/bed/office/studio-apartment, only to be helplessly whisked away by a dump-truck. Every episode this happened – and what had always worried me was how TC got back to the alleyway for the beginning of each subsequent episode. Did he jump out the back of the truck? And if so, did he drag his bin with him? Or did he ring Benny, Choo Choo, Brain (with his Droopy Dog eyes) and the others, and order them to come and get him?

Similarly, when Fred Flintstone got locked out of the house by his sabre-toothed pussycat at the end of every episode of

The Flintstones, did he resign himself to a night's sleep on the rock-hard doorstep? Wasn't there a back door he could resort to? Didn't Wilma get pissed off (or just *pissed*, as they say out there) at the regular-as-clockwork cries of 'WILMAAAAAA . . . !' every evening as she applied her curlers and prehistoric mudpack?

I was later to find out that, at least in this instance, popular consensus has Wilma open the door, while only one person believed that Fred started his next sunny day in Bedrock cruelly unshaven and bleary-eyed on the doorstep of the Flintstone household. But that afternoon I was alone with only my own questions for company. After a few hours of contemplation, I got up off the floor, fixed myself an iced tea and scanned the television pages for episodes of either cartoon, but found neither. If I'd wanted to, I could have watched four *Creature from the Black Lagoon* films all in a row, but I'd seen them the day before. So instead, I started preparing a salad and waited for Stephanie to get back from the city.

•

'Wilma let him in.'

'You reckon?'

'*Totally.*'

Steph took another spoonful of Fuzzy Munch, dipped her spoon into the tub of Furry Slop Pops and put it into her mouth, one hand under her chin to catch the drops. The air in her kitchen was warm and tangy.

'And that's your last answer?'

'Yup!' Little did I know that she would be the first of many people who believed as much.

'I think . . .' I started to reply, but then paused dramatically as I reached for the chopped-hazelnuts sprinkler. 'I think that if anything happened – and that's not to say that I'm convinced as to what *did* happen – then she left him on the doorstep. For the whole night. On purpose.'

'Oh come on, Jeremy!' A few beers never did any harm to Steph's sense of indignation.

'I mean it,' I said. 'Pass me the crushed-biscuit topping can you?'

She slid it across the table saloon-style, knowing that only my American relations are allowed to call me *Jeremy*, just as I never, ever, ever use the word *cookie*. 'Almost every show had Fred and Barney screwing things up. Betty and Wilma were always saving their asses . . .'

'Betty and Wilma fucked up too,' I replied. 'I can think of plenty of their scams that went wrong.'

Steph put down her ice-cream and handed me the phone.

'Call Jackie! See what *she* says!' she challenged.

As it turned out, Jackie (Steph's sister) was at an architects' dinner downtown, at a conference centre somewhere on Van Ness, and although the ringer on her cellphone had been switched to SOOTHE mode, it hadn't been turned off entirely and I might as well have gone right in there and played a drum solo.

'Waddya mean: "What happened to Fred at the end of *The Flintstones*?"' Jackie hissed down the line. 'Do you know what you've done? My phone just went off in the middle of Jay Szymanski's speech! In front of two hundred architects!'

I later discovered, after an intimate conversation with a beautiful designer called Alexis Vanek, that Jackie had disembowelled her handbag in her haste to find her bleeping phone and in the process managed to spill two bottles of wine over the curator of the Powers Institute and the visiting Chief of Police sitting on either side of her. And though Jay Szymanski, acclaimed designer of both Rosenfeld Memorial

8

Museums (Chicago and New York), might not have blinked an eyelid at the digitised *Fur Elise* that sounded out from amidst his seated audience, he hadn't been able to ignore the SWAT team of waiters that rushed to clear up the spreading mess and had needed to pause in the middle of the word *psychogeography* with an eyebrow impatiently raised.

I quickly summarised the terms of the dispute. There was a moment's silence at the other end of the line, if you didn't count the scurrying of waiters or the faltering voice echoing in the background.

'Wilma let him in. Of course she did. Now can I please hang up?'

I put the phone down. Steph was already stretched out on a sofa with a bottle of Chablis and looking at the ceiling.

'I told you so.'

Indeed she had.

'Steph? When you were a kid, did you ever stare up at the ceiling and . . .'

●

Over the weekend and the following week, I searched the TV listings for a glimpse of Fred or TC, something to jump-start my memory, but they didn't seem to be showing either cartoon in that part of the state. That left me with only raw human data, so I asked almost everyone I met what they thought, as long as it didn't seem obvious that the person in question would be offended. Steph, when I asked her, couldn't remember the end of *Top Cat* but claimed she did remember that at the end of every show she'd had to turn over as soon as possible to catch the end of *Wacky Races* because they'd clashed. Jackie wouldn't budge from her position, not even under duress, and I was still undecided. A few people couldn't remember seeing, or had never seen, both cartoons (which is to say that I asked my uncle and my grandmother next). But most had some recollection of one or the other and even a fair number of Jackie's architect friends offered me ideas on the subject and were no end of fun after I brought the whole thing up one evening, in a lobster restaurant on the top floor of the Embacadero Centre. I hadn't been sure how such a line of questioning would go down, but after a few rounds of tequila their answers had been prolific and many of them spent the rest of the evening trying to impersonate Fred and Barney or the giggling of Betty and Wilma, much to my and Jackie's surprise. Even the *maître d'* had a theory. Citing Fred's virility as his principal evidence and acknowledging with a shrug that it was Wilma's *duty* to let him in, he lingered by our table and solemnly expounded his belief that surely '*Monsieur Fleentston*' would have gone out for a big night of gambling and drinking with Barney and his other buddies from the quarry. 'A man az no uzzer course of action,' he added, with a brief smile for Ms Vanek who was sitting next to me (and whom he later escorted home), 'when a woman doz no return iz lov.'

In a way, it was good to know that there were other people like me out there, people troubled by the little things as well as the big. But what wasn't so great was that I was starting to get the same answers after a while. For every gem there were turkeys. For every 'Fred went on a bender' there were several people who gave Wilma the benefit of the doubt. Even my aunt, after presentations by both Steph and myself, concluded that Wilma was the key to the situation (all this said in a hushed tone you understand, with a sideways glance at my slumped uncle who was busy watching Jerry Rice receive his millionth pass for the 49ers that quarter). Did everyone think that Wilma let Fred back in? It seemed like it when I finally collated the results of my survey so that I could make some kind of sense of them.

They went something like this.

90.48% of the people questioned could remember seeing *The Flintstones*. 100% of these could remember the ending (I guess shouting 'WILMAAAAAA' at the top of your voice grabs attention) and of that figure a staggering 84.21% believed that Wilma let him in. Of this percentage, 71.88% were women. Incidentally, 0.026% of people who had seen *The Flintstones* confirmed the best of my suspicions and thought that it wasn't necessary 'to find closure for that particular narrative sequence as its meaning/outcome was formally, as well as arbitrarily, convened/deferred', that there was 'no necessary reason to make logical/chronological connections between the credits sequence and the main body of the narrative' and that the credits were 'a repeated syntagm anyway'. As it happened, 0.026% of people who had seen *The Flintstones* was a Doctor of Literature at Santa Cruz, an old college friend of Steph's that I met on my third weekend in America. And every time 0.026% got to a '/', she said the word 'stroke', which I thought was pretty sexy.

The other side of the coin was a much tidier affair. Of the people questioned, exactly one-third had seen *Top Cat* (23.81% had seen both) yet only 50% could remember the credits sequence. The overwhelming majority view – 90.86% to be exact – agreed that TC was cool. Very cool. Positively low temperature. After this, opinions varied with most – 57.14% – opting for the calling of the gang, although 0.00% of these couldn't remember any of their names other than Brain, Benny and Choo Choo. The Doctor of Literature, now 0.071% of all *Top Cat* viewers questioned, did her little bit as well and after dialling us a pizza from her bedside telephone, decided that TC was so cool that on reaching the depot, he simply had his trash can put on the next truck back to the alley ('he was under no pressure . . . he probably had a mini-bar in his trash can and kicked back with a highball') none the worse for the experience.

11

3

Start to finish, I was in San Francisco for six weeks. Enough time to learn to stop asking for 'twenty Marlboro' at the fag shop, to stop calling fags *fags*, to look in the right direction when crossing the road, to know that a *Café Borgia* was the brightest possible way to start the day. The best thing I'd seen, or nearly seen, had been a species of Amazonian fish in the aquarium at the California Academy of Sciences. It was so brazenly vile that it was prohibited from sharing a tank with any other creatures, and the little plastic sign above the tank (which had been empty for unspecified and wholly ominous reasons) informed that the fish had been known to attack straying cattle. Even schools of piranha were considered a soft target, and after looking around at the rest of the fish and a few belligerent octopi, I reckoned *that* fact alone made it the Leader of the Pack. The Big Chief. It was illegal just to own one in the State of California.

On my last day in America, I was still thinking about this absent fish and preparing to watch my last episode of *Maria!* – an episode about shark attack – when my mother called.

'Is Steph there?' she asked, after I'd enquired about the kids and reassured her that I'd visited my grandmother regularly.

'No. She's at work.' My mother would have known that Steph was at work, it being a Friday morning.

'That's a shame. And how are *you*? Have you packed?'

I paused, looking at my suitcases stacked by the front door. The last thing I wanted on my final morning in San Francisco was another 'I-never-liked-her-Are-you-feeling-better?' speech, however well intended.

'Mum?'

'Yeeess . . . ?' It is a peculiar trait of my mother's that she often sounds like Bela Lugosi's butler.

'Do you remember the end of *The Flintstones*, when Fred gets locked out?'

'Yes I do.'

This didn't surprise me. My mother is one of those people who, in spite of displaying many of the undesirable symptoms of prolonged parenthood, has a firm grasp of who Adam West and Burt Ward are and holds a healthy torch for the mercurial Jim Rockford.

'Well . . . what do you think happens? How does Fred get back inside the house? Or do you think that he sleeps the night on the doorstep?'

My mother didn't answer for a while and I guessed that she was thinking. But after a few minutes she still hadn't answered and I suggested that she thought that Wilma simply let Fred back in the house.

'Oh no!' she said in a tone of voice that I'd only heard her use once before. It was when I had accused her of preferring The Beatles over The Stones because she was soft. ('Oh no!' she had said, 'I just didn't like Mick Jagger's lips.')

'Oh no!' she said down the telephone. 'What I think happened was that while Fred was banging on the door, the director shouts, "Cut!" Fred then goes back to his trailer, gets into his normal clothes and drives home. Why do you ask?'

•

After I put the phone down, I pondered my mother's genius. Her answer took some beating. A moment of pure class. Even my Doctor of Literature friend couldn't have matched that. I thought about it again, thought of good ol' Fred marching back to his trailer, to his cellphone, his cigars, a cocaine habit, an LA Rams cheerleader or three and all the rest. 'Hey!' he would

13

shout, 'this champagne ain't cold. Waddya all . . . *amateurs?*'
before steaming off the lot in his red sports car.

Such a statement provoked questions beyond 'Would Fred's
feet stick out the bottom of his Buick Wildcat?' Surely it raised
all sorts of issues with regards TC and his stray gang of cool
cats. What was the truth about Choo Choo's pink fur and
cream polo-neck? Why were Brain's eyes so droopy (and why
was he so aimless?) and how long would it be before Dibble
cracked and confessed certain shocking truths about rehab, mere
tabloid speculation up until then, to his Latin-American fans
on *Maria!*?

I had little time to think about it that day. My plane was
due to take off in a few hours and Maxine (Doctor Cigliuti to
you) had been kind enough to offer to take me to the airport
at around one o'clock. I'd be a liar if I said that things weren't
a little awkward as we drove along the freeway to San Francisco
International, and though we both cheered up after I'd given
her a hug and said some nice things to her once we'd got out of
the car, an uncomfortable silence returned while I was pulling
my cases out of the trunk. I lit a cigarette to give my hands
something to do and was looking up at the fading summer sky
when she finally spoke up.

'Can I ask you something?'

'Sure. Anything you like.'

'I'm embarrassed.'

'Don't be.'

I turned to face her and saw hesitation in the pools of
her eyes.

'It's just that I wanted to know if you were being serious.'

I took one of her hands in mine. I'm a shit when it comes to
conversations like this. A real shit. Even my ex-wife will agree
with me there.

'Are you referring to us sleeping together . . . ? I mean . . .
sort of . . . seeing . . .'

Her mouth spread wide in a smile.

'No, dumb-ass! I meant about *The Flintstones*.' She punched
me on the shoulder. 'And *Top Cat* too.'

I replied that I'd been serious.

'That's good. I'm glad. It's just that I never had a chance to
ask you if you get a show called *Magnum P.I.* in England.'

Magnum! I thought of Thomas, Rick, Higgins and the other
TC. In my mind I saw a titles sequence that included leopard-
print bikinis, magical Hawaiian sunsets, grass skirts and a big
red Ferrari.

'It's one of my favourite shows,' Maxine added and I looked
at my watch. There was still thirty minutes until check-in and
there was a Bagel Counter through the swing doors near to
where we were standing. I hurried her over and said it was my
turn to buy.

THE COMFORT ZONE

And this is where we wait
together, regardless of age,
our carts stocked with brightly
coloured goods.

Don DeLillo, *White Noise*

1

I often think back to a moment during the first round of THE GAME. Moll and I were standing by the delicatessen counter in the supermarket, staring at the tubs of shivering food on the other side of the glass.

'Look at the Calamata olives!' she said, pointing. 'They look like the gleaming husks of beetles!'

After three years together, I was used to Moll's prosodic reaction to many things, including bad computer games, the word *cunt* and egg mayonnaise. But she knows that I'm paralysed by insects more than anything else (along with injections, dentists and failure): *was she being deliberately mean?*

'Don't put me off . . . I'm concentrating!' I replied as I surreptitiously bit on another Chicken Penang Bite. 'I need to score at least another ten quid in the next few minutes if we're to stay in contention. I just saw Chip and Suki on their fifth packet of chocolate raisins over in aisle 26 – and Chip wasn't even looking green.'

'But they do! *Look*!' She pointed again. 'Imagine eating a quarter-pound of beetles, the crack of the shells as they split between your teeth, the writhing thoraxes . . .'

Suddenly it was me who was starting to turn green as Moll asked the girl behind the counter for a half-dozen scotch eggs.

'What do we actually want to pay for?' I asked.

'Some beers, some wine, some crisps – the others can pay me back when they come over tonight. But please don't get any cakes or biscuits. I've had enough of sleeping next to you

19

after you've got so stoned that you pass out without brushing your teeth.'

'What do you mean by *that*?' I asked, and it was then that Moll snapped.

'We all fall asleep in our clothes once in a while but you seem to be turning it into a ritual. If you're not careful, you'll have to go to the dentist before the end of the summer, something which *you* despise and I despise hearing about.'

●

Once again, I'm left with the feeling that I'm learning too little too late. When had that sour note of frustration crept into her voice? Had it been there all summer? Or longer?

At the time, I put Moll's combative manner down to the content of her reading. The latest issue of *Sassy!* magazine had run a feature article entitled 'How To Argue!', the journalist citing 'Taking Turns', 'Calm Honest Responses' and 'Eye Contact' as the necessary components of any 'serious discussion', big ticks splashed on to the page next to photographs of a couple engaged in all three activities. Conversely, the journalist had also cast a damning verdict on such male tricks as the 'Looking-to-the-heavens-What-did-I-do?' response, the 'Hands-up-You-win' approach (typically employed within sixty seconds, with eyes widened) and the 'Glassy Stare'.

So there in the supermarket, I only imagined that Moll had simply been taking the opportunity to implement some new Agony-Aunt theory that she'd recently fixated on, as she often did and usually out of the blue. But now I realise that she was trying to tell me that she was ready to leave, that there wasn't anyone else (even if there seemed to be very soon afterwards) but that she'd had enough of *me*.

But if that's the case, then why did she stay around to play THE GAME?

•

Of course there are a multitude of theories discussed and dismissed by all of us involved with THE GAME, a 'shitload of reasons' (as The Doc might phrase it) as to why we had a competition to see who could steal and eat the most food from the supermarket. 'Swashbuckling in an age of microwave meals, CCTV and slow-motion replays,' Jefferson suggested when I raised the issue just the other day, perhaps seven months later when most of us were sitting in the pub watching Wimbledon knock Manchester United out of the FA Cup.

'I get bored shopping,' said Chip, 'always have done. When I eat meat what I really want to have done is looked the fucker in the eye and ripped out its throat with my own teeth.' Which separates him, I suppose, from those who simply said that they'd had nothing better to do.

'*We* did it because we knew that we were championship material from the start,' said The Gooners, who then started dancing around the TV room of the pub spilling their lager everywhere and singing their 'Oh-to . . . oh-to-be . . . oh-to-be-a . . . GOONA' victory song until a newsflash that Leeds were one-nil up at Highbury sent them humbly back to their seats.

'I also think we got carried away by the Euro '96 feelgood-factor,' said Jefferson.

'Bullshit. *You* got involved 'cos you're a thievin' scouser. It's in yer blood,' said The Doc.

•

As for me? Well, parts of me identified with most of those answers. But if anyone asked me why I played THE GAME, I would tell them it was because of Gazza and the inspiration of a simple trajectory one Saturday afternoon last June (remember the perfect turf and the Wembley weather, the ball looping up

21

through the air from his left foot to his right, Scots defenders on the floor or nowhere to be seen, the Dentist's Chair celebration, those Tears-in-Turin finally and thankfully a million years away from *that* Saturday afternoon at Wembley). I never felt like explaining it in any other terms.

'I think witnessing such moments of genius always stirs people up a bit,' I said to Calamity Claire, for example, during a retrospective moment by the jukebox. 'We all see it and want to get *out there* and achieve something.'

•

Of course Moll wasn't in the pub on the night Marcus Gayle's headed goal knocked United out of the FA Cup, or at least not in the same pub as us. And even though we talked about it a lot at the time, I still don't have her reasons.

2

It all happened during the summer of '96. Moll and I were living in the basement of my Aunt Jocasta's house in Chiswick and getting our rent paid by the Housing Benefit office because I was claiming the dole. Although a year had passed since we'd left university, I still wasn't working, was still unable to decide what-I-wanted-to-do-with-my-life: everything I could think of seemed not important enough to be a life's work, but too important to be merely a hobby.

It was a time spent in frantic apprehension of the dentist's chair (a real one), in fearful dread of the 'Butcher of Burlington Gardens' and his array of mouth-pumps, his arsenal of hypodermic weaponry, his oral torture-machines. It was the summer of the European Championships, a magical three weeks when everyone went football crazy. And it was a summer spent floating into the dole office with a portfolio of rejection letters painstakingly procured by a combination of careful targeting and contrived helplessness.

Did I have what it takes to be an On-Site Analyst for leading blue-chip manufacturers of FMCGs? Was I a team-playing, self-starting writer of 'Advertorials'?

I am aware of my lack of experience in the field of Industrial Liaison, I would write on bluntly worded application letters, *but believe that my interpersonal skills and an aptitude for quick learning will more than compensate.*

Out with the databased mailshot and in with the rejection letters. *You have not been successful with your application in this instance,* the companies would reply, leaving me with no other option than to surrender the evidence of my enterprise at the job centre once a fortnight and duly collect my winnings.

•

So there I was (and I wasn't the only one), spending the summer mixing records at parties and clubs for a little extra cash to supplement my giro and selling three-gram eighths of hash for the same reasons. Moll had recently started some part-time work-experience at a VT editing suite in Euston and the result was plenty of empty days for me to do whatever I wanted – which invariably meant watching the football whenever it was on, sunbathing in the park with my comics and smoking single-skin joints while I doodled down ideas (but not really) for the novel I was planning to write called *The Year I Stayed In.* Also, Chip from next door had pretty much taken to letting the part-timers run the off-licence which he managed ('you don't need to *sell* alcohol – *it sells itself,*' he would chortle) and the both of us would get high and meander along the High Road in the sunshine, stopping off at beer gardens and record shops as they passed us by, paying visits to the library with its cheap video rental and to the supermarket with its bright colours and its air-conditioning.

●

'Just because I'm a bit slack in a personal sense at the moment doesn't mean that I have to stop caring about the planet,' I said, handing the joint to Chip and taking a jam jar out of the white plastic bag. 'And anyway: listen to this . . .'

We were standing by the recycling skips at the back of the supermarket car-park. I pushed the jar through the little spyhole and we heard the smash as it broke on the other side.

'Weird, isn't it?' I said.

'The sound reverberates inside the skip.'

'It's sort of violent . . .'

'. . . yet benevolent.'

'An action that's satisfyingly propitious . . .'

'. . . yet rewarding at a destructive level.'

'A morsel of cheap fulfilment . . .'

'. . . just when it was least looked for.'

'The crucial issue remains: do they plan it that way?'

'Of course they do.'

Chip took a large Ribena bottle out of the carrier bag. The sound of the smash was even louder.

'It's good to help the environment.'

'Let's go. The Germany–Czech Republic game starts in an hour and we've got shopping to do.'

The recycling skips were only the first round in the supermarket's continuity of cheap thrills. All I needed was four bottles of Budweiser Budvar as an excuse to be in the building in the first place (Grolsch if it was Holland playing, cans of Carlsberg Ice for Denmark and so on) and if high-velocity skidding along the polished aisles on my own wire trolley wasn't sufficient entertainment then I could always examine everyone else's shopping.

•

There were plenty of other options if I needed them.

I could slip haemorrhoid cream through the bars of another customer's trolley or into their basket when they weren't looking and then watch them squirm when they arrived at the checkout. What were they going to do when they eventually noticed the offending tube (in their minds, it was the size of a courgette)?

Usually they either tried to hide it amongst the magazines by the till or else ran back to the Home Remedial shelves to replace it. Some tried to claim that they were the victim of a practical joke, resulting in much entertainment on the part of the cashier and other customers. And occasionally (and best of all) some just paid for it, trying to keep a straight face and not draw any attention to themselves. I even played the trick on my bank manager when I saw him buying groceries one lunchtime and watching *his* poker face cloud over as the cashier-girl passed the tube through the infra-red was a moment to savour.

•

If I wanted, I could search out Sonia, the prettiest girl out of all the supermarket staff, who usually worked at the cigarette counter. Talking to her was as easy as buying a scratchcard or a packet of Rizlas and she would occasionally ask me for a couple of eighths for her friends, which never hurt.

•

And sometimes there were free samples on offer at a makeshift counter in the supermarket entrance and I could nibble on a small cube of whatever cheese it was that was on trial, or perhaps sip on a thimble of some newly developed Chardonnay and see how many times I could get away with going back and asking for more.

•

But if all this got boring, or didn't suit the mood of the day, then I could simply stand there in the crowd that slowly divided itself over the tills and marvel at everybody: the pensioners with their frugal baskets of chocolate mints, ready-to-bake spotted dick and own-brand custard creams perched on top of four crates of cat food; the students with their cereals and tinned tomatoes, their economy pasta and special-offer wines; the Range-Rovered wives with two heaped trolleys and a clutch of food-and-wine magazines, credit cards poised and primed. The price of a four-pack bought me the right to check everyone out at the checkout, the parade of packets, tins, bags and boxes on the black rubber conveyor-belt telling its own story, divulging the details of other lives.

I would often find myself treading water in the sluggish queue at clocking-off time, amazed as people's shopping formed its own account of someone else's immediate future. *There they went*: one bake-in-the-tray Broccoli Mornay; one bag of apples; one tube of Rolos; one jumbo-size packet of crisps. I'd take a mental inventory of the shopping as it rolled down towards the chaos of plastic bags at the far end and I'd look up to see some gently perspiring first-jobber in a grey polyester suit (nineteen years old and now already half a decade younger than me) trying to pay and pack at the same time and evanescing bedsit vibes, an evening-in-front-of-the-TV and a late-pint-round-the-corner before the early night under the inevitably frayed duvet and another day's duty at the filing cabinet. *There they went*: the single rotund slab of Barbary Duck; the 365g jar of Gourmet à L'Orange Sauce; the black plastic tray of Sugar Snaps (already topped and tailed). I'd look up to see an opera-swilling, fringe-theatre-loving Chiswick dilettante waiting with open carrier bags, a copy of *Aria* poking out of an authentically scuffed leather satchel and a red spotted hankie spilling from his breast pocket.

Eventually I wondered if there was something intrusive about this point-of-sale voyeurism and I soon asked Chip if he analysed other people's shopping.

'Of course I do. It's a late-twentieth-century condition.'

Chip said it was called 'Social Profiling'.

'I do it all the time at the off-licence . . .'

'When you're there . . .'

'When I'm there.'

'Chip – you *work* there. You're the manager for fuck's sake! We're just customers here and we're still looking over our shoulders at everyone else's shopping.'

'They plan it that way. It may be a cheap thrill, but it's a thrill nonetheless.'

•

The problem with cheap thrills, of course, is that they can soon get expensive. The European Championships meant that there was an average of three hours of football programming each day to shop for and all of us were partial to the odd snack as we wheeled around amongst the tamarillos and galia melons. To start with we presented the empty wrappers, packets and Tetrapaks of the items that had fallen foul of our impatience to the disapproving eyes of the cashier-girls. After all, we weren't *criminals*. We were just bored. And *peckish*. But it didn't take long before the empty wrappers, packets and Tetrapaks stopped ending up on the conveyor-belt and started ending up in our pockets, in our record-bags, on the floor or stuffed under the mounds of glistening grapefruit.

'I could get used to this,' said Chip, as he deposited an empty Hot 'n' Spicy Pepparami wrapper behind the columns of toilet-paper in aisle 5.

'I think we already are,' I countered.

'Still this . . . this *grazing* lark,' he continued (Chip and I

27

were pleased to have discovered the official terminology for our particular style of snacking), 'it's not *all* bad. I mean it takes *application* to know where to stash all this . . . *debris*.'

'It's a skill,' I suggested.

'You could almost turn the whole thing into a sport.'

Now *there* was an idea.

3

'Do you have any work to declare?'

'No.'

No way. Another fast-track-entry into the-world-of-media-sales had been denied me (O.T.E. rumoured to be *blah–blah–blah*) and my misspelt application to become a 'recriutment copyriter' for Paine, Toyle & Loss on Hammersmith Road had also met with rejection. I dutifully pushed my rejection letters across the desk down-at-the-dole-office, while a young black guy was going through a similar process at the adjacent signing-point.

'Have you worked at all this last fortnight?'

'No,' he replied, signing his name and smoothing out the creases of his hundred-pound Dolce & Gabbana jeans with the pale undersides of his fingers. I followed the line of his legs down to the floor where his feet lay cosseted in a sparkling pair of box-fresh Filas and he turned his head and winked.

A minute later, we were both pushing through the swing doors and stepping out into the street. As soon as we were out of sight, we shook hands.

'How's it going, Tevin?'

'Not bad, as it happens.'

'Where did you get your new trainers?'

'A mate's shop down in Tooting. He imports. I can sort you out if you want.'

'Not at the moment. I'm a bit skint. You got time for a drink?'

Tevin nodded and soon we were skinning up in a beer garden along the High Road and drinking Red Stripe from the bottle, talking about football and pot and records.

'Tevin – can I ask you a question?'

'Sure,' he said.

'How come you aren't like your brother or some of the other boys you roll around with?'

'What do you mean by that?' Tevin asked, flicking weed seeds off the table-top and on to the floor.

'Your brother and your other mates all dress *down* when it comes to signing on. They're probably in the multi-storey right now changing out of their Hilfiger and Ralph Lauren. But *you*? You go into the job centre with your big trainers, a new Armani jacket and all-the-rest and tell them blatantly that you haven't worked.'

•

Tevin, along with his brother, Reesey, and his cousins, used to serve-up in an area that spanned west from Shepherd's Bush Road as far as Hanwell, never straying further south than the river and never further north than the Hanger Lane Gyratory after a run-in with the Martin Family up in Wembley a couple of years back. Ounces, wraps of coke, pills, pagers, smart-cards for mobiles, SIMMs and SCSIs, satellite receivers – they were happy to deliver it all. And when it came to signing-on day, they'd leave their Golf GTis in a car-park nearby and change into six-year-old Air-Maxes and worn-out 501s before showing their faces. Sometimes they'd even take it in turns to sign on for each other. *We all look the same to them*, Tevin said on one occasion, *which is fine with us.*

•

'Yeah. I guess you're right.' Tevin cupped the joint and lit it. 'The thing is . . . I ain't really like Reesey or the others.'

'In what way?'

'Well . . . like I'm older than them, right?'

'Right.'

'An' they're all happy signing on and making the extra dollar selling. But *me*? I don't want to be signing on no more. I got my music and my screensavers and my HTML skills and all that. I don't want to still be serving up pills in a year's time. I will if I have to . . . *but that's different.*'

Tevin took another sip of his beer.

'So I guess I just front up to the system to remind me who I am, to remind me who I want to be . . . *and to give me a kick up the arse.*'

We drank up. Tevin wanted to show me the new hands-free kit he'd 'found' for his car. He also had a new Zoom Tube so we climbed in and went for a spin down the M4 as far as Heathrow before turning back, putting some old '92 Vibes 'n' Wishdokta on the tape-deck so that I could check out the bass.

'How's Chip?' Tevin asked as we sailed past Junction 2. 'Is he still running that off-licence or what? Every time I go in there looking for him, he ain't there.'

'He's not working much these days.'

'Enjoying the sunshine, is it?'

'Something like that. The both of us are trying to start something up at the moment.'

'What's that then?'

I told Tevin about our out-of-control snacking.

'So we thought we'd have a competition. We're sorting the

rules out at the moment and looking for possible competitors. You interested?'

'Reckon so.' Tevin laughed. 'It sounds . . . *interesting*.'

●

Supermarkets. Think about them one way and they're just shops, just *big* shops, just another fantastic convenience. Think about them another way and suddenly you're in the realm of Loyalty Cards and Reward Points, the land of absent clocks, artificial light and data-tracking.

'It's called a "Comfort Zone". They set their environmental controls at a steady 23°C during the summer,' announced Suki, Chip's girlfriend. Two days later, Moll, Chip, Suki and I were eating a meal that I'd made. Cooking for the four of us had become my duty on the days I cashed my giro.

'Because of the humidity problem that comes with air-conditioning,' she continued, 'they have to overcool the air and then re-heat it to the appropriate temperature.'

'That sounds good for the environment,' I said. 'And how the hell do you know that anyway?'

Suki shrugged.

'Part of me *loves* going to the supermarket. I feel so free,' said Moll. 'There's so much choice. I know that the reality is otherwise, of course, but never when I'm actually in a supermarket.'

'I was horrified when I noticed that they don't sell single-litre bottles of any of the major soft drinks any more,' said Suki. 'It's just an attempt to force us to increase our dosage.'

'The supermarket is like the Federation of Planets in *Star Trek*,' Chip chipped in. 'It doesn't matter who you are or what you look like − you can still be a member of the institution. All you've got to do is obey the rules, which is to say that you dutifully spend your money there . . .'

'Which is where *we* come in,' I interrupted.

Chip and I had both mentioned our preliminary ideas about THE GAME to Suki and Moll. And now we pushed our plates to one side and addressed the task of forming an official list of rules.

'Are we going to have teams?' asked Chip.

'We could have a mass free-for-all,' offered Suki, 'just get everyone we know to walk into the supermarket at the same time and start stealing.'

'What if someone gets caught?' asked Moll.

It took almost two hours of discussion before we came up with a set of ideas that looked even vaguely feasible. But eventually I had it all written down and made another pot of coffee before summarising everything back to the others.

First, we were going to put all of the teams into a hat and then make a draw which placed them in a knockout competition. Teams were to consist of two players – one doing the actual *eating* while the other acted as a look-out and general *aide-de-camp* – with *both* players permitted to conceal food packaging and price labels around their person. After all, we were going to score each game by totalling the cash-value of goods consumed and needed some easy way to keep a record.

The length of each leg of the competition had also been a difficult issue. An hour? Half an hour? Forty-five minutes? In the end I suggested twenty-two and a half minutes (half the length of half a football match) which seemed satisfactory, and it was agreed that both members of the team had to join the 'Five Items Only' queue before such time had elapsed.

'We'll get someone trustworthy to sit on the old people's benches behind the checkout line with a stopwatch,' I said, 'so that all you have to do is be seen to join the queue within the allotted time. That way, competitors can't be penalised for the sluggishness of other shoppers in the queue before them.'

'What?' objected Chip. 'We have to *buy* something as we go round so that we can get out at the end?'

'It seems inconsistent with the general premise, I know, but I can't see any other fair way of implementing closure on the GAME process.'

Suki suggested that if Chip was so worried about it, he could try buying some fruit. It was cheap, she told him, and might even be good for him.

•

And so it was that we had the basic format of THE GAME. Unsurprisingly, a lot of suggestions were discarded. The idea of a Vegetarian League was just one example. And though it seemed fair to allow contenders to take a tin-opener and items of cutlery in with them (the range of foodstuffs that it would have been possible to eat would have been too limited otherwise), a line had to be drawn at plates, bowls and similar receptacles, otherwise this would have made THE GAME 'ridiculous'.

4

Once the initial rules were decided, it was a matter of forming the teams. Tevin checked with Reesey and then logged in officially by mobile phone. Jan and Steve-from-up-the-road called in from up the road the following day. Chip and Suki already seemed to have devised a ten-aisle strategy.

A few days later I called The Doc and Calamity Claire. The Doc answered.

'A thievin' competition,' he concluded after I'd run through the details with him.

'It's not exactly *thieving*.'

'What is it then? How's it diff'rent?' The Doc sniffed

disdainfully. 'Just so's I know, y'know?' He'd been mixing records at Two Smoking Turntables until six that morning and I'd woken him which always made him a little bit haughty.

'It's different because we're not criminals,' I told him, 'we're not desperate. Nor are we trying to *gain* anything.'

'Y'what?'

'*Theft* means that the thief wants to *possess* or *consume* the thieved object for some reason generated by either the thieved object itself or by a value system to which the thieved object is linked. There's also the issue of the evasion of the economic system of sacrifice, of payment, of having the ready cash.'

'Yeah?'

'What we're engaging in is a totally different sort of exercise: a contest of mental agility and gastronomic fortitude; a head-to-head-single-leg-knockout-cup-competition requiring consumer knowledge and progressive moralities.'

The Doc blew his nose.

'Soun's like the diff'rence between thievin' and a thievin' *competition* to me. Not that I give a shit . . . I'm in.'

'Great. What about Claire?'

I heard him turn over and prod her. A muffled 'fuck off' came back in response before The Doc returned to the line.

'Make that both of us.'

So that was The Doc and Calamity Claire booked. I put the phone down, walked into the living-room and sat down next to Moll who was watching Turkey vs. Denmark.

'The Doc says that he and Claire will play,' I told her.

'I heard. Through the door.'

Moll looked tired. I thought that maybe the late nights she'd been working recently were getting to her so I tried to make her laugh.

'Did I tell you about the time Gazza told the President of

the Danish Football Association that he could speak Danish and then proceeded to do an imitation of the Swedish Chef from *The Muppet Show*?'

'Yes.'

'Smile if you like me . . .' I poked Moll in the ribs but she grimaced.

'Get off!'

'Who's winning?' I asked, starting to roll a joint, even though I knew that the game had only just kicked off, even though the score was displayed in the top left-hand corner of the screen along with the time.

'They've only just kicked off.'

We didn't say much for a while, just the odd comment on my part with regard to the Danish number two being 'surprisingly handy' and the observation that the Turkish centre-halves were sluggish in stepping-up-on-the-opposition-forwards. Moll was still being quiet and I wondered if she was having second thoughts about THE GAME.

'You want to play, don't you?' I asked.

'Want to play *what*?'

'THE GAME.'

'You sound like you're asking me to come outside and kick footballs at cars in the street after our homework's done.'

I looked across at her, trying to work out her mood, but her eyes just reflected back the twinkling lights of the television screen. I could just about make out the white dot of the ball pinging back and forth.

'It'll probably be just as much fun,' I ventured.

'I don't know if I really want to get involved.'

We both sat in silence again for a few moments, and then Moll turned to me and said that she'd play, that she'd be my partner for the whole competition.

'I just want to say, for the record, that I didn't like your definition of theft. Okay?'

•

(*How come?* I hadn't even been bullshitting! How else could one respond to that supernatural array of goods, mass-produced and beamed in from a multitude of different elsewheres, those vast corridors of food suddenly coming into being as I came in off the street, bored and stoned?)

•

'I just want to say, for the record, that I didn't like your definition of theft. Okay?'

I shuffled in my seat.

'*Okay.*'

'I thought it was limited and simplistic.'

'*Okay.* Jeez – I was just messing around.'

Okay. No problem. That was fine. Or was it?

Moll was subdued for the rest of the day and then left for another night shift over in Euston. Soon after, Jefferson arrived to drink a few bottles of Nastro Azzurro and to watch Italy vs. Germany. I thought about talking to him about Moll's increasingly erratic moods but remembered that he never had any good advice when it came to women and told him about THE GAME instead.

'I think I'll be good at this,' he said.

'What makes you say that?' I asked, but then had to wait until after we'd watched a replay of Zola scuffing a penalty before I got my answer.

'The *wanker* . . . he had the Germans at his mercy!' Jefferson shouted in disbelief before the conversation resumed. As it turned out, Jefferson had spent a couple of years at a boarding school up in Cheshire where he'd developed a flair for gluttony. 'They used to ration our tuck,' he said, 'with draconian precision. We were allowed, for example, *four* cans of Coke for each half of the term, *six* packets of crisps, two packets of Fruit Chews, two bars of chocolate and so on. Well, you can imagine what everybody did. The "four cans" rule meant that everybody brought back four 500ml supercans. The "six packet" rule for crisps meant that people arrived at the beginning of term with those huge multi-packs, or else six large cash-and-carry sacks – and I mean *sacks* – of Bar Snacks and Bombay Mix.

'It totally defeated the object of the rules. The school didn't want two hundred boys running about with unlimited sweets. And what did they get? Two hundred boys with a zero-level of patience devouring this unholy amount of *trash* in the first two hours of term, getting totally out of control on caffeine, tartrazine and e-numbers and then throwing up the first of their Christmas-sized bars of Dairy Milk just as they were climbing into bed.'

'So you're confident then?' I asked. 'Who's going to be your partner?'

'It'll have to be Jam . . . and *he* can do the eating come to think of it. I saw him eat twenty-two packets of Monster Munch . . .'

'What? At school?' I asked. Jam, along with guys like Dr Rob and Wavy Dave who now lived down Fulham Palace Road, were all childhood friends of Jefferson's from Liverpool.

'No. Last night, after we beat the Dutch. After we *thrashed* the Dutch. He says he was so stunned, and not just by the ten pints he'd drunk throughout the game, that he doesn't really know what came over him. Can't say I'm surprised. I mean, we beat them! Four-one! Their worst defeat in thirty-six years and *we* gave it to them. Didn't everyone go a little crazy last night?'

Thinking about how Moll had been acting, I wasn't sure. There were some things in life that I knew I could take for granted, some things that were as blatantly obvious as Danny Blind's foul on Paul Ince as he arrived in the penalty box at about twenty-two minutes past eight the night before. These included the fact that we had, indeed, *thrashed* the Dutch. We'd *tonked* them. We'd *battered* them. Choose your own combination of words out of *spanked*, *humiliated* and *humbled*. Over the ninety minutes, we'd delivered a football showcase that even started to absolve the pain of Turnip Taylor's final days and The Koeman Incident, with perhaps the third goal being the exhibition piece (Gazza taking the ball off Adams after a mistake by Ronald de Boer, exchanging the ball with *both* Anderton and McManaman before *strolling* into the box and slipping it to Sheringham who feints then passes to Shearer who gives it the-doomsday-treatment-off-the-bootlaces). That much was certain. *But what about Moll?*

After the game I'd travelled out to Vauxhall with my records. I'd been asked to mix a set at Bam Bam's, a small club near the station, by a friend-of-a-friend-of-a-friend for forty quid. Moll hadn't been sure if she was going to come because she thought that she might be called in to work at the last minute. But in the end she wasn't needed and tagged along with Suki.

•

Have I said how beautiful Moll was? Forget about turning-heads-in-the-pub or looking-good-on-your-arm or wolf-whistles-in-the-street – Moll was always too striking for any of this to be sufficient (however much she protests that her nose is too big or chest too flat). And it was that night, the night England put four past the Dutch in front of a packed Wembley, that I realised she was changing, that it was as if she was growing even more beautiful by the day.

I'm not talking about the-sunshine-bringing-out-the-best-in-people – what I saw was more than just a tan. Nor am I talking

about a few beers and a night of historic football lending my
contact lenses a rosy tint. Amidst the noise of the nightclub, the
beat pounding four-to-the-floor and the-crowd-going-wild as I
dropped another piano-break into the mix, my radar picked up
on the way women narrowed their eyes at her before turning
away to chat in groups at the bar. I registered, even across the
distance of the dancefloor, the hormonal rustle filtering through
the crowd of men that loitered near to her and Suki, and I asked
myself if it had been always been that way.

I realised it hadn't. It was as if she'd started to effuse some sort
of aura into the space around her, some sort of signal, some sort
of sound (I faded a dub into the after-echoes of the piano-break).
When had *that* started to happen? *And why hadn't I noticed?*

Later on, maybe as late as three or four in the morning, I was
still pondering these same questions as the three of us slid back
home in a mini-cab. And when Suki let herself in next door,
leaving Moll and I fumbling for keys on our doorstep, I took
my cue.

'You look beautiful,' I said, remembering what I'd seen from
behind the turntables.

'Hurry up and let us in. It's got cold . . .'

'I mean it. You look beautiful.'

'Do I?'

'I think so.'

'But you're drunk.'

'So?'

'So . . . you're making me embarrassed.'

I looked for a glimmer of irony in her eyes but couldn't find
it.

'What do you mean, *I make you embarrassed*?' I asked.

There was a pause. One of us managed to open the door and
we went inside, both of us walking into the kitchen.

'I didn't mean anything by it,' Moll said, standing with her back to me as she poured herself a glass of water. 'I'm tired. Sorry. It came out wrong, that's all.'

'"Embarrassed" means *embarrassed* however tired you are, doesn't it?' The conversation wasn't going as I'd planned.

'I've apologised, haven't I?'

'Yes . . .' I let my voice trail off, trying to defuse the situation, and Moll said that she was going to get changed.

I sat down on a chair, not knowing what to think for a few minutes, and then walked along the short passage to our bedroom to find Moll already in bed, curled up in a ball and facing away from the door. I took my trainers off and curled up behind her.

'Are you asleep?'

'No.'

'Don't you think it's stupid when people say "Are you asleep?" and the other person says "No"?'

'Take your clothes off, brush your teeth and get into bed.'

'Are you okay?' I asked.

'Fine. I'm tired and I've probably got to work tomorrow.' A hand reached back and squeezed mine. 'Sleep well.'

•

I couldn't sleep for ages. And then, like I've said, the next day I called The Doc and Moll snapped at me afterwards leaving me even more perplexed. *What was the matter with her?* Over the next few days I cooked for her and did her laundry. I cleaned up and even sold some old records at the Music and Video Exchange on Goldhawk Road and spent the money on a new pair of trainers for her. It seemed to cheer her up a little bit but she still seemed to be avoiding me. Was it THE GAME that was making her anxious? I offered to cancel the whole project but she told me that she still wanted to take part.

And then one evening she came home from work and suggested that we go for a walk along the Thames. For a moment my heart yelped because I wondered if she had some bad news to tell me. But she seemed happier and talked about the commercial she'd been working on that day and even bought me dinner in one of the pubs on the towpath. There, we talked about things that had happened at university where we'd met and afterwards, as we walked back arm-in-arm through the leafy streets, she told me that we were celebrating.

'What?' I asked.

Moll told me she'd been offered a full-time editing job and I wrapped my arms around her and congratulated her.

'That's amazing.'

'I'm sorry I've been a bit *serious* recently,' she told me, 'I guess I've just been a bit tense because my work-experience was coming to an end and I wasn't sure what was going to happen.'

'That's alright. And there was me thinking that it was something else, THE GAME perhaps . . . or *me*.'

She squeezed my arm and kissed me.

5

A few days later, I awoke to find that Moll had already left for work. Having nothing else to do, I pulled on some clothes and wandered down the High Road with a joint.

It wasn't just the supermarket that set my pulse racing. The empty days often propelled me to the local Our Price where I'd loiter by the house CDs and leaf through the cases admiring the artwork, imagining what it would be like to be a world-class DJ and putting the shop-staff on edge because they all thought I was going to start shoplifting or removing the inlay booklets.

If I was feeling particularly brave, I'd take the bus up to the sports shops in Hammersmith or even into the West End and just gaze at the trainers. Up in the West End, they've got them all. All the sizes in all the colours: a trainer for every occasion. The latest Reebok Odyssey Hexes in white, black and Rio red for those days when you felt like you needed some 'front'. White Nike Tour Pluses in classic tennis-shoe design with the swoosh tastefully rendered in oxidised green for when you felt like you were 'on-top-of-things'. ('postmodern Green Flash,' I suggested to my brother when I told him about them on the telephone: I told him that wearing uncomplicated trainers was the same as being secure in your own sexuality).

•

But once THE GAME got under way, the importance of these minor distractions dissipated. The draw, for instance, caused a stir of excitement as one would expect.

Competition hot-spots obviously included a first-round derby between the Chip–Suki team and Moll and me. Reesey and Tevin facing Farid and Danny had to be what football commentators liked to call 'the plum tie' and having the Jefferson–Jam team drawn against The Gooners was a satisfying nod to those Liverpool–Arsenal confrontations that have thrilled-audiences-down-through-the-ages.

•

'Friggin' scousers!' said The Hood, the designated 'eater' for The Gooners, when I rang him to let him know the results of the draw. 'They've got to be the favourites to win a stealing competition.'

'You Gooners, you're all the same.'

I told him he was just trying to start some of that good ol' siege-mentality that the Arsenal were so famous for. And when it came down to it, Jefferson and Jam *weren't* favourites. The unofficial book that Farid had started priced Chip and Suki as the most likely champions, with Reesey and Tevin as next strongest contenders.

•

Whatever the prices, whatever the odds, we decided that an official training-period was out of the question.

'People could just compile shopping-lists and then graze to a GAME-plan,' argued Chip. 'There has to be an element of spontaneity otherwise there's no fun to be had.'

'That's easy for us to say,' Suki suggested. 'We've been thinking about this for a lot longer than some of the others.'

'Some of us have to work and don't have as much time to prepare,' Moll added.

I mused for a while. 'There's also a problem with people just going back and eating the same old things round after round,' I said. 'I think the solution is that people can't eat the same product in more than a single round. If you've taken your chances with

Bali Satay Sticks in the first round, for instance, then you can't eat them in any of the subsequent rounds. That way, it doesn't matter if you've prepared for a lifetime, you'll still have to come up with other methods of scoring.'

'It'll be less boring,' Suki added and we all nodded.

Thus it was agreed that the first round would be played in two days' time, with each subsequent leg due to take place at three-day intervals so as to avoid unnecessary suspicion, and we duly called everyone to let them know.

6

'Have you got the stopwatch ready?'

'Yes. For the fourth time.' Moll brought it out from inside her t-shirt as proof.

It was the day of the first round. She'd decided to wear a light trench-coat as it could hold a large quantity of empty packaging without looking too out of place and she'd even stayed up a couple of hours the night before, stitching plastic carrier-bags into the linings of the pockets to prevent any staining. With a similar nod towards tactical thinking, I'd chosen to wear a pair of Adidas Scatbacks (in white, poppy and black with white traction pads and a three-stripe speed-lacing system) for extra-agility-in-the-field.

'Where's my penknife?' I panicked. I'd brought along a Swiss Army penknife with fork and spoon attachments that Aunt Jocasta had given me one Christmas, a present that I'd never thought I'd have any use for.

'It's in the back pocket of your jeans.' Moll put a hand on my shoulder. 'Look, don't start getting nervous or we'll never get anywhere.'

We were standing outside the main hall of the supermarket,

Me, Moll, Chip, Suki and Seb, who had been chosen to adjudicate the whole competition.

'Right people,' Seb said. 'I want to see fair play. Any questions? Yes? No?'

Moll, Chip, Suki and I all shook hands and wished each other luck.

'Right!' said Seb. 'Get set . . . *go!*'

Chip and Suki disappeared immediately.

'Where have *they* gone?' I asked.

'Never mind them,' Moll replied. 'We've got our own GAME-plan, haven't we?'

I nodded.

•

Which was really to run away from the truth of the matter. But Moll's small moment of reassurance seemed to do the trick. Later that afternoon, with the curtains drawn, Moll and I lay on our bed and reviewed our opening performance.

'I've never seen you quite so fired up, not even when you're mixing at the club,' Moll said as she stroked the swollen curve of my boiling stomach. 'The way you got started on those Belgian Chocolates . . . *brilliant!* We were already on a scoring ratio of £3.99 per 250g while Chip and Suki were messing about with chocolate raisins and Boasters.'

'In retrospect, I felt they lingered too long in the confectionery aisle,' I suggested. 'They got caught-in-possession . . .'

'You looked like Dan Akroyd in *Trading Places* when you stuffed all that Cooked Topside of Beef into your mouth.'

'Did I?'

The warm flush of success gradually crept through my veins as the gastric convulsions subsided little by little.

•

We'd won! We'd actually won!

•

'I thought it looked in the balance for a while,' I said to Moll. 'Chip can consume Lonza Stagionata like no other human being on the planet. How much do you reckon he ate?'

'I think he weighed in at about 400g. Suki admitted that he's been scaling down the amount he's been eating at home over the last few days.'

'On the sly?'

'On the sly.'

'That would explain his seven mandarin tartlets then . . .'

'*And* the six ready-to-eat chicken thighs oven-roasted with brown sugar . . .'

'– the four-pack of Yop Drinking Yoghurt . . .'

'– the whole pears canned in syrup.'

'He displayed nice technique on the tin-opener,' I concluded. As the victor, I had no problem with magnanimity. And there was no doubt about it: Chip and Suki had played to win right from the start. Chip had eaten big, looking for those big scores, those one-hundred-and-eighties, those royal-flushes, those golden-goals while we'd initially floundered.

'It just goes to show what you can do if you put your mind to it,' Moll suggested.

She was right (when *wasn't* she?). It had looked in-the-balance for a while. And with ten minutes left-on-the-clock, Chip and Suki had seemed ready to sprint-for-the-line while Moll and I argued by the delicatessen counter, acres-of-ground to catch up, a bag of Scotch Eggs and Vegetable Pakoras next on the menu and little else but straws-to-clutch-at once they'd been dealt with.

So how had we won?

•

I'd taken the healthy option. I'd gone for Lactobacillus casei

Shirota. On it's own, it only measured 2×10^{-3} millimetres long. Encountered in packs (packs of seven 65ml bottles of Yakult for £2.49 to be precise), it still didn't amount to much more than a mouthful.

I'd drunk nine packs – and washed them down with two jars of DeLuxe Goat's Cheese suspended in Grapeseed Oil (£3.49 per jar) for good measure. After that, there was no stopping me.

'The Yakult was a moment of inspiration.'

'Chip thought he'd already won . . .'

'He got complacent . . .'

'– his eyes–were–bigger–than–his–stomach . . .'

'– he thought victory was his . . .'

'– he saw tomorrow's headlines a–day–too–soon . . .'

7

The first two rounds were completed without anyone getting arrested. Which is not to say that they passed without incident. Both teams of Scousers (Jefferson/Jam and the Wavy Dave/Dr Rob combo) were knocked out immediately, leading to much banter, while local boys, the Gillespie Brothers, represented West London with great style – or so *they'd* have it.

•

'DKNY innit?' Mark Gillespie said to me the day after the second round had been completed.

'What do you mean?'

'Me an' Sy go in there in our DKNY and our 'enri Lloyd and we're immediately intimidatin'. No member of starf's gonna challenge us when we're so well dressed.'

•

It was a similar line of thinking that had propelled Jan to wear his suit. But fashion choices hadn't constituted the only variety of attack-as-the-best-form-of-defence tactics he'd used. Jan had walked around the supermarket carrying a dictaphone and a clipboard, trying to behave in a manner that he described as 'conspicuously furtive'.

'I invaded their space with technology of my own. The authorities that run the supermarket, they're like an old prize-fighter gone soft, they're like America in Vietnam,' he'd confided. But then Jan was the sort of guy who claimed that NASA cleaned the space shuttles with Coca-Cola.

'Oh yeah?'

'Yeah. They're the fat cats that have got too used to being top dogs . . .'

I'd raised a hand to interrupt but Jan was on a roll.

'– controlling *their* environment with *their* surveillance systems,' he'd continued, '*their* bar-code readers, *their* weighing scales. Me? I walked into *their* yard with technology of my own . . .'

'With a dictaphone . . .'

'Yeah, a dictaphone. And *their* control system couldn't cope with it. I was a guerrilla-warrior marching into their HQ with a belt of hand-grenades taped to my body. I was a new type of Klingon Warbird de-cloaking off their starboard bow. I could have been *anyone* . . .'

'Are you sure?'

Jan took a breath.

'Well, the original idea was to look like some kind of store-detective or independent consultant taking notes on staff-performance levels and other business-operations criteria.'

'I see. *Conspicuously* furtive. And do you think it worked for you?'

'We wouldn't have made it to the second round otherwise. In the first round, I thought me and Steve-from-up-the-road were busted for sure. One of the shelf-stackers turned a corner and bumped into me just as I was trying to finish off a mouthful of Flavoured Surimi Shapes.'

'What happened?'

'I swallowed, cleared my throat and asked her where the Ferrero Rocher were, cool as a demi-cucumber. One look at my clipboard and she virtually went and bought them for me.'

•

All this talk of guerrilla warfare surprisingly bore some relation to reality. A day before the semi-finals, for example, Tevin and I were sitting in our usual beer garden and having a civilised drink in anticipation of the following day's clash, when he told me what had happened in his last tie.

'Y'know how you've got to be real careful, right, when you're eating the stuff and everything?' he said. 'Well, I was standing by the bubble-bath and some girl was chatting up Reesey over by the hairsprays when I see this guy in a beard staring at me.'

'Who was he?'

'I didn't know. So I started walking and got Reesey to take the girl's number and say that he'll call her later 'cause I think the guy's a store-detective or undercover police or something like that. But a few minutes later I bump into him again and this time I don't know what to think 'cause I catch *him* looking out for *me*. D'you know what I mean?'

I nodded. 'I think so.'

'And then we see him outside the store. *Outside the store*! I ask Reesey if he looks like five-oh and Reesey says that he has to be because of the shit haircut he's got and the shit clothes he's wearing and the both of us are getting ready to run for it when he comes right up to us and says: *Are you boys brothers?*'

'You're joking?'

'No joke!'

'So what happened?'

'He grabs me by my hand, tells me and Reesey that he's from Freedom Against Retail Tyranny, a coalition of "culture-terrorists", and that he's been in the supermarket spiking luxury ice-creams with laxative solution and a syringe. And then he asks what group *we're* from.'

'You what?'

'No joke! I almost pissed myself. He says that he's seen me and Reesey creeping around the supermarket and he wants to know what pressure-group we're working for.'

'What did you say?'

'I told him to watch out in case he did someone an injury . . . and Reesey sold him some skunk.'

•

In spite of these near-misses (and others), these false-alarms and cries-of-wolf, many things became clearer over the first two rounds of THE GAME, such as the need for certain tactical revisions. For instance, most teams in the second round opted to send the second member to get one of the numbered delicatessen tickets as soon as the clock started running while the designated 'eater' got busy with some solo scavenging around the yoghurts and desserts, or failing that, the pastry shelves.

Another general trend was to leave the consumption of liquid produce to the workings of biological necessity rather than to-go-out-and-try-and-win-THE-GAME by guzzling a couple of gallons of Ocean Spray Cranberry Juice. As 'Lord' Bund put it: 'After a dozen Kabanos, a brace of Mini Spring Rolls and a jar of Pitted Morello Cherries, you've *got* to drink a litre of Florida Breakfast Juice. It's not even a choice.'

Innovation also proved to be a valuable commodity. Teams that relied on easy manoeuvres like Parma Ham and Amaretto Truffles without recourse to adequate Plan Bs and Cs often found themselves getting in each other's way in a mutual race to snatch such items, or else stuck for good ideas when it came to the second round. Conversely, those teams that could execute that special move as and when THE GAME dictated usually found themselves with nothing but open road between them and the chequered flag.

And ultimately, as Moll and I found out, it all came down to each team's will-to-win. In our second round, we simply walked out into the supermarket and set about winning the tie, no-questions-asked, while The Doc and Calamity Claire allowed their minds to wander. While we were busy eating Gourmet Nut Selections and even managed to open and drain a bottle of Châteauneuf-du-Pape while no one was looking, they ended up tasting all the cheeses on offer at the delicatessen counter and eventually couldn't be bothered to compete and paid for most of their shopping anyway.

8

And then the day of the semi-final arrived.

Moll and I got up late and drank tea in the kitchen while she munched on toast and flicked through a magazine. After that, we wandered out into the park across the road from the supermarket where we found Tevin and Reesey and Seb along with a few of the others who'd turned up to watch.

'Semi-final day,' concluded Tevin. 'We've got a crowd.'

'Shall we get going?' asked Seb.

The five of us left the others in a circle on the warm grass and trooped off towards the supermarket, Seb leading the way. In the entrance, he turned to face both teams.

'Right. You all know the rules.'

We nodded.

'See you in twenty-two and a half minutes then.'

He pulled his stopwatch out and held his thumb dramatically over the button.

'Get set . . . *Go!*'

Moll and I headed straight for the smoked salmon.

'An unoriginal manoeuvre, I know,' I told Moll, 'but we've been saving it. And as Bill Shankly said: "You've got to win THE GAME before you play THE GAME."'

'Stop talking and eat up.'

A supermarket manager strolled by as the blade of my penknife slipped along the greasy plastic but Moll got him to show her where the bin-liners were and I sauntered off in the other direction, rolling the slices into the smallest shapes possible before placing them in my mouth and swallowing, jamming them into mashed balls of pink flesh before gulping them down. A packet of Ocean Sticks followed, my hands squeezing the white slivers of reconstituted-non-specific-fish-product out of the polythene wrappers and straight down my throat. Moll returned with a delicatessen ticket.

'Should be about six minutes. We're fourth in the queue. Here . . . I got you a carton of Grape and Peach Juice.'

'Thanks.' I took it and put it inside my jacket. I'd rigged up a tube system that ran up from my inside pocket and down my left sleeve so that drinking a litre of fruit juice was only a matter a few simple scratches of the nose.

'We've made a good start, haven't we?' I asked Moll.

She agreed, but we then wasted the next six minutes entirely. I'd stripped a bunch of white seedless grapes into my outer pockets and was able to keep grabbing handfuls, but I was still only looking to notch up 99p for the whole lot.

'We need a big score soon. What are we going to go for?' I asked Moll.

'What about confectionery?'

We walked over to aisle 26 but two shelf-stackers were right in the middle of it, refilling the Pick 'n' Mix selection from huge cardboard boxes of sweets. At the other end of the aisle, we could see Reesey and Tevin standing there with matching expressions of disappointment.

'Let's hit the delicatessen counter,' Moll said decisively.

Our number came up just as we reached it.

'You order here while I raid the bakery,' I told Moll and tripped off and selected myself a Dairy Cream Fruit Choux Bun (a bit of a mouthful, I know, especially when you're chewing a mouthful of cream, glazed fruit and choux pastry and *especially* when you're doing this while your head's dipped into the cold blast of the freezer lockers so that it looks as if all you're doing is scrabbling for a Famous Fisherman's Pie). When I found Moll again, she'd filled a basket with a bottle of mouthwash along with the wrapped items from the delicatessen counter.

'For cover,' she explained, 'as well as for later. How do you feel?'

'Not too good – but I'll manage. What else have you got in there?'

Moll showed me and I gulped. A tub of Mushroom à la Greque, a tub of Isle of Skye Salmon Pâté and a thick wedge of Roquefort.

'Wasn't there anything else, anything less . . . *fragrant*?'

'For chrissakes, there isn't a lot left in the supermarket that's eligible. I did the best I could.'

The tub of Mushroom à la Greque slipped down easily enough and I told Moll it was a good choice. But then she unwrapped the other items and I had another moment of doubt.

'I can't do those,' I moaned, chorusing along with a sudden vicious gurgling that originated from somewhere within my stressed innards. 'I can't do them . . . I can't . . .'

'Why not? The cheese is £6.68 for a quarter. Another few mouthfuls and we've added 92p on to that . . .'

'I've eaten enough seafood to . . . to . . .'

'*Be a man!* You want to win, don't you?'

I stared at the food. What was it to be first? The pink translucent slush or the slab of soured cow's milk? More than ever before, I realised why people talked about being sick to the pit of their stomach.

'Quickly,' Moll urged. 'There's no one about.'

'But it's so big,' I complained.

'Of course it's big. That's why it's so expensive. That's why we'll win.'

A quarter of Roquefort cheese: eight (large) mouthfuls. I

took the first two relatively easily but the rest needed some courage.

'What if I throw up all over the floor?' I burped horribly, feeling a wedge of creamy cheese caked against the roof of my mouth. 'Does that disqualify us?'

'I don't know. I wouldn't have thought so. I think you said we have to be discovered playing THE GAME and vomiting wouldn't *necessarily* result in us being caught. Why? Are you about to?'

I gulped down some air. It tasted of bacon rinds and washing-powder.

'I don't think so.'

I didn't even bother to get out my spoon for the salmon pâté, instead dipping my hand into it and dredging out the pink paste with my fingers, wiping my hands on my t-shirt when I'd finished.

'You're swaying on your feet!' Moll pointed out.

'We still need a big score . . .'

'You've gone green again!'

'We still need a big score.' My mouth was on automatic for a few seconds, words just falling out of it. I took another sip of Grape and Peach Juice but it did little to help.

Then a quick look at the stopwatch told us we had about eight minutes left. Six pots of Flintstones Fromage Fraïs later and we still had four minutes to get to the checkouts. This gave us just enough time to deal with a jar of Fruttibosco Antipasto (£5.50), another hi-scoring product that we'd been saving for such a moment. The oil felt as if it was lining my throat, as if it was forming viscous reservoirs in the bottoms of my lungs, as if it was sealing up each and every blood-vessel.

'I don't feel very well. I don't think I can eat any more.'

Moll took hold of my elbow and guided me to the check-out. Reesey and Tevin were already there, Tevin looking equally troubled.

'I think he's payin' the price for the last two rounds,' Reesey said to Moll who agreed that THE GAME was a test of endurance as much as anything else.

'Are you alright?' I hissed at Tevin. I was virtually doubling up from stomach cramps.

'No.'

•

Seb met us on the other side of the tills and the five of us walked out of the supermarket, across the High Road and on to the grass where Jefferson, The Doc and the others were waiting.

'How did it go?' asked Chip.

'Anyone get caught?' asked Jam.

'You don't look very well,' Calamity Claire told me.

Tevin, Reesey, Moll and I emptied our pockets into two different piles and Seb made a list of what was in each before returning to the supermarket to verify the prices. In the meantime, the others milled around, everyone smoking joints except for Tevin and me who couldn't even manage a smile. I lay back and stretched myself out on the grass and closed my eyes, trying to focus on anything except the torture in my abdomen.

'You shouldn't lie down. It won't help your digestion.'

I opened my eyes. Moll was sitting next to me.

'I can't help it,' I said.

'Are you nervous?'

'I don't know. I don't know what I feel at the moment. Everything's numb.'

'Take deep breaths,' she said, stroking my hair.

And then Seb returned and sat down on another bench some distance away while he finished his lists, his notebook in one hand and a calculator in the other. All of us waited. After a few minutes he came over, a huge smile on his face.

•

'Who won? Who won?'

•

He put the two lists down on the ground and everyone huddled round. It took a few moments before I could get close enough to see them.

Moll/Me

Scottish Smoked Salmon	£9.95
White Seedless Grapes	£0.99
Mushroom à la Greque	£0.95
Roquefort Cheese	£6.68
Ocean Sticks	£1.05
Cape Grape & Peach Juice	£1.19
Fruttibosco Antipasto	£5.50
Flintstones Fromage Fraïs	£2.79
Isle of Skye Salmon Pâté	£0.92
Dairy Cream Fruit Choux Pastry	£0.69
Total	£30.71

Reesey/Tevin

Haribo Kola Bottles	£0.47
Dairy Cream Fruit Choux Pastry	£0.69
Kinder Surprise x 2	£0.84
Scottish Smoked Salmon x 2	£19.90
Bloom's Cooked Chicken Salami	£3.19
Frijj Drinking Yoghurt (Strawberry)	£0.75
Lemon Soufflé	£1.99
Lemon Sorbet	£1.39
Piel de Sapo Melon	£1.49
Total	£30.71

'I don't believe it!' said Suki.

'Double salmon! Nice tactics!' Jan congratulated Tevin and Reesey. Reesey explained that he'd watched Moll drag away the nearest manager and Tevin had stepped in and maximised his scoring potential.

'What do we do now?' Moll asked.

'A replay?' suggested Calamity Claire.

Seb reckoned that there had to be a period of extra-time and most agreed with him.

'Five more minutes and then we'll count up and see who's in front,' he said and Jefferson reckoned that we had to go back in there with all the empty packets and wrappers that we'd collected so far still in our pockets.

'It's an important fatigue on your competitive abilities,' he said and everyone else nodded.

•

Back we trooped, across the grass and back to the supermarket.

'I still can't believe this,' I said to Reesey. 'I feel *fucked*.'

'Are you ready?' Seb asked.

I looked across at Tevin and he smiled back weakly.

'Get set . . .*go!*'

This time Moll and I set off at a slower pace, going straight for the Special Selection shelves in aisle 1.

'I can't remember what we've already eaten from here.'

Moll *could*, however, and pulled me out a tray of Ackerman's Luxury Plain Chocolate Discs, some Rakusen's Chocolate Digestives from the Kosher shelves and I forced them down amongst a crowd of housewives milling around by the Fresh Meat and Gravy Powders. It took a while but Moll assured me it was worth it.

'Trust me,' she said, 'they're expensive.'

After that, we had seconds to get to the tills and I snatched a Single Mull of Kintrae portion from the Fancy Cheese Selection for good luck, while Moll grabbed a can of Coke so that we had something to pay for.

'Can you see Reesey and Tevin?' I asked and Moll shook her head but they soon came ambling up behind us, also with a solitary can of Coke.

'Are you lot having a picnic or something?' the cashier-girl asked.

'Something like that,' we all replied.

•

'I don't believe it!' Suki exclaimed yet again when we were back outside in the park five minutes later.

'Me neither. What is it with you lot? Are you all *gluttons* for punishment?' said The Doc before collapsing into a fit of laughter.

We were all standing around Seb's scrawling handwriting . . . *again*!

Moll/Me

Ackerman's Luxury Plain Chocolate Discs	£3.95
Rakusen's Chocolate Digestives	£0.90
Small Cheese Portion	£0.19
Total	£5.04

Reesey/Tevin

Cream Slices Double Pack	£1.09
Ackerman's Luxury Plain and Mint Chocolate Discs	£3.95
Total	£5.04

'You must have passed us as you came back from the bakery shelves,' Moll told Reesey.

Tevin and I were already staggering back across the grass towards the supermarket, the lowering sun streaking across our faces.

•

'I admit it,' exhaled Moll. 'I'm stuck. I can't think of anything else that you could eat.' We both stood motionless in the centre of the supermarket.

It had been decided that the 'penalty shoot-out' would take the form of a five-minute, one-product-only binge. Each team was to pick one product and eat as much of it as it could within the time allotted.

'I wish we'd left the Yakult until now. At the very least, it might make me feel better,' I said.

'I doubt it.'

Standing there, I could feel Moll sensing the-pressure-of-the-clock, but was helpless. I couldn't think of anything else either, not *then*, not as we stood in the central aisle surrounded by bustling shoppers. I looked about, my gaze taking in the shelf-stackers with their crates and sticker guns, the wheels of the trolleys, the signs that hung from the ceiling and labelled each aisle: Frozen Foods/Pastes & Spreads . . . Frozen Foods/Table Sauces . . . Canned Cat Food/Packet Cat Food . . . Canned Dog Food/Packet Dog Food . . . Tights & Socks/Home Remedials . . .

•

'Can you see anyone?'

'No not yet. What's holding you up?' Moll asked, watching my hands struggle with a family size jar of Vitamin C tablets.

'It's these childproof lids . . . I can't get them open quickly enough . . .'

'I'm not surprised . . .'

'Don't start . . .'

Moll put a hand on my shoulder. For a moment I thought she was comforting me. But then she spoke.

'Don't look up . . . but I can see one of the managers, standing at the end of the aisle by the tights and socks.'

Her voice was suddenly quiet, urgent.

'He's looking at us.'

'Are you sure?' I pretended to cough and upended another jar of tablets into my mouth. They were chalky and bitter but seemed good value at £5.50 for a few moments' nausea.

'Keep an eye on him,' I whispered, reaching for another bottle. 'These jars are worth a small mortgage. We're going to win, we're okay, we're going to win.'

'*There are two of them now.*'

'What are they doing?' (Another jar gone. I was sure that I had the white dust all over my face and looked like some out-of-control-gangster crazed on cocaine.)

'They're both looking at us and talking to each other . . . wait . . . Now one of them's speaking into a walkie-talkie.'

'Shit, shit, *shit*.' (And then another jar. Perhaps I was getting good at this . . .) I coughed. I was starting to gag but forced myself to keep on swallowing.

'What are they doing *now*?'

'There's still only two of them. They're just standing there. I think they've got us.'

'What about the other end of the aisle? Can we get out . . . ?'

'Yes . . . *no*! There's two of them there as well.'

I was starting to feel faint and the ground began to move in front of my eyes.

'I don't think I can manage another one,' I croaked weakly. 'I don't think I could manage *anything*.'

'It's too late. One of them's walking this way . . . the others are sealing off each end of the aisle.'

'That's it then . . .' I felt like I was about to suffocate in the air around me, in all 23°C of it.

'We're finished . . .' I said.

'Kiss me!'

'You what . . . ?'

'*Kiss me* . . . *NOW*! Maybe we'll embarrass them . . .'

'You reckon?'

'I don't know, do I?'

●

Like runaway lovers who've ducked into a side-alley during a chase sequence in an old romantic comedy, our arms slid around each other.

●

'I'm sorry about my breath,' I whispered, seconds before my lips met hers, 'I didn't manage to brush my teeth after I last ate.'

●

Moll's hands were at the back of my neck. I could see tears welling at the corners of her eyes as the space between us narrowed, then disappeared.

●

'That's okay,' she said. 'Lady had the same problem with Tramp, and that was on their first date,' she whispered between her immaculate teeth. 'Remember? In the alley behind the Italian restaurant?'

●

I wanted to laugh. I could see the two store managers approaching with a wary but determined gait and I wanted to laugh, but my lips were silenced by Moll's.

9

Unsurprisingly, there was the whole tap-on-the-shoulder routine to follow, a sordid débâcle in the manager's office and then in the interview room down at the local cop-shop after that.

No one at the supermarket bothered searching us until the

police came and when they did they were confused to say the least.

'Are you ill?' the constable asked me, sifting through the mound of litter on the table (it looked as if someone had taken a rubbish-bin from off the High Road and upended it on to the manager's desk).

'Actually, I feel a little bit better than I did a few minutes ago . . .'

'I don't mean *right now*,' he interrupted. 'I meant *in the head*.'

I shrugged my shoulders. The constable ran his eyes over the crumpled packets, the scooped-out pots, the empty wrapper for the Roquefort. He picked up the four empty jars of Health Care vitamin tablets and stared at them for a while.

'Are you a drug addict?' he tried.

'I don't think so.'

Moll fared similarly at the hands of a WPC before we were led outside and put in the back of the squad car. I wanted to make a joke about Mini Metros but didn't (Moll was unlikely to see-the-funny-side-of-it and I knew I'd just get in more trouble later) and in the distance I could see Reesey, Tevin and the others standing in the middle of the park as we were driven off down the High Road.

•

At the police station, we were officially charged, released on bail (Moll paid for both of us out of a savings account that I hadn't known about) and then sent out on to the streets with a clutch of Legal Aid forms, both of us due to appear at West London Magistrates' Court within a few months.

'I'll get us a taxi home,' I said when we were standing on Hammersmith Broadway

'Oh *will* you.'

I knew Moll was upset because she was chewing the butt of her cigarette and I tried to slide a conciliatory arm around her waist.

'Get your hands off me!'

I snapped my hand back.

Buses were streaming in and out of Hammersmith Station – 27s, 319s, 220s, 190s – but in the end KAB Cars saw us right and got us home for a fiver.

'I hate the way they do that,' I said, once we'd got home and let ourselves in.

'Do what?' Moll asked.

'I hate the way they drive you home at twenty-nine-point-nine miles per hour and then make attempts on the land-speed record once you've paid your money. It just doesn't seem fair. Anyway, where are the Rizlas? I'll roll a joint . . .'

Moll pulled the soggy mush of a Silk Cut out of her mouth.

'I'm going to go and pack my things.'

'What?'

'I'm going to go and pack my things. I've had enough. I'd appreciate you giving me an hour of space so I can sort it all out.'

•

Twenty-two minutes and thirty seconds later I went into the bedroom to try and talk to her. I'd smoked my joint but Moll hadn't come back into the kitchen. I had to talk to her, didn't I? Wasn't this all something that could be straightened out?

•

'Bored of being stoned already?' she asked when I knocked and opened the door. Black rubbish bags of clothes were lined up by the bed, a few crates already filled with books and videos. 'Anything I'm not sure is one hundred per cent mine I've put in the corner over there. You can have a look through it all and I'll take what you don't want when I come back to get the rest of my things.'

'Is this about drugs?' I asked her.

'Yes, that's right. I've turned into a moron moralist over the last two hours just because I've been arrested for shoplifting. *Is that how you think about me?*'

I sat down on the edge of the bed.

'Why are you going then? This *is* because of what happened this afternoon, isn't it?'

'No.'

'So you're coming back?'

'No.'

'So why are you going?' I asked after a deep breath, my head spinning.

'I don't need this . . .'

'We can talk about it later if you want. Just don't go now . . .'

'I don't mean that I *don't need this NOW.*' She paused. 'I mean that I don't need *this* . . . *any* of this . . . *all* of this . . .'

'You mean *me.*'

'Yes.' Moll lit another cigarette.

'But *you* said that you wanted to take part in THE GAME. It was *you* who wanted to play,' I said and quickly regretted it. It was the typical sort of mistake I make in arguments of this type.

'I think we're going backwards here . . .'

'Are we?'

'Look. Let's get one thing straight. *Yes*, I said that I'd take part in all of this. But I was doing it for you . . .'

'So this *is* about THE GAME.' I was starting to tremble with frustration.

'No. This is purely about *you*, about *you* and *me*, about *me* doing things for *you*.'

'Like what?' I asked.

'Like standing about and watching you mix records at night-clubs for hours on end . . .'

'So this is about DJing?'

'No. It's still about you.'

'What else . . . ?'

Moll sighed. 'You don't seem to be doing anything for yourself. So it's about you avoiding everything. I've been doing it too – until recently.'

Her anger suddenly seemed to drop. She came and sat next to me on the bed, though she made sure that we weren't touching each other. 'I'm to blame as well,' she said.

'For what?'

'*Can't you see*? We're both missing out at the moment, missing out on so much. I love the things you think. I love the things you talk about and the way you talk about them.'

'So what's the problem?'

'All of . . . *this*.' Moll gestured around the room. 'It can't go on. It just can't.'

'Like what?'

'Like you being on the dole. You put more effort into getting turned down for jobs than you do in looking for something that you *want* to do . . .'

'That's *my* choice isn't it?'

'Yes. It's *your* choice the same way it's *your* choice to let Housing Benefit pay the rent, the same way it's *your* choice to sell hash so that you can get stoned all day and afford new records and trainers. It's even *your* choice to spend all this time on a stupid competition that's ended up with us getting arrested.' Moll lit another cigarette and I noticed that I wasn't the only one trembling. 'It's all so *comfortable* for you isn't it, not having to work, not having to do anything.'

I paused. 'It's been fun for you, hasn't it?'

'I don't know. I still want things to change even if it has. I still want a change . . . starting with us. *Fun* isn't so important any more to me, or at least not *your* kind of fun. I'm sorry if that's sounds hurtful but it's the truth. I've got a new job and it's something that I actually want to do. You've got to find the same.'

Sitting there on the bed, I wanted to say that I could change. I wanted to say that between the two of us we could make things different. But Moll was looking directly into my eyes and the words wouldn't come.

'You haven't noticed how you've stopped talking to me about what I'm interested in, or what I want to do unless it's the same as you,' she said. 'You're also scared of the future and now I'm convinced that it's you that's been holding yourself back rather than anything else. You'd rather just idle your time away and I've been suffering as a result. Just look at what happened today.'

•

'Convince yourself back the other way then?' I tried. Moll shook her head.

•

'Can't.'

•

Her voice was quiet, a whisper.

'I would say that there's a part of me that still loves you. But that's not the point. And it should be obvious anyway.'

10

We only spoke once on the telephone between the day she left and the day of our appearance in court. Legal Aid had suggested to me that incarceration was out of the question because it was my first offence but this only made me more worried.

'What if they've gone through their surveillance tapes and seen how much stuff we've stolen over the whole summer?' I asked Moll.

'They won't have. Don't be so paranoid.' There were voices and music in the background on her end of the line.

'How do you know? *And what if they have!* We won't be first-time offenders then, will we? We'll be more like *tenth*-time offenders. And it's not is if we can explain THE GAME to them.'

Moll told me that she was prepared to accept whatever happened. 'After all,' she concluded, 'it was *us* who committed the crime.'

I didn't have an answer to that and she said that she'd see me in court before hanging up.

•

Eventually our big day arrived. Moll turned up with private legal representation of her own (she'd borrowed the money from 'a non-mutual friend'; I wanted to accuse her of doing it just to hurt me) and we both apologised-to-society in front of anyone who'd listen. In return, we were sent away with £100 fines and criminal records. We'd also been made to pay the full cost of the produce we'd stolen

'We *must* have made a good team,' I said to Moll outside the doors to the building. She'd had her hair cut in a style I hadn't seen before and was wearing some new clothes including a new jacket that looked worryingly unisex. Some new boyfriend?

'I'm not coming back,' she said.

'I was talking about not getting seen on the security cameras at the supermarket. We must have been a good team otherwise they would have spotted us on tape and we wouldn't have got off so lightly.'

'I came here today prepared to take full responsibility for what I did.'

'Are you sure?'

'As much as I can be. I've still got some things round the flat, haven't I?'

'I've put them in boxes for you.'

'Thanks. I'll come round when you're out sometime next week. Leave a message on my answerphone to say when that'll be okay.'

'Okay.'

11

That was the last time I saw her. A few days later, I returned home to find her boxes gone and her key hanging on the hook magnetised to the door of the fridge.

And now, usually late at night, I often find myself thinking about the first time I saw her. It was in the checkout line at the supermarket in Fiveways, perhaps halfway through our first term up in Birmingham. I joined the queue behind her and started to unpack my basket before I noticed her. Then I looked up and saw her face, her green eyes scanning a page of *Madame Bovary*. My heart palpitated. It flipped and flopped like a fish stranded on the wrong side of the waterline and gasping for oxygen. I looked away, but by then I knew that she'd noticed me noticing *her* and I stared down at her shopping sitting on the conveyor-belt in front of us, all the time hoping I wouldn't blush. Red onions, cos lettuce, a stick of celery, radishes, V8 juice, a gigantic pot of Marmite, clementines, a box of camomile tea, a granary loaf, a tub of natural yoghurt. A healthy selection, I thought to myself (healthier than mine). But amongst these were some anomalous choices: a jumbo bag of Monster Munch, the two packets of chocolate biscuits, Pom Bar Snack Teddies, fish fingers, a quarter-pound of peanut brittle.

Later I would learn how these items fitted into her life. The Snack Teddies were a habit that she'd picked up during a gap year spent living in France. The peanut brittle was something she only ever indulged in when she reached the halfway point in whatever novel she happened to be reading. She adored the strange, idiotic aliens on the TV advertisements hence the Monster Munch (pickled onion was her favourite flavour), and for a while there was nothing she liked to do more than stay up all night with me and watch parts of our combined video collection with a plate of fish fingers on her lap, the orange breadcrumbs smeared with thick-cut marmalade. We'd get stoned and watch my Cary Grant tapes (*Notorious, People Will Talk, Bringing Up Baby, North by Northwest*), or else watch her Russ Meyer collection – *Vixen, Supervixens, Beneath the Valley of the Ultravixens, The Lust Seekers, Beyond the Valley of the Dolls* ('Valley of the Molls,' she'd whisper into my ear).

•

As for THE GAME?

It turned out that Moll and I would have won our semi if we'd not been caught because Tevin had been forced to retire. His stomach had given up and he'd eventually been carried home by Reesey and The Doc. So Moll and I hadn't needed to eat a morsel: we'd have won the tie by default. To add insult to injury, The Gooners capitalised on the weak opposition to romp home to victory in the final three days later.

●

So that was it for Moll and I. Another semi-final lost on penalties, just like that other match, the semi-final between England and Germany that took place a few days later and placed England as tragic losers yet again.

●

But that's what happens, isn't it? Sometimes you win, and sometimes you're left with a bitter taste in your mouth. Does it help to cry over spilt milk?

HIGHER SOCIETY

What pleasure can it be for a
man of culture to see a
splendid beast impaled on a
huntsman's spear?

Marcus Tullius Cicero, *Ad Familiares VII*

1

First Saturday of the Christmas hols.

Usually I bound straight down the main stairs, not stopping for more than a second's glance at either the portrait of Granpa Charles in his regimental colours (painted just before he died at Passchendaele) or at Great-Granpa Nigel's hunting trophies. But tonight I stop and stare at the grim collection of stuffed heads mounted on the wall and I feel my skin prickle. *Is it because I turned sixteen a fortnight ago and I know what's coming?* I pause on the landing and look at them all closely for the first time in years. There are fifteen in total and though they're all different shapes, sizes and colours, some with straggly long hair and some with fearsome teeth, there's something uniform about all of them. Is it the expressions on the animals' faces, something about the muted colours of their preserved hides? Or is it because when I look at the collection closely, the animals don't seem to look so different, not once I've taken in the delicate tissue of their nostrils or their sad black eyes?

The sound of my mother interrupts my thoughts, her voice piercing through the thick oak door into the dust and silence of the hallway. She's in the kitchen, on the telephone, and I sit down on a step to listen when I hear her mention my name.

'Yes Timmy's back for the holidays. How's he getting on? Splendidly! Absolutely splendidly!'

Her voice drops a register for a couple of seconds, adopts the tone all mothers use when they're confiding in someone that they think they're going to get their way.

'They've all had to start choosing their universities and he's

having a few flutters about Oxford, says he wants to study . . .
now what did he call it . . . *Development*. What is it? God knows!
Something about Africa anyway and apparently one simply can't
do it at Oxford. Says he's going to have to apply to Southampton
or Reading or some other awful *town*. Can you imagine it? Me?
Dragging *my* mother to Southampton for his graduation?'

There's a pause while she laughs and I imagine her holding
the receiver in her right hand and making her palms-up 'I'm at
a loss (but not really)' gesture with her left.

'Well, Pru,' she continues, back at full volume, 'that's *exactly*
what I said. I said: "With an Eton and Oxford education, you'll
never look back in this world." Yes, it *was* brave of me . . . no,
they don't like being contradicted at that age . . . but I had to
say *something*! One simply can't lose sight of reality in life. "Go to
Oxford," I said to him, "and do something sensible like History
just like your father did. It's not as if it can do you any harm. If
you're still interested in Africa in a few years' time, then we'll
pay for you to go on safari in your gap year just like we did with
Simon and Rupert." *Simon and Rupert?* They're fine, absolutely
fine. Simon's doing very well . . . probably already spent his
entire Christmas bonus on Daisy! And Rupert will be back
from Bosnia on Christmas Eve. He's doing wonderfully . . .'

●

The eavesdropping continues throughout dinner. Mother, Father
and I perch at one end of the dining-table, a couple of candles
sending our restless shadows slithering all over the ceiling, and
I let my parents' voices wash over each ear for an hour.
They mostly chirp away about Simon and Rupert, both of
them concluding that Simon's firm will ride through the latest
'nervous time for the City' and that people in Bosnia 'don't
know how lucky they are to have people like Rupert keeping
their peace'. At the end of the meal, Father puts his knife and

fork together and leans back in his chair and I watch as he picks at a piece of meat between his teeth, preferring to dig it out with a fingernail than use a toothpick.

'The problem with your average Slav,' he says, 'is that he's as stubborn as a mule. Absolutely intractable. Rather play silly buggers just to make a point than find a solution. Always been the case, right through history.'

Mother agrees and then sighs. 'Yugoslavia was always such a beautiful place.'

They pause, having exhausted all the usual topics of conversation that they find it easy to agree upon (namely the successes of Simon and Rupert) and then turn their attention to me. Mother takes another sip of the heavy claret and asks me to explain 'Development', tells me that she 'really wants to get to the bottom of it'. Father duly answers her, lighting a cigar.

'Useless idealism,' he says, a cloud of smoke appearing in front of his face, 'nothing more than the intellectualisation of hand-outs.'

A predictable chain of events ensues. Before too long, the two of them have ticked off the Third World for being both 'irresponsible' and 'lazy' with regards debt repayment, asked what would have happened if '*we*' hadn't bailed them out' and *tut-tutted* about 'the grunge contingent' who were 'always trying to change the world from the job centre'. Father laughs loudly at this as if he's never told this joke before, as if it isn't a predictable part of the same old hideous ritual that he forces everyone else to endure every time he has an audience. (For instance, I remember Simon bringing home a vegetarian literature student for Sunday lunch during *his* Oxford days. With much embarrassment, she'd had to decline not only the roast but also the vegetables because all of them had been doused in meat stock at some stage of their preparation and Father mercilessly took this as a cue to make her squirm throughout the meal as he tumbled through a routine of jokes about the 'grunge contingent', 'herbivorous job-dodgers' and 'giro revolutionaries'.)

'Another thing about these provincial universities,' he continues, 'is that they're a breeding ground for hunt saboteurs and the like.' He *hurrumphs*, taps his cigar over the ashtray. 'It's little wonder they don't offer Development at Oxford or Cambridge. I don't see Oxbridge graduates wasting their time with such nonsense. Too busy working all the hours God sends, too busy driving towards success, too busy making the economy function while these surly, unwashed longhairs waste away their time grazing on tax-payers' money and spoiling respectable people's legitimate sport.'

Mother nods her head in agreement. She says that she sees them at the supermarket at the weekends. 'I have to hold my nose when I'm behind one of them in the queue for the checkout,' she says and adds that it's the children she feels sorry for.

•

Of course, the conversation strays from hunting to shooting as it always does at this time of year, both of them telling me how much I must be looking forward to my 'big day'. Luckily I'm able to escape before they get too involved by offering to clear the plates and I leave the both of them in the dining room talking about 'that dreadful Keith Sliney', the man Father's invited to the Boxing Day shoot so that he can be persuaded to operate corporate events on the estate.

Later I'm upstairs in my bedroom listening to The Smiths and leaning out of the window to smoke a cigarette so that my room won't stink. *Could dinner have been worse?* Sometimes my parents hardly speak at all, instead taking turns to make short statements to each other across the dinner table, eyes not engaged with life in its present tense, both of them happy to let the other's grunts serve as agreement, as punctuation, as indication to speak, breathe or swallow.

What are their intimate conversations like? I wonder. *Do they have any?* It's hard to believe that they still try. It's also hard to remember a time when they used to talk to each other with any degree of tenderness, without being suspicious that my memory is loaded with childish idealism. What I *can* remember is Rupert's 'surprise' trip home from Sandhurst one weekend maybe six years ago. The two of us played a few frames of billiards in the library on the Sunday afternoon and then went for a walk down through the herb garden and out into the orchard. It was late September, fallen apples carpeting the orchard floor, sluggish wasps quivering amongst the craters burrowed out of their brown, pulpy flesh. Rupert looked terribly serious and I wondered what was the matter.

'Father's been seeing a woman,' he said once we'd made it as far as the first of the sheep fields, and then named her. She was a family friend and I remembered how a couple of years earlier I'd once overheard her whisper to another woman, during tea at the village cricket match, that she was 'the latest in a long line' to find out that my father 'had the biggest cock in Wiltshire'. At the edge of the orchard, sitting on the fence, I almost wanted to laugh at my earlier innocence and tried to look terribly serious too. *Is he . . . moving on?* I asked. Rupert shook his head. He seemed to tower above me, his hand ruffling my hair. 'There's nothing to worry about,' he said. 'Everything's going to be fine.' Mother and Father were staying together and all that the three of us had to do was to be good and to be brave.

2

The next morning I wake up just before eight and I'm sitting up in bed stretching when I hear Mother knock on the door.

'Don't be too long!' she calls out and tells me that Alan's already waiting for me.

'Won't be,' I reply, already pulling on some old cords and a jumper. Downstairs, Father's sitting at the table in the kitchen, newspaper in one static hand, triangle of toast in the other, the serrated edge of a half-moon bitten out of it, butter oozing around the teeth-marks. 'Don't be late for Alan,' he says, his eyes never leaving the newsprint, and I grab a piece of toast and a mug of coffee, swallowing them both down in a couple of mouthfuls before heading out of the back door.

Alan's waiting by the Land Rover, its engine already running. 'Morn', Master Timothy.'

'Morning, Alan.'

'How was your term? You working yourself hard?'

I say that I have been and he nods and then tells me to help him load the guns into the back.

'You forgotten all the things I taught you during the summer?'

'Of course not, Alan.'

'Good.'

We both climb into the front and drive off, trees and fields soon rattling past, the green curve of the horizon bouncing up and down on the other side of the mud-spattered windshield.

'This morning,' he continues, 'I'm going to take you up to Bleadon's.'

Bleadon's Copse: one of nine different drives on the estate

and the one reserved for the family's traditional Boxing Day Shoot. Father believes that this is one of the reasons he's going *to screw a fortune out of that bastard Sliney*. 'All these wide-boys, Yanks and Nips want to do,' he often says, 'is to pull on a Barbour and yomp around the countryside. All *we'll* do is cart them round from drive to drive, make them feel we're going to a whole lot of trouble, let them plug away at some cheap game and send them back to London with a brace and the bill.'

Alan is a little more economical in his reaction to Father's plans. 'Your father, Master Rupert and Master Simon,' he says to me, raising his voice so he can be heard above the sound of the engine, 'their first shoots were special occasions. Nothing makes me more proud than the sight of one of you youngsters joining the grown-ups. But after this year . . .' He breaks off and sighs.

'At least you'll get *your big day* before everything's changed. After this year, it'll all be different.'

•

I think back to the first Boxing Day after Rupert turned sixteen (he's ten years older than me so I must have been six) and I remember how I stood in my thick dressing gown by a window in the drawing-room and watched Alan drive Father and Rupert away in the first Land Rover, the rest of the cars falling into line behind them with the other guests on board.

'When can I go with Rupert?' I asked Mother who'd waved them all off from the doorstep before coming back inside, holding hands with Simon who followed behind her, the cheated adrenaline not quite faded from his face (he'd desperately wanted to join them).

'When you're old enough.'

She explained that since the end of the Civil War, every Lovington man has traditionally gone up to Bleadon's for his first shoot on the first Boxing Day after his sixteenth birthday.

'It's Simon's turn next,' she'd said. 'You'll have to wait a while for yours.'

With each passing year, the pattern of the day's events grew more and more familiar, the men arriving mid-morning and standing around on the gravel for a while before setting off, swigging sloe gin from silver hip flasks while they chatted, letting cigarette smoke and freezing breath mingle in the morning air. Rupert, sensible as ever, would always spend the time checking over the equipment, his eyes bright with excitement, while Father moved from friend to friend, always ready with a jovial slap on the back and a Christmas joke. It became routine to watch the convoy disappear up the drive, to spend the day reading in my bedroom as the faint echo of gunfire drifted as far as the house, to run small errands for Mother in the kitchen as she supervised the preparations for tea and for dinner. The men would return mid-afternoon, their boots caked with dirt and blood, Father sitting down in the rocking chair by the oven to pull off his Hunters and letting out a sigh as he lit his first cigar of the day, a wired tension in his eyes slowly subsiding, the corridors of the house full of the mouth-watering smell of the cooking meat, the sound of chattering voices and footsteps echoing through the corridors as guests returned upstairs to their bedrooms to bathe and change clothes. And a couple of years later, Simon duly joined them and it became just as habitual to listen to his and Rupert's bantering as to which of them had been the most successful as it was to open presents the day before.

•

And now? To be honest, now that it's bearing down on me, I don't want 'my big day'. It's all anyone seems to want to talk to me about (unless they want to lecture me about Oxford) and all I want to do is run away. Over the last few winters, I've been able to shut it out of my mind. But then one morning, halfway through the summer, Alan set up the targets as I always knew he would, and I reported to him each day afterwards, my heart throbbing with increasing fear.

I started with 'manners' (as Alan calls them), lessons on the correct way a 'sportsman' carries a gun, how he cleans it, how he stores it and so on. Then I started shooting with a four-ten, learning how to break the breech and load the cartridges and letting off rounds at targets stuck in the ground fifty yards away. Soon, after a fortnight, Alan graduated me on to a twenty bore. 'This is what you'll use when it comes to the real thing,' he said, letting me balance the weight of the gun between both hands. 'It's a bigger gun,' he'd said needlessly, 'not as big as your father's, but certainly enough for now.'

From the last two weeks of August up until the beginning of term, I practised almost every day with the twenty bore under Alan's scrutinising gaze, needing a recoil pad for the first few days until my body learnt to accept the pounding kick of the butt. By the time I went back to school to start my A levels, I had a dark bruise on my right shoulder. Other boys had similar bruises and would show them off to each other, brag about the size of gun they were going to use over the approaching Christmas hols, about how many they were 'going to bag' when it came to their first time. *Me?* I tried not to join in and would shrink away from any gathering of my contemporaries when they were talking enthusiastically about 'letting them have it with both barrels', hands miming the action of lifting the gun-muzzle and pulling through with the target while their fingers squeezed off imaginary rounds at the imaginary game their minds seemed intent on obliterating. By the end of term, a first shoot fast approaching for all of us who had just turned sixteen, the levels of anticipation amongst many of them had reached a wild intensity. *You have to drink the blood of your first kill* was one rumour that was produced by this gory whirlpool of conjectures. *You become a sex beast* was another rumour touted by a boy in my Geography class. He was convinced that a successful day's shooting transformed you into an uncontrollable ravisher of women. 'My elder brother told me,' he claimed. 'He says the killing releases something inside of you,' though nothing I'd experienced at home seemed to verify this. Sure, there was a certain exhilaration that I could sense in the air when the men returned from Bleadon's, but that was all it was, surely?

Thus it wasn't hard for me to be scornful of such unruly fantasies. But as the term drew to a close, I realised that I was one of very few who were dreading the impending hols. To keep me from worrying about it, I tried burying myself in my schoolwork. I wrapped myself around the intricacies of my English Literature papers. '*Macbeth* is Shakespeare's most mature and profound vision of evil' was one essay topic I covered. 'Discuss how *Measure for Measure* investigates the tension between the Old Testament value of justice and the New Testament ideal of mercy' was another. I also threw myself at my piano lessons, practising for a couple of hours every day, but it didn't help. My fingers seemed to move automatically while my mind remained free to think about the dulled crack of the ammunition inside the muffled vacuum of the ear-protectors, about what kind of damage the spreading pellets could do to live flesh. And now I'm up on Bleadon's.

●

'That's where they'll come out,' Alan explains.

Up on Bleadon's, Alan and I take up a position eighty or so yards away from the edge of the trees, the ground dipping in between and giving me a clear shot across the whole width of the copse. 'There . . . there . . . and *there*,' he points with his finger and we set up targets on the same spots.

84

3

The days roll by, Christmas getting nearer and nearer.

If asked, most of the family prefer the summer when the sun seems to hang in the sky for ever, saturating everything with glowing colour from early morning until the doves return through the twilight to the dovecote just as dinner is served under the rhododendron tree. In contrast, I've always preferred the winter. The estate and the surrounding countryside seem particularly beautiful at this time of year and normally I spend much of my time outside. In the mornings, I can look out over the fields, crows wheeling through their twisted patterns in the crystalline air above sheets of groundfrost, my breath always carrying with it that brittle edge that lets me know I'm *alive*. Late in the afternoon, the world gets even colder, the sun lost behind clouds over Salisbury Plain, the white haze of the horizon awash with diffusions of pink and cold purple until suddenly there is no more light and everything is lost to the darkness.

This year I feel differently and as soon as I've finished practising with Alan, I spend most of my time inside listening to the radio, or else reading the books set for the following term's classes: *Journey's End, Far from the Madding Crowd* and a collection of Yeats' poetry. One evening, in the middle of the week before Christmas, I'm reading 'Leda and the Swan' when I hear the sound of engines coming down the upper drive. I look out of my window and see two blue lorries come to a standstill in front of the house, a logo emblazoned across their sides in white letters. *Cavanger & Sons of Warminster*. Father's game dealers. Tom Cavanger, the eldest of old Will Cavanger's three sons and current proprietor of the business, climbs out of the cab of the first lorry. There's the sound of the back door being unbolted before Father and Alan stride into sight.

'Mr Lovington. How are you, sir?'

'Very good. Now what have you got for us?' Father asks briskly.

'A hundred. Young and healthy.' His voice billows with deference. 'I know you often have a special day here at Everleigh Hall this time of year so I've got you the best, no sad flappers, just healthy young'uns with a lot of life in 'em.'

'Good!' Father replies. 'We don't want them to collapse the moment they're released.'

'We certainly don't,' Cavanger replies. From the treacle in his voice it's clear that Cavanger already knows about Keith Sliney and that he might be returning to Everleigh Hall more than his customary once a year if things go as Father's planned.

Alan gets into the cab of the first lorry and leads the other to the game-pens while Father takes Cavanger inside the house. They come back out ten minutes later, Cavanger repeating to Father that the animals he's brought are top grade, that all he has to do 'is ask' if we ever need anything *more reasonable* in the future and Father *hurrumphs* before he shakes his hand and walks back inside.

●

Over dinner, Father can't decide whether he's offended or delighted by Cavanger's over-familiarity. He calls him an 'obsequious little shit' several times and spits that he won't be propositioned on his own land – but also concludes that he's glad that Cavanger's 'on board'.

'We can get some real lame ducks for next to nothing,' he tells Mother. 'Take the margin up to something respectable.' Afterwards, Mother goes upstairs early and Father goes to his study to make some telephone calls while I pull on a coat and walk down to the game-pens.

Some families, like that of my friend James Biddestone who lives over in Tidcombe, are indiscriminate as to what they'll shoot. 'As long as it can move,' I've heard James' father declare and the game-pens on his land bear out this belief. They're simple breeze-block igloos, the concrete floors awash with rotten straw and congealing excrement. The animals they buy are little more than zombies. Many of them are malformed or have missing limbs or missing eyes, atrophied vocal cords (where do they come from?). Once delivered, they're kept manacled to the sides of the shelter on short chains that allow them to do nothing more strenuous than huddle together for warmth under the shredded rags that lie around amongst the toxic puddles. And when it comes to the morning of a shoot, the Biddestones' groundsmen hose them down before carting them up to the drive and then use the same hoses to scour down the pens later in the day. Father, on the other hand, claims to have the most humane facilities in the county: insulated sheds with gas-fired air heaters and concrete latrines at one end. The animals, allowed to roam freely around their spacious cages, even get mashed oats and milk twice a day and are let out into a stockade for an hour each morning and afternoon.

I open the door to the first pen.

There are maybe thirty of them inside. Many are sleeping, the sound of their ragged breathing joining with the faint background roar of the gas flues. In the orange glow of the heat lamps, a few skip and scrape across the floor, stopping every so often and looking about, bending to sniff the feeding troughs and each other. I walk inside, shut the door (I gag for a second at the smell. It may be 'clean' in here but it still stinks like a pig shed) and make my way down the central aisle between the two cages on either side. Some of them jerk their heads around at my intrusion, eyes holding me for a second. And then one of them, a female, comes closer and stoops towards me, her dark eyes looming close through the wire mesh. She has a blanket pulled around her shoulders that's scarcely large enough to cover the jutting spars of her ribcage and the pale curves of her small breasts, and when she bends her head to one side to look at me, she exposes the soft flesh of her neck.

'Hello,' I say in a soft voice, returning her stare. I realise that we're both probably the same age and we stay like that for a few moments, the two of us facing each other.

'Hello,' I say again, 'You're a beauty, aren't you.' I wonder if I can reach my hand through the wire and stroke her hair, her skin, but she looks me up and down one more time before scurrying back across to the far corner where I see two bodies churning amongst the straw. She crouches, sniffs the back of one of the writhing animals, grunts, runs her hand and then her tongue along its spine before sliding herself amongst the grappling pair.

•

The next morning Mother exclaims that she is horrified.

'Do you know what happened over in Fosbury last night?' she asks over breakfast.

She goes on to tell me that the Marshwoods woke up this morning to discover that their game-pens have been raided by saboteurs. Apparently fifty animals have been released and the authorities are still combing the countryside for some of them.

'Camilla's been crying her eyes out to me on the telephone already this morning. The police and Alasdair are agreed that it's likely to be an inside job as one of the groundsmen they took on at the beginning of the autumn can't be found. They're resigned to the fact that he must have been an infiltrator.' She sips her tea and straightens her cardigan. 'These ghastly *people*,' she sighs, as if they didn't deserve to be labelled as such. 'You give them a job. They accept your food, your money and they take lodgings from you. To make things worse, the bugger stole some of their possessions: silver, money . . .' She trails off, confident that her point has been made. 'Can you imagine if anything like this ever happened to us? I'd feel *violated*. When I heard, I thanked God that we have such trustworthy staff.'

I wrap up half of the croissant I'm eating in a napkin, stuff it into my pocket and tell Mother I'm going outside to look for Alan. Eventually I find him by the game-pens fixing reinforced padlocks to all the doors and gates.

'You heard?' he asks, nodding to me as I approach before focusing his attention back on his tools.

'Yes. Mother's just been telling me.'

'Well I've got to fix the pens up, make sure they're all secure. I want you to pace round the stockade and check the fence, make sure there aren't any gaps or weak points. If there are, remember where and tell me in a minute. We can go up to Bleadon's and practise after that.'

The steel-mesh fences, twelve foot high and topped with razor-wire, seem secure. The animals on the other side are out getting their morning exercise, eyelids twitching in the sunlight, and I see now that many of them are the same age as me or younger. As I pace my way round the stockade, my eyes search for the female that I was looking at last night and eventually I see her and walk around to where she is. A couple of feet away from the wire, she's amongst a whole trembling crowd of males and females and most of them draw back as I approach. But she stays where she is, her black eyes bright and curious, nostrils faintly rippling. *Does she recognise me?* I check that Alan's not watching and then break off a bit of croissant and poke it through the fence. She arches her head away from my outstretched fingers so I toss the piece through the fence on to the grass in front of her and for a moment it looks unbelievably stupid, a torn piece of patisserie lying there amongst the leaves and the grass. But then she crouches down (I notice the rangy muscles running up the insides of her thighs, the wild jute of her scrambled pubic hair), and sniffs at it before picking it up and putting it in her mouth. I wait to see if she swallows it or spits it out and feel relieved when she chews. *What are you thinking?* I wonder when our eyes meet again. Her lips part, her tongue trembles in her mouth, and she lets out a soft warble. I step a little closer, only half aware that I'm pressing my face against the fence, and hold out another piece of pastry. This time she moves her face towards it. *Will she take it?* My skin anticipates the soft embrace of her lips and tongue closing around my fingers and I feel her warm breath on my fingertips as they approach the damp cavern of her mouth.

●

Mother drives me over to Ludgershall so that Dr Sputtinger can clean up the wound. After a few swabs with cotton wool and disinfectant, it looks no more serious than a couple of paper cuts. 'What happened?' Sputtinger asks, fixing a bandage around my hand. Mother answers.

'For some reason, he decided that one of my *pains-au-chocolat* would make a good breakfast for one of the animals. Unfortunately the young thing wanted his fingers too. I can't believe he's been so silly. Lucky he's got quick hands or who knows what might have happened!'

Sputtinger chuckles along with her, jokes that if I want a girlfriend then I should go to some parties and then gives me a jab 'just to be on the safe side'.

This isn't the end of my humiliation. Later in the day, Father returns from a shoot in Bishopstone and booms with laughter as Mother furnishes him with the details of my day. And a few days later, on Christmas Eve, Simon and Daisy arrive mid-morning in a new Coupé, brandishing smiles and bottles of Scotch, and Mother fills them in on the family news including an account of my 'escapade' while they place a pile of wrapped presents under the tree in the library. Then she goes through the whole story again when Rupert arrives in the evening.

'Looks like someone needs a girlfriend,' he jokes and Father asks what's wrong with the girls who work down at the pub. 'I hear they'll fuck anyone for Babycham,' he guffaws, too drunk to take any heed of Mother's hisses of feigned offence, and I cringe behind my consommé. Luckily I've drunk enough wine by the end of the meal so that I can go to bed early without need of an excuse. And upstairs, I lie on my bed, going through the motions of smoking a cigarette, the spinning of the room soon blending seamlessly with the onslaught of my dreams until I'm hideously lost as to what's true or false. At some point I'm on the front doorstep of the house with the whole family, Daisy included, polishing the guns and waiting for the Biddestones to arrive so that we can draw lots to see who gets to shoot each other first. At other times, it's *me* that's writhing around on the ground in the game-pen, *her* fingernails tearing strips out of my back, my windpipe choked by knotted clumps of her hair.

4

Christmas Day is either a tragedy or comedy depending on one's point of view. It starts with breakfast, all the main players assembling in the kitchen one by one. The rest of the family are hungover having stayed up drinking long after I went upstairs and are in the middle of a second round of Bloody Marys when the taxi arrives with Granpa Humphrey. Half an hour later Great-Aunt Gillian arrives with Great-Uncle Benjamin and we all make our way to St Francis's in the village, Simon pushing Humphrey's wheelchair and me pushing Benjamin's, the four of us falling some way behind Father and Rupert who talk about tomorrow the whole way down to the village, Mother, Daisy and Gillian walking maybe twenty yards in front of them.

Inside the church, we take our usual places near the front on the left side of the aisle, Father grandly shaking hands with the several offered in his direction. And as usual, Humphrey's emphysema makes him cough approximately once every ninety seconds, a succulently venomous gurgle that makes me want to pull out a handkerchief and wipe my hands. Father Peter deals with this repeated interruption with huge doses of pious understanding. 'This festival, inspired by a birth in the village of Bethlehem two thousand years ago, is a festival of life . . . of forgiving,' he intones halfway through his speech, pausing immaculately as Humphrey's lungs sound out another report and testing my resolve not to laugh. 'A festival of . . . understanding . . . and compassion.' This is by no means the entirety of the floorshow. Great-Uncle Benjamin is prone to bouts of nervous twitching that cause him to flinch every so often as if he'd been poked in the kidneys. This wouldn't be such a problem in isolation, but the spasm also comes with a sound effect like a compressed, high-pitched hiccup. *Only ten times louder.* By the time we're all kneeling to say the Lord's Prayer, Humphrey sounds like a twenty-gun salute while Benjamin froths about in his wheelchair doing his best imitation of a broken accordion being used as an occasional football.

After the service, Mother, Gillian, Daisy and Simon return to the house with Benjamin and Humphrey while Father and Rupert go to The Fallen Sparrow for a 'traditional pint' and insist that I come along. Many of the local men in the pub will be beating tomorrow and Father makes a big show of introducing me to them all and buying them a drink, playing his Lord-of-the-Manor role with consummate ease. A few of them track me with sideways glances, especially the teenagers loitering around the pool-table who've already left the local school and have started work on the farms or in the local factories. Their eyes seem to ask what makes me so different from them and when Father announces that it's time to go, I'm only too happy to leave and barely pause to mumble a polite goodbye.

•

By the end of lunch everyone's drunk again. Humphrey and Benjamin still persist in punctuating everything with some kind of visceral accompaniment (they add clipped belching and syrupy farts to their repertoire) and once we've all moved to the library to open presents, Gillian falls asleep in an armchair, the rumble of her sherry-soaked snores supplying a rolling timpani to this concert of emissions and squeaks.

We open presents for the next hour, those of us still awake either faking surprise at having been given a present we wanted (and knowing in advance that we were going to receive it), or else faking gratitude at having been given something we didn't want. I have to do the worst of both, Mother and Father having given me a brand-new shooting jacket, leather cartridge-bag and ear-protectors.

'All from Holland and Holland,' Father tells me, 'the *best*.' Humphrey takes a rest from his spluttering to tell me that 'they'll last a lifetime' and I almost find myself *hurrumphing*.

I spend the remainder of the day watching Mother and Father grow increasingly brusque with each other, watching Simon and Rupert play billiards with a bottle of scotch each, watching Daisy grow more and more uncomfortable as the Lovington clan descends into increasing disarray.

'I remember,' Benjamin bellows, burying his snout into a

93

cauldron of port, 'your – *heech* – Great-Uncle Giles' first shoot. Must have been – *heech* – back in 'thirteen. Absolute lion of a man, went on to be a fine racquets player too until they carted him – *heech* – off to Ypres. He bagged thirty-three that year, amazed everyone, never been bested. And then there was my Uncle Cranston. One of the rascals hid in a tree and jumped out at him – *heech* – and had his hands around Cranston's neck before any of us could do a damned thing about it. Had to finish him off with his hunting knife, right bloody mess everywhere. And did I tell I about – *heech* – you Great-Uncle Giles' first shoot . . . ?'

5

That night, I sleep for a few hours, my body creased up with nervousness, and I wake up at about five, my spine stiff, my stomach boiling away. When I get out of bed to be sick in the washbasin, I think to myself that it's going to be okay, that I've got the flu. But my head clears as I rinse my mouth out and I realise that there's nothing wrong with me and I lie down on my bed again and stare uselessly at the ceiling.

Half an hour later I get up again when I hear noises outside. I put on a dressing gown and tiptoe up to a bathroom on the floor above where there's a better view and I see that the sound is coming from the game-pens. The doors are open, the glow from the heaters effusing a milky orange nimbus out into the night. Through this walk the animals. It's too far to make out anything but the vaguest of shapes but even at this distance I can see their lean figures padding out into the stockade. The night air carries across the echoes of gamekeepers' shouts, the rattling of chains and barking dogs. The sound of engines heaving into activity coincides with the distant glare of headlamps suddenly piercing through the darkness and a wave of fear ripples through the crowd of shadows. Soon there's the metallic clanging of the lorries being shut up and locked, the shifting of gears as they pull away and up the track to Bleadon's.

•

Mother tries not to look too pleased with herself when I appear in the kitchen in my plus-fours and waistcoat.

'Oh Timmy darling! You look so grown up. I'm very, very proud,' she gushes and then busies herself pouring me a coffee and dishing out a plate of kedgeree that feels like sand and sawdust in my mouth. A few minutes later Father walks in and says that Keith Sliney has just called from his car to say that he's five minutes away and would I come out to meet him. I nod, pushing my knife and fork together, and follow him outside.

'Everything ready?' Father says as we both wait on the gravel.

'Yes.'

'Are you nervous?'

'No.'

'It doesn't matter if you are. I was. Rupert *wasn't*, of course, but Simon *was*, even if he'll never admit to it. You'll get over it once the action's started.'

Sliney's car glides down the drive and comes to a halt in front of us, a midnight-blue Porsche with tinted windows and cream upholstery.

'Gaudy little shit!' Father grunts and then suddenly puts on a relaxed smile as Sliney climbs out of his car.

'Mr Lovington. Nice to meet you finally.' He offers his hand and Father takes it, telling Sliney to call him 'Edward'.

'I've brought a friend,' Sliney says. 'I thought it'd be okay.'

'Absolutely,' Father replies, eyes sweeping over her fur coat and highlights. 'The more the merrier.' The blonde that gets out from the passenger seat introduces herself as Carol and Father says he's delighted to meet her before leading us inside. Over coffee in the kitchen, Father and Sliney talk about how long it takes to get to Everleigh from London and both of them agree it's an easy journey while Mother is left to gossip with Carol. 'What a nice place you have here,' Carol says to her and I notice Mother wince.

'Did you see *her*?' she asks minutes later, shutting the kitchen door behind her once they've been shown to their room. 'He could have let us know about her in advance. I mean, really . . . it's as if he's just picked her up in a nightclub, exchanged her heels for wellingtons and asked her to tag along. And *him*? He looked very mail-order.'

'He's a shit,' Father agrees. 'So what? We show him and his floozy a fantastic time until tomorrow morning when we get shot of them, a good job done.'

•

By ten o'clock, everyone's arrived. There are the regulars like Harry Aster, old 'Jock' McKinney and Andy Tretton who turn up every year. And there are the less frequent faces, men like Will Connell and Tom Shipton, old school friends of Father's whom he only sees once every few years. They all pat me on the back and shake my hand, many of them wishing me luck, others even going as far as saying, 'Well done!'

'You ready, Master Timothy?' Alan asks, coming up beside me and placing a heavy hand on my shoulder.

'Yes, Alan.'

'You're not going to forget everything now, are you?' he asks, the corners of his mouth breaking into a smile, and I say that I won't.

'Good lad. Well it's time.'

Father nods and everyone climbs into their allotted vehicle, Sliney coming in the first Land Rover with Father and me, Alan up front in the driver's seat. On the way up, Father makes conversation by telling Sliney about the tradition of the Boxing Day shoot 'here in Everleigh', pointing out other drives as we pass them.

Up on Bleadon's, I can't help but notice how quiet it is. The air is motionless. I'm given the fifth and central gun as a matter of course, while Sliney and my Father take the positions either side of me, the others then drawing pegs and taking up their positions to our left and right. Rupert comes up to me and wishes me luck and at some point I hear Alan remind me to enjoy myself.

'Don't get nervous and snatch at the shot,' he whispers soothingly and then retreats a few feet behind me.

The last thing I hear before I put on my ear-protectors over my cap is the sound of rattling cages and chains, of the dogs barking somewhere on the other side of the copse. Then everything's reduced to a muffled blur. Alan hands me my gun and as I slot the two cartridges into the breech with uncertain fingers, I can see out of the corner of my eye the other men watching me as they sit back on shooting-sticks, lifting hip flasks to their mouths one final time or else grinding cigarettes out in the mud with their boots.

Standing there, the gun heavy in my hand, I focus on the dense wall of trees eighty yards away, trying to shift my mind away from my heart that's beating a countdown, from the inside of my gloves where I can feel the sweat soaking into the lining. Down the shallow hill, Bleadon's is nothing more than a dark impenetrable mass in front of me. And then suddenly, amidst its rambling texture of greens and browns, I can make out the odd figure flitting from behind one tree-trunk to another. I gulp, almost swallow my tongue, remember Alan telling me to *wait until they clear the edge of the copse.* My body stiffens as they get nearer, pale arms swinging wildly as they run through the trees towards us.

Then the first naked body appears. Then *another . . . and another . . .* bare feet flashing through the mist that's hugging the ground. My stomach flips. I feel the hairs rise on the back of my neck. As I flick the safety-catch, I almost look around at Alan but I know he'll just narrow his eyes and nod.

Now one of the animals runs towards me, clearly in range, and if I don't shoot then he'll soon be ridiculously close. I raise my gun and shut my eyes for a second, the first trigger giving way to the pressure of my finger with oiled exactness. When I open my eyes again, I see that the first round has missed completely and the animal, now only forty yards away, has broken sharply to my left. The barrels follow and the second trigger gives way as smoothly as the first. Another pounding kick of the butt. The figure, up until now more like a ghost, suddenly becomes substantial. It catches the load above the left buttock and topples sideways into the mud. To my right, I see Rupert raise his gun and let off both barrels with casual efficiency, his hands moving as easily as if they were lighting a cigarette, and behind him the muzzle flash and gunsmoke stretches out in a line.

Then I freeze completely. I can't do it. I can't go on and I cradle the gun uselessly against my chest. Father notices and I see him mutter something to himself before swinging his hulking twelve bore up into the air and firing another thunderous burst. This goes on for half an hour, wave after wave of animals released into the copse only to come out the other side to be slaughtered. On the ground in front me, the bodies stretch out towards the treeline, some lying still, others thrashing about, eyes white with pain, hands clutching at the gaping tears in their flesh. Then for a few seconds, the air becomes still again and I realise that everyone's stopped firing. From the other side of the copse, a red smoke flare soars up towards the turbulent clouds and I don't see who's the first to suddenly charge forward, but I think it's Harry Aster, snapping his breech shut and darting towards the trees. Father and Keith Sliney advance too, their eyes seething with frenzied determination, and I find myself straggling along behind them, all of us surging forward in a line over the falling ground, feet trampling over dead and wounded. Amidst the confusion, I can make out Rupert at the front of the crowd, understandably the quickest over the uneven ground, and I watch him kneel perhaps twenty yards from the trees and let off at least four rounds before the next nearest person draws up alongside of him. Soon the whole group has formed up in a tight wedge in front of me and I watch them loose off load after load as the animals stumble into range. I'm not sure how long this goes on for because my mind relays its images in time with the muted roar of the guns. But eventually the barrage stops and I see Father, Alan and Rupert enter into a short discussion before leading us into Bleadon's in a line. As we stalk through the copse, we find most of the animals quivering with fear. Some have climbed the branches, looking for some kind of escape route that doesn't exist. Others simply cower on the ground and the men take turns to fire from short range. Next to me, Simon paces forward, his face spattered with blood and when one of them springs out from behind a fallen tree-trunk, I see his eyes flash as his first round catches the animal squarely between the shoulders and catapults it into a ditch.

An hour later Father raises a hand and calls our advance to a halt. He consults Alan and then signals that it's time to head back towards the house.

It's over.

Soon the Land Rovers come into sight as we all trudge back out of Bleadon's and I take off my ear-protectors to find that the air is full of the dull groans of the animals that lie on the ground waiting for the last pulses of life to drain out of them, though these are soon drowned out by the chatter of the men as they gather in the centre of the clear ground.

'How many?' I hear Rupert ask Simon as I walk closer.

'Not sure. Fifteen? Sixteen?'

Harry Aster hands around cigarettes. 'Better than last year?' he asks the group, swigging from his hip flask and wiping his mouth on his sleeve before handing it to me. 'I saw you get *your* first one, Timmy. Congratulations, young man.'

I don't say anything but take a sip of sloe gin. Sliney, Father and Alan walk up and soon we're all assembled in a circle. Harry Aster repeats that he saw me get my first one.

'Yes,' Father replies, 'he did.'

Looking down, I suddenly realise that we're all standing by the corpse of the female that bit my finger, liquid weeping from her ruptured midriff, limbs splayed, one eyelid half-closed, the other wide open, blood seeping through the grooves of her white teeth. Her mouth is a clotted cylinder of chipped teeth and blood.

'Time for the *blooding*,' Father says.

'Blooding?' I ask, taking a step backwards but finding myself blocked by a stout wall of tweed.

'To celebrate you first kill, Master Timothy,' says Alan, almost grudgingly. 'It's traditional. A rite of passage.'

I look around the ring of faces and they stare back at me almost hungrily.

'Alan,' I hear my father say, 'I believe the honour falls to you.'

'Yes sir.' Alan strides into the centre of the circle. 'Master Timothy?'

I don't move but the wall of tweed and leather closes around me and I watch, horrified, as Alan crouches down beside the body of the female and saws at her wrist with a hunting knife until her right hand comes free. 'Here we are,' he murmurs as he walks towards me, raising the sopping hand and swiping it across my cheeks.

•

Alan drives us back. Rupert rides with me and Sliney and they talk about SA80s and the different types of ammunition used by the Army as we roll down the hill. Father, however, sits in the front and doesn't look at me once or say a word to me. Back at the house, Alan collects the guns for cleaning, his hands invisibly accepting tips from each guest, but when I hand him my gun, he thanks me but refuses my folded twenty-pound note.

'No need for a tip, Master Timothy.' He pauses and looks at the ground. 'Not on your first time.'

In the kitchen, Mother puts down her glass of wine and asks me if I've enjoyed myself. I reply that I was nervous, not sure whether I should tell her the truth, just as Father and Sliney walk through the kitchen door.

'Ever been on safari?' Father's saying to him. Sliney shakes his head. 'You should be our guest next summer,' Father says, slapping him on the back and offering him a drink. 'Nothing like chasing those jungle-bunnies across the plain from the back of a jeep, the hot wind in your face, the African sun beating down.'

I hover by the stove where I can smell a game pie cooking away in preparation for the hunt dinner later on. 'Did it go well?' Mother asks Father.

'It went fine,' he replies, looking at me but saying nothing more.

Mother tells Sliney that Carol went up to their room half an hour ago, that she is waiting for him, and Sliney says to Father that they can talk later and takes his drink upstairs with him. Father then announces to Mother that he's going upstairs too. He pauses after he says it, making eye-contact with Mother for a couple of seconds before turning and leaving the room. Then the door shuts and Mother sighs, a hand moving to her hair.

'You said you were nervous.'

I nod.

'You won't be,' she says, 'as you get older.'

She lingers for a moment longer and then tells me that she's going upstairs to talk to Father. And once she's left, I'm alone in the kitchen.

I sit down in the rocking chair by the stove to soak up the warmth, to let my breathing settle. I let my body slouch, let my head come to rest on the back of the chair and shut my eyes. It takes a little time to get the images out of my mind, the crippled slump of the bodies as they fell to the ground, the sight of the dogs scrabbling at the throats of the wounded. It seems to help when I imagine the rooms around me, familiar images of home, and I let my mind drift out beyond the kitchen to the four corners of the house. I can hear noises coming from the garages, the spluttering of the pipes in the basement, footsteps on the gravel somewhere outside. I let my mind wander out of the kitchen door and up the main stairs, past the portrait of Granpa Charles, past the bloodless stares of Great-Granpa Nigel's trophies hanging on the walls (the animals don't seem to look so different, not once I've taken in the delicate tissue of their nostrils or their sad black eyes), up to the bedrooms where I can hear the sound of adults talking, the opening and shutting of cupboards, the running of baths and showers. After a while I can pick out the fainter traces of background noise, light footfalls on carpet, the distant murmur of carols being sung on the World Service somewhere on the top floor, the metallic sound of bedsprings and luggage being unzipped, the shutting of doors and windows. These sounds are distant, like the whisper of rhythmic breathing, like the faint wind outside the window, almost as faint as the gentle creaking from down the corridor where fresh game has been hung in the pantry, toes dangling towards the ground and swaying inches from the sawdust.

INK

What's done cannot be undone.
To bed, to bed, to bed.

William Shakespeare, *Macbeth*

1

Jack awoke to the sound of the Westerkerk clocktower booming out over the rooftops of Amsterdam. Where was he? Whose house was he in? The bells that had shaken him out of his dreamless sleep, a dark and shapeless blackout from which he emerged thirsty and nauseous, fell silent and Jack started to remember the night before just as his hangover burst into horrifying life.

I'm in the shit, he thought to himself immediately as he twisted on to his back, his face peeling away from the pillow, a hand moving to his forehead: *I am definitely in the shit!* Now there were hazy recollections of his drunken arrival at Johanna's house the night before: the way the door had pitched and yawed in front of him as he stretched out a hand to ring the bell; the sound of Coco's anxious voice saying that she'd been worried to death and asking him where he'd been; the disarray of his gurgled answers. Her tone had hardened when she'd smelt the alcohol coming off his breath in thick waves and she'd shrieked later at the sight of his bandaged arm. By that time, Jack had been incapable of anything but sprawling across their bed and listening to her repeated insistence that she 'just didn't understand' while the ceiling spiralled dangerously above him.

Jack raised his throbbing limb and contemplated the dressing and the translucent quadrant of surgical tape. The material was blotted with small rosettes of blood that were fringed by yellow rings the colour of clouded urine. The flesh underneath ached and caused Jack to exhale, to remember both the whirring of the tattooist's needle and how *it* had looked when freshly completed, the black ink glistening amongst droplets of blood the colour of strawberry cordial.

He got out of bed and stumbled towards the adjacent bathroom where he drained off the ball of heat in his bladder and then deposited himself under the falling spray of the shower with his right arm extended into the dry air. When it came to brushing his teeth, he was obliged to swipe at his gums uselessly with the toothbrush in his left hand and afterwards he dried and dressed himself with the same awkwardness. After that there was nothing else he could do but go downstairs and face her.

Negotiating the steep ravine of the staircase, Jack shuffled into the kitchen and saw Coco crouched by the open dishwasher. She didn't look up and didn't say anything. So Jack didn't say anything. The Silent Treatment. All things considered, this was probably best. He opened the fridge door, pulled out a bottle of water and sat down at the small, round table where he watched Coco load dirty bowls and mugs in between the plastic spokes. Finally she spoke as she wiped the table in front of him.

'Does it hurt?'

'What?' Jack asked, half mesmerised by the ebb and flow of his hangover. The nausea now seemed tangible, *muscular*, organised in waves of contractions.

'Does it hurt – the tattoo?'

'A little bit.'

Coco's eyes stayed fixed on the surface of the table where her hand moved in circular motions.

'Does it need re-dressing?'

'The guy told me to leave it for two days. Where's Johanna?'

'She's gone out to have breakfast with some friends.'

Of course she had, thought Jack, how discreet. 'And Marie?' he asked.

'In her room getting ready. I thought we could go to the

Rijksmuseum this afternoon and then have lunch in Vondelpark. And then I want to take Marie shopping.'

'Sounds good,' Jack croaked as Coco lapsed back into silence and proceeded to make a small breakfast for him. Without another word, and with her back to him, she buttered toast at the counter and poured his tea before setting it down in front of him and going upstairs.

•

Half an hour later The Silent Treatment had been temporarily suspended in favour of The Talking Torture. Jack, Coco and Marie walked south along Prinsengracht, Jack and Coco always a yard apart and not holding hands, talking about anything except the night before or why Jack had been so late arriving at the house or what he'd been doing. At one point Coco pointed out a small chest of drawers outside an antique shop and asked Jack if he thought it would suit their bedroom back in London.

'That's what I love about Amsterdam,' she said. 'You walk down these canals and you can't tell if some of these houses are museums or galleries or shops or just *homes*.' Then she told Jack how her work had gone in Amsterdam the last few days and what she and Marie had done in the evenings, all the time not looking at him as she gave him the list of names, times and places.

'We got to Schipol an hour late and the train service to Centraal Station had been suspended . . . it was so muggy . . . Marie was ecstatic to see Johanna again . . . she took us to this amazing Indonesian restaurant called Temple Doeloe . . . Marie and I had rijstaffel . . . on Tuesday we met our opposite numbers at TRS . . . the night before last we went to the Muziektheatre . . . Marie and Johanna spent the afternoon at Anne Frank's House . . . Paul Scheider told me yesterday that he wants me to think about heading the new team.'

Jack listened, struggling to inject enthusiasm into his murmured replies. 'Mmmm,' he agreed. 'Really?' he sighed (inside
he winced at another internal lurch, another visceral plea
for help). It was hard to know what to say if they weren't
going to talk about *it* – and it was hard to know where to
look, especially with his eyeballs pulsating so ferociously. Jack
definitely didn't want to look Coço in the eye and settled
for focusing on Marie as she hopped and skipped a little way
ahead of them, her pigtails flapping behind her. Occasionally
Marie paused to take a photograph of a houseboat with her
new camera or to turn around and wave at them. At least *she*
was happy.

A few bridges further on and the three of them stopped at a
canalside café for bagels and a drink. Marie sat twisted in her
chair so she could reach over and stroke a cat that dozed on
some nearby steps, singing the words of a nursery rhyme as she
ran her fingers through its fur. And Coco was still talking and
Jack was still hoping that the fresh air and the breakfast he'd
eaten were going to make some kind of impact on the way he
was feeling. *Wasn't that the point of forcing down the food and the
liquid?* he asked himself. Wasn't that the reason for being outside
and upright when he should have been in bed with a joint and
the television turned down low: *that it was all meant to make him
feel better?* Jack didn't feel better. He felt worse. For brief spells
the vertigo would fade and his head seemed to shrink back to
its normal size only for the pressure behind his eyes to return
minutes later. His face itself felt numb and bloodless, the skin
stretched into a grimace as if he were freefalling towards the
ground, his heart not so much beating as *sobbing*, each breath
a source of hope as his stomach clenched and crumpled. And
Coco was still talking.

'Look at those houses . . . that's what I love about it here . . .

so open . . . the Dutch never bother about net curtains or any of that *English* crap . . .'

'Really?' Jack picked up his coffee cup but put it down again. His hands were trembling too much. He'd spill it all over himself.

'It's a pity . . . the rubbish in this city is enough of a problem as it is without there being a strike . . . hasn't been collected since Monday . . . piled up in the streets everywhere . . . there isn't even going to be any transport for the whole of *next* Monday . . . we'll have to get a taxi back to the airport . . .'

'Mmmmm,' Jack agreed, rubbing the bridge of his nose between his thumb and forefinger and wishing that he could be transported through time, either forward to the next day or back to the day before, it didn't matter, anything not to be sitting right *there* and right *then*. And Coco was still talking, and not talking about *it* but wondering whether they should see the East Wing of the Rijksmuseum first or a special exhibition of medieval carvings she'd read about in the *Financial Times*. 'I think it's already been shown in London so this might be our last . . . *will you look at that!*'

Jack wearily turned his head to see what Coco was pointing at. On the ground near the edge of the bank (and near another pile of rubbish sacks) lay a solitary leather boot, a small size that suggested it had belonged to a woman. In a way it looked no more extraordinary than the beer cans and junk-food cartons that lay around it, just another piece of flotsam left over from Amsterdam's Friday night.

'What kind of girl loses one shoe?' Jack heard Coco say, but didn't pay her much attention as his eyes desperately searched the cobbles for the boot's partner. 'Probably the sort of girl who wears shoes like that,' she said. 'Look! It's got little feathers *glued* to the sides at the heel. How *naff* . . .'

Jack couldn't see the other one anywhere, just the right half of the pair a few yards away from them. It stood the right way up, its buckle straps broken and hanging down loosely at its sides, the toe pointing out over the canal as if marking the spot where its wearer had taken a final step before flinging herself into the water. 'Losing both shoes you could put down to carelessness or drunkenness – but to lose one?' Jack heard Coco ask. 'It makes me think something more *disturbed* has happened . . . I mean, who loses one shoe? Who would want to take off *just one?*'

2

Coco had first mentioned the trip to Amsterdam back in March five months earlier. After another stagnant day at his word-processor, Jack had collected Marie from school as usual and walked her home through the drizzle across Brook Green. Back inside the warmth of the flat, he let her watch cartoons for an hour (and watched them with her) before she started her homework on the kitchen table and Jack started on a vegetable stew. Her class had been set the task of writing 'a story' describing their mothers.

'How do you spell *slissiter?*' Marie asked at one point, chewing her pencil.

'S-O-L-I-C-I-T-O-R,' Jack replied, coring the seeds out of a red pepper.

'And what about *cumpny?*'

'C-O-M-P-A-N-Y,' he replied, crushing garlic and rock salt into a paste with a flat butter knife. 'I thought you knew how to use a dictionary?'

'I do.' Silence. 'How do you spell *ryter?*'

112

'W–R–I–T–E–R.' Jack couldn't resist seeing what she'd written and wiped his hands on a cloth as he peered over her shoulder.

my Mummy is called Coco and is big with brown hair and brown eyes. my Mummy wears a soot and wears ear rings and is a soliciter. She works in the city. Sometimes she is very seriuss and very tired. Usually she is fun and tels jokes. She works for a company. my Mummy is french and english. Jack is english and he is a writer. Jack also does cleening and cooking.

'Well done,' Jack said, 'but you need to check your spelling.' He was writing out a list of corrections on a piece of scrap paper when Coco came through the door and looked to see what they were doing.

'A fat grouchy prostitute,' she whispered in his ear once she'd read Marie's piece. 'You told her what to write, didn't you!'

Marie made her amendments, gathered up her things and took them up to her bedroom while Coco poured a glass of wine from the open bottle in the fridge and sat down at the table. It was then that she told Jack about her trip to Amsterdam.

'The firm want me to go over for the third week of July and help wrap up the merger. Anyway, you know how I hate staying in hotels . . .'

Jack had nodded.

'So I rang Johanna to see if I could stay with her and she said that it was a great idea and also suggested I bring Marie with me for a holiday so that they can spend some time together. Do you think it's a good idea?'

•

Johanna was Maarten's mother and Maarten was Marie's father. Coco and Jack had 'done' the subject of Coco and Maarten the second night they'd slept together because they'd been 'doing' the whole subject of Coco and Marie at the time and you couldn't talk about one thing without talking about the other. Lying in her bed at her flat in Olympia, Coco told Jack how she'd met Maarten while they'd studied politics together at the Université de Lyon almost a decade before, both of them shunning other simultaneously casual relationships to move into a bedsit together on the north bank of the Saône, under the shadow of the grey cathedral. 'It was pretty grimy really,' Coco had admitted, 'just a mattress, a sink, a couple of gas rings and no heating in the winter. It sounds like a cliché, I know, but that's how it was!'

It *did* sound like a cliché, Jack thought as he listened, but it also sounded better than his three years in Nottingham spent trying not to get beaten up by the local metal fans (Nottingham still had them – *why?*) and only getting laid once every two and a quarter terms when everyone else seemed to be getting a couple of 'bunk-ups' a week. And Jack imagined how grimy it had been, whole weeks at a time spent in frowsy orgasmic bliss with nothing but more sex to keep the cold away, their room a caramel glow of candlelight bouncing off tumblers of wine and upturned copies of Spinoza (Maarten's) and Mill (hers). There would have been the beautiful spring mornings and the suffocating heat at siesta-time during the summer, the cloudy skies of tragic autumn afternoons, the leaves falling as the two of them walked through the dark streets back towards their bed.

'My parents came to Lyon to visit me but it was really to check out Maarten of course,' Coco had told him. 'They expected the worst so they saw the worst. One look at my mother's face told me she was praying that we'd split up. Which of course we did though perhaps not in the way she expected.'

Coco discovered that she was pregnant four months before her final exams and Maarten had disappeared from Lyon two months later.

'Just gone! I arrived back at the flat to find that all he'd left was a copy of *Ethics* with a note scrawled inside.'

'What did it say?' Jack had asked.

'I don't know. Once I saw his handwriting all over the inside cover I got so angry that I threw the book out the window. I went down half an hour later to look for it, after I'd stopped crying, but someone must have picked it up and walked off with it. It's funny to think that a complete stranger in Lyon has a copy of *Ethics* with Maarten's message to me written inside.'

Astonishingly, Coco passed all her papers first time and Marie was born four months later. At the same time, Coco's English mother separated from her Corsican father and moved back to England. Coco followed her, wanting to put Lyon in the past, and moved into the same house in Barnes and plans for postgraduate studies were dismissed in favour of re-training in the law which ultimately led to her job at Scheider & Rex.

'And now I'm here,' she'd said, wrapped in Jack's arms.

•

Jack's friends were impressed when he first introduced Coco to them at a pub the following Friday night.

'Not bad, Jack, not bad!' Al had said while Coco was at the bar buying drinks.

'Italian?' Chris had asked.

'She's really nice – not like the miserable poets you usually go out with,' Sophie had observed. 'She tells jokes and talks to us rather than sitting in the corner consumed by angst.'

'How old?' Geoff had asked.

'Thanks . . . err Corsican actually, or at least her father's Corsican and her mother's English . . . she's thirty.'

'*Thirty!*'

'Thirty.'

'She'll want a kid,' Chris tutted into his pint.

'I don't think women reach thirty and suddenly want chil-dren,' Jack replied. 'It's not like a deadline. And anyway, she's already got one. A seven-year-old girl called Marie.'

'Where's the father?'

'Somewhere in the Far East – Indonesia or some place like that. He flew the coop just before Marie was born and only shows up every couple of years.'

'And you've met her?'

'I've met her.'

'*Already?*'

'Why not?'

His friends hadn't had an answer and Jack was pleased that their surprise at the five-year age gap between him and Coco and at her having a seven-year-old child had been revealed as the hollow product of twentysomething foolishness. Maybe she *was* five years older than him. Maybe she was a solicitor and earned five times more than he did (at the time he'd been working part-time at Cinemaniacs Videos on the Uxbridge Road while he attempted to finish his first novel) – but weren't these material concerns meant to be irrelevant? When he moved into Coco's flat three months later, Jack fielded another round of enquiries as to the suitability of the relationship. Was he ready to settle down? Was he ready to play the role of a father?

'What can I tell you? I love her, and Marie. Isn't that all that counts?' He and Geoff and Al were in the pub a couple of nights before he was due to move out of his bedsit. 'And as for *settling down*, it wouldn't seem so strange to everyone else if it was *her* that was moving in with *me* or if it was me that had the better-paid job.'

•

'Do you think it's a good idea?' Coco had asked him. 'Marie and I would fly out on the Monday night and you could have the week here on your own, get some writing done and fly out on the Friday afternoon. You said you were going to finish around then so maybe this all works out for the best?'

Jack *had* said that his book would be finished by the end of July. That had been last August when he'd moved in and when he'd reached a halfway point in his novel. The problem was that he was still only halfway through. He was only *ever* halfway through and though there were occasional flashes of progress, Jack sometimes felt that he was doomed to never continue beyond the first hundred pages. He'd given up the drudgery of the video store to write at home in the day and look after the flat, to accompany Marie to and from school, to increase the stability of his life so that writing would become easier instead of harder. But by the time Coco and Marie were packing their cases for Amsterdam, Jack was still looking at the same passages that he'd been toiling over at Christmas, still sensing the same flaws, the same problems, and was too ashamed to admit to Coco that he was still stuck.

'Take care and see you on Friday,' she'd said to him, the taxi waiting in the road behind her to take her and Marie to the airport. 'Hope your work goes well. We'll call.'

The taxi had driven away down the road and Jack had gone back inside the flat and slumped down on the sofa where he spent the next few days scrupulously avoiding the word-processor, instead getting stoned (usually he was never allowed to smoke in the flat) and watching *Teletubbies* and cooking programmes, or else the black-and-whites they showed on Channel 4 during the day. Was Coco getting frustrated with him? Or was he projecting his own frustrations on to her? he would ask himself. Would she understand how or why he was finding it difficult to write? Or was that an impossibility given that he himself had few or no answers? Coco telephoned twice over the next few days, briefly letting Jack know that she and Marie were well, and Jack would lie to her, saying that he was making progress. And then Friday had arrived and seemingly before he knew it, Jack was rushing to the station to catch his train to Gatwick.

•

At Schipol Airport, Jack arrived to find the train service to Centraal Station suspended on account of engineering works being carried out on the line.

'You can take a bus to Zuid WTC and proceed by metro from there,' the ticket clerk told him from the other side of the glass.

Jack anticipated the journey taking an extra hour as it always did when this kind of thing happened and he only had a few hours to himself in Amsterdam before he was due at Johanna's house: his plans to spend the afternoon in a coffeeshop looked as if they were doomed and he'd probably not get another chance. But then the replacement bus service delivered him to the metro connection in no time at all and in the hot carriage, his travel-bag clamped between his legs, Jack pulled out a map and realised that he could recoup some of his preciously planned afternoon by getting out at an earlier station rather than going the whole way to the end of the line. At Nieuwmarkt, the escalator brought him up into the sunshine and into familiar territory. The coffeeshop he'd planned to go to, Basjoe, a small place run by three Surinamese brothers, was only five minutes away. Smiling, Jack crossed over the cobbled square, past a Chinese supermarket and benches where men slept in the baking heat, their breathing heavy from early-afternoon drinking, and walked down the side of the wide canal. He looked at his watch. It was a little after a quarter past two and he'd agreed to be at Johanna's on Prinsengracht at five. It would take twenty minutes to get across the city from

Basjoe so he had a whole two hours to idle away. He'd lost no time at all.

Basjoe seemed unchanged since he'd been there as a student a few years earlier: the same advertisement on the cigarette machine in the corner, the same newspaper racks mounted on the brown walls, the same indolent dub on the hi-fi system. From his table, Jack asked for a couple of grams of Silver Haze and a 7up and once he'd rolled a joint and lit it, he pulled out his copy of *The Long Goodbye* and began reading.

I drove back to Hollywood feeling like a short length of chewed string. It was too early to eat, and too hot. I turned on the fan in my office. It didn't make the air any cooler, just a little more lively. Outside on the boulevard the traffic bawled endlessly. Inside my head thoughts stuck together like flies on fly paper . . .

Damn right! sighed Jack putting the book down and taking another drag on the joint. It *was* hot and it was hard to read and not be distracted by the people outside walking past the window in front of him, the girls wheeling past on bicycles, their summer dresses flattened against their bodies (*cling! cling!* the small bells on the handlebars sounded), the taxis and cars slowing to make the turn right outside the door to the coffeeshop. Jack picked up the book and tried again.

I drove back to Hollywood feeling like a short length of . . . it was no good. There was too much noise inside as well, the sound of the bassline and the chattering voices. Four Americans sat at a table near the counter talking about which had been better, the Bubblegum at Grey Area or the Crystal at Abraxas. At another table sat a couple who weren't talking but staring down at their orange juices with ditched eyes, the boy every so often the victim of a bout of violent coughing. Two locals sat at the table nearest the door talking in Dutch and on a stool at the counter, a girl in a leather jacket and short black dress sat on her own, drumming her fingernails on the wood. Jack took another drag on his joint and turned back to his book.

I drove back to Hollywood feeling like a short length of chewed string. It was too early to eat, and too hot. I turned the . . . this time Jack closed the book before laying it back down on the table. He wasn't going to be able to read and decided to put the book back in his bag, determined to enjoy getting high while the world passed by outside. He looked down at his watch. Ten to three. When he looked up again he saw that the girl at the bar had moved to the table directly next to his and that she was staring at him.

'What's wrong?' she asked. Her voice was American.

'Pardon me?' Jack looked at her again to check that he didn't know her. He didn't.

'I asked, "What's wrong?"'

'What do you mean?' Jack replied.

'You're sat there looking at your watch and re-reading *The Long Goodbye* . . .'

'How do you know I'm re-reading it?' Jack interrupted.

'The cover's all beat up.'

'I could have bought it in a second-hand shop.'

'Yeah, you could have. You telling me you bought it second-hand?'

'No. I'm re-reading it. You're right,' Jack smiled.

The girl smiled back.

'So what's wrong?' she asked as she got up from her table and sat down at his. 'No one re-reads *The Long Goodbye* unless there's something going wrong in their life. Chandler's self-pitying enough at the best of times – *but in that one?* Sheesh! You got Terry Lennox: the human ghost, the lost soul who isn't lost, the murderer who isn't a murderer, the suicide who isn't even a suicide! And what does Marlowe do? Gets himself beaten up and thrown in jail for the guy . . . when he's not too busy lighting up cigarettes and pouring spare cups of coffee as a tribute to the guy's memory!'

'You think Marlowe's a . . .'

'A *chump?*' she interrupted. Jack passed her the joint. 'No, not really.' She took a drag and held it in for a few seconds. 'I guess I love *The Long Goodbye*,' she said, smoke signals appearing in front of her lips. 'I mean, *anyone* would fall for Terry Lennox.' She took another drag – more smoke signals. 'I would.'

Jack looked at her more closely. She looked as if she was in her early twenties, maybe a little younger. And if anyone looked like a human ghost, it was her. Her skin looked as if it had been violently and repeatedly scrubbed, bleached except where the skin mottled into dark rings around her eyes. The small black dress skimmed the tops of her thighs, revealing the spokes of her legs which crossed at the bony points of her knees before disappearing into cavernous motorcycle boots. On each boot, Jack noticed, were glued two small feathers that slanted backwards and upwards from each side of her heel.

'You seem to know a lot about Raymond Chandler. Do you study him?' he asked.

'I went out with a college lecturer for a while. Back when I lived in Los Angeles. So anyway, you haven't told me what's wrong yet.'

'Do I really look that miserable?'

'Maybe. The name's Wilma. Hi.' She extended a hand.

'Jack,' he said, shaking the hand and feeling the bones of her fingers.

'I'm sorry I kind of grabbed you, Jack,' she said stubbing out the joint in the ashtray and starting to roll another from a small ziploc she pulled out of a pocket. 'To tell you the truth, I'm a little bit tense.'

'Why's that?'

'I'm about to have a tattoo. At five o' clock. I just came in here to have a smoke and relax but I guess I'm too nervous. That's why I came over. You looked like you couldn't concentrate anyway.'

'I couldn't,' Jack said. 'I don't know why I even tried.'

'You want a drink?' Wilma asked. 'I need a beer.'

'Sure. A beer would be good.'

'I know a coffeeshop near the tattooist's where they serve alcohol. Why don't we smoke this on the way?' They were silent for a while as Jack watched her raise the cigarette paper to her mouth and run her tongue along its gummed edge. After that they walked out of Basjoe, turned right and walked along a short street to the Achterburgwal where they turned right again, lighting the joint as they walked past the Amsterdam Grand and a couple of coffeeshops with tables scattered out over the pavement. Still not talking, they took a left over another bridge, passing the joint between them. These streets were busier. Around them milled groups of men in football shirts with carrier bags stacked with cans of lager, kids with backpacks slung over their shoulders and dreadlocks tied back in bunches, black guys in dirty shellsuits standing in groups at the street corners whispering, 'Coke? Ecstasy? Coke? Ecstasy?' or else saying nothing at all but staring at everyone with wild eyes as they walked past. Then Jack followed Wilma deeper into the red-light district, past the sex shops and theatres advertising 'live shows'. From the steps, brutish men with shaved heads and expensive suits called out to the people passing by while prostitutes in Lycra bodystockings and high heels looked down on them all, impassive behind the glass doors of their cubicles. Occasionally Wilma acknowledged an acquaintance and returned a greeting with a turn of her head and a brisk 'Hiya!' or 'How ya doin'?' Then they turned left again and walked down a street lined with nothing else but cubicles and at the end they came out on to Warmoesstraat. 'In here,' said Wilma before ducking into a coffeeshop called Green Peace.

Inside the sound system was blaring out Pink Floyd's *Wish You Were Here*. Where else in the world do they still play Pink Floyd albums in bars? Jack laughed to himself as his ears hummed with the sound of ambient synthesizers. At the bar he ordered a couple of pints from a wrecked American who air-guitared with twitching hands while the glasses filled. When he was sitting back down with Wilma at a table by the huge window, she started talking again.

'You see over there?' She pointed through the glass at a shop-front across the street. 'That's where I'm having it done.'

Jack looked over at the huge posters in the windows with small images dotted over them like nursery wallpaper and the name of the place painted in large letters on to the glass: Victor's Body Shop.

'Is this your first tattoo?' Jack asked.

'No. My sixth.'

'Sixth?'

'Yeah. You'd have thought they'd get easier, that you wouldn't get so nervous. But you don't. Or at least I don't.' She sipped at her beer. 'Maybe it's because after your first time, you know how much pain to expect.'

'Where have you got them? If you don't mind me asking.' Jack looked across at her. He couldn't see any tattoos, just her piercings: the two rings through her left nostril, the stud in her tongue that flashed and bobbed as she spoke, the bar through her right eyebrow, the graveyard of crosses that hung from her earlobes. Who knew what lay underneath her jacket or her dress?

123

'I don't mind. I'll show them to you if you like.' Wilma bent down and slid her right ankle out of its boot. On the pale skin sat the black shape of a reptile, about four inches long. It looked as if it was climbing up her leg, its tail whiplashing behind it.

'A lizard?'

'A gecko,' Wilma replied. 'This was the first one I ever got done, in LA when I was sixteen. Thought it wouldn't hurt, but it hurt like *shit*. The vibrations from the needle sent shockwaves all the way up my shin-bone and into my kneecap . . . took an hour and a half. See the way the guy did the claws and everything?'

Now Wilma pulled off her leather jacket revealing the long spindles of her fleshless arms. On the outside of her left bicep was a figure of eight lying on its side. Infinity. 'I got this one done next. It hurt less because of where it is but took three hours. You see how thick it is and how neat the curves are?' The loops were as thick as one of Jack's fingers. Wilma twisted in her seat and bared the outside of her other bicep at him. Marked on to the skin was the cartoon face of Wilma Flintstone, her hair marked out in a spiral above the triangular face and the points of her eyes. 'You get the show in England?' she asked.

'All the time.'

'Got this one done at the same time and at the same place, on Haight in San Francisco. Turned out the guy was a cartoon freak and loved all those old Hanna-Barbera shows. He kept shouting 'Wilmaaaaa!' every so often to make me laugh. My mom named me after her.'

'How long did that one take?'

'Another hour and a half. This one hurt worse. It's all outline which means the needle cuts slightly deeper. *As for this baby . . .*'

She turned her back to him, gathered her hair into a bunch over her shoulder and told him to unzip her. As Jack's fingers took hold of the metal tag and started to move downwards, he thought of Coco in a business meeting with her colleagues. He imagined that they would be sitting around a table in a boardroom, everyone in suits and talking about . . .

'Not the whole way!' Wilma laughed, interrupting his thoughts. Jack pulled the zipper down perhaps six inches, perhaps a little more, and the black material parted to reveal the white surface of her skin. Christ! he thought. He'd almost lowered his mouth and kissed the back of her neck. A reflex, he told himself, it was just a reflex. You unzip a girl's dress and your instinct's going to start taking over.

'What do you think?' Wilma asked. Across her shoulder-blades there was a set of four concentric rings, two black and two white (the bleached pink of her skin), each band half an inch wide. In the middle was a black circle perhaps one and a half inches in diameter.

'Put your hand on it,' Wilma said. Jack put his hand on it and stretched his fingers apart. The whole design was as wide as the distance between the tip of his thumb and little finger. What was it? A target? A black hole? A dark sun? Or just a set of concentric rings around a black circle? Underneath, the skin felt cold.

'That must have been painful,' he said.

'Painful! I wish it'd been that simple.' She was still turned away from him and Jack let his eyes wander down from the top of her neck to where her spine jutted out like a knotted rope. Again there was the urge to bend down and place his lips against her skin and again he thought of Coco . . . and *Christ!* They were in a coffeeshop in full public view and he had to be at Johanna's house in an hour. It would take half an hour to walk across town which meant . . .

'I was in the chair for eight hours,' Wilma said, still leaning away from him, 'at a place called Barbarians in Greenwich Village. I almost blacked out from the pain about four times and had to stop after five hours.' She now sat up straight which Jack took as a cue to zip up her dress. 'Almost didn't go back to have it finished.' She swivelled on the seat and was facing him again. 'But I did.' She drained her beer. 'I couldn't lie on my back for a fortnight afterwards. I got one more around my belly-button, a snake eating its own tail. I got it done at Victor's but I guess I can't show you that one without stripping off.'

Now Jack and Wilma both started rolling joints. Wilma went up to the bar saying that she needed something stronger and asked the wrecked American for a bottle of vodka from out of the freezer which he gave her and which, Jack noticed, she didn't pay for.

'You ever want one?' she asked when she returned to their table.

'What?'

'A tattoo?'

'I did once, but I never dared to take it any further.'

'Why not?'

'A combination of things really. I'm shit scared about pain and I could never think about what I wanted. I mean, they last for *ever*. I know people have them lasered off and so on, but essentially they're permanent. I toyed with the idea of having a seahorse or something but I could never find an image that made it seem worth facing up to the pain.'

Listening to himself, Jack felt a little cowardly. He'd wanted a tattoo since he was sixteen but he'd been frightened. And here was this girl who'd spent *days* under the tattooist's needle. He almost expected Wilma to laugh at him, but instead she told him that he should take a look in the window across the road.

'If you want one then you should get one,' she said to him.

126

'Even if it's only small. It would only take half an hour.' She laughed and smoke spurted out her nostrils. 'Easier than a trip to the dentist.'

'I couldn't,' Jack replied, suddenly feeling like he could at least take a look through the window. He looked at his watch. It was a quarter past four. Why not go across the street with her and take a look? He wouldn't see anything he wanted and he had to be making his way over to Johanna's in fifteen minutes in any case. Why not go over and take a look and then say goodbye to Wilma and return to what suddenly felt like normal life?

'Why not?' Wilma asked.

'Why not *what*?' Jack asked, forgetting what she'd last said.

'Why couldn't you get a tattoo?'

'My girlfriend would freak.'

'That's not a reason.'

'Yes it is,' Jack replied, suddenly a little indignant. Wilma knew nothing about him and Coco. Yet it was the first time he'd mentioned Coco all afternoon.

'No it's not. You just said you wanted a tattoo since you were sixteen. How old are you now? Twenty-four? Twenty-five?'

Jack replied that he was twenty-five.

'So how long have you been thinking about this?' Wilma continued. 'Nine fucking years.' She refilled both their glasses, Jack suddenly realising that he'd emptied his. 'All I'm saying is that you should come across the street with me and see what it's all about. I bet you've never even taken a look at a tattooist's.'

This was true. He'd thought about getting a tattoo many times, but never been anywhere near a tattoo parlour.

'Okay,' he said. 'We'll finish these joints and these drinks and I'll come and take a look.' In his mind, Jack told himself that he'd walk across the street with her and politely inspect the place and by then it would be four-thirty and time to say goodbye and walk through the city to Johanna's house where he'd find Coco and Marie waiting for him.

Now they sat in silence, both of them smoking. Every so often Jack sneaked glances at her, the way her throat rippled as she swallowed more vodka, the way her dress gripped her pinched torso (*cling! cling!* trilled the bicycle bells in the street outside), the faint camber of her breasts lying above the tapered angles of her ribcage and waist. In five minutes they'd finished their drinks and smoked their joints down to the roach. Then Wilma shrugged on her leather jacket and picked up the bottle which was now only half full and slotted it into the inside pocket before they cut through the ambling bodies that swayed up and down Warmoesstraat and came to a standstill outside Victor's Body Shop.

'What are you going to have done this time?' Jack asked Wilma as they stood facing the glass looking at the sample designs on the other side. He realised that she hadn't told him.

'I got the image in my pocket. Here! Take a look.' From a breast pocket, Wilma pulled out a folded piece of paper. It was a photocopy from a textbook of some sort, two columns of text around a picture of an African carving.

'It's a juju doll,' Wilma said. 'Come on, I'll introduce you to Victor,' and without another word she pushed her way inside. Jack stood in the street for a second and looked at his watch. 4.29. He had a minute before he was due to set off, he thought as he followed her through the swing doors.

The inside of the parlour was spacious and brightly lit. Wilma and Jack leaned on the small counter and Wilma rang the bell. Out of a doorway appeared a tall blond man who recognised Wilma with a smile.

'Hi Wilma.'

'Hi there, Victor. How ya doin'?'

'Okay. Had a lot of tourists in today.'

'Meet my friend Jack. He's thinking about having his first.'

'Hiya,' Jack nodded and Victor nodded back.

Victor was as pale as Wilma, and almost as skinny. Long, gangling arms sprouted out of his faded Motorhead vest, his skin a swirling tangle of colours and shapes. Every inch of his arms was decorated with some kind of design: twisting curlicues in black, green and red whose overall pattern Jack couldn't determine; an eagle on his left forearm pictured in a steep dive, its talons outstretched; a series of five bands that ringed around his right bicep; an approximation of the internal bones mapped out across the backs of his fingers and hands. As he ran one of these through his hair, Jack could see that even the shaved mound of his armpit had been tattooed with a pop-art explosion, the word *BLAM!* skewing out its centre.

'Do you know what you want?' Victor asked. 'We've got plenty of examples that might help you decide on something if you haven't.'

'I'll take a look.'

Jack left Wilma and Victor talking and wandered over to the large black ring-binders that sat on the small shelf running around the perimeter of the room. Telling himself that he'd say goodbye to Wilma as soon as he had a chance, he opened one and leafed through its laminated pages. The sample designs were arranged thematically as far as he could tell: a selection of skulls stared back up at him and a variety of cowled Grim Reapers beckoned towards him with skeletal fingers; a series of moons and stars came next followed by a crowd of naked women with muscular breasts and hips, some of them leaning back over the bonnets of hotrods, others astride huge motorcycles. *Blowtorch*

Bitch . . . Bad Motherfucker . . . Born to Lose. There were pages of superheroes: Superman, Spiderman and the Silver Surfer as well as a whole page of Batman designs and Bat-signals. Another folder contained pages of miscellaneous symbols: the zig-zags of lightning bolts; the variegated stripes of a barcode, the fused apostrophes of *yin* and *yang*; the Star of David; the symbols for radiation and for pi; the black sphere of an eightball; an apple with a bite taken out of it; a spider's web; an *ohm*; Thor's Hammer; a marijuana leaf; a handprint and two footprints. At the back was a section containing the Celtic Runes and their translations and examples of Arabic and Indian script: *Peace . . . Strength . . . Inner Fire.* Chinese characters followed: *Dragon . . . Tiger . . . Warrior . . . Truth.*

'Anything grab you?' Wilma was now looking over his shoulder.

'Not really,' Jack replied. 'I guess I wouldn't choose anything I'd seen here because . . . .well, it wouldn't really seem individual.'

He looked down at Wilma's boots, the feathers slanting back from the anklebones, and then glanced at his watch again. It was ten minutes to five.

'No it wouldn't, but maybe something you've seen's inspired you?' he heard Wilma reply. If he left straight away he'd only be twenty minutes late. Coco could be running late too, what with her colleagues inviting her to join them for the inevitable round of drinks . . .

'Victor says his brother Frank is free for the rest of the afternoon. You could have a small one done at the same time as me. It's up to you.'

Jack looked at his watch again but realised this was avoiding the real issue. He suddenly knew as he looked down at Wilma's legs that he wasn't frightened of the pain. Christ! He'd have a small one, high up on his upper arm where it had to be least painful. *How would Coco react if he came home with a tattoo?* She'd be shocked at first, he admitted to himself, but she'd soon adjust, wouldn't she? It wasn't as if she was a prude and *everybody* had tattoos these days. You saw them *everywhere*. Even people at Scheider & Rex had them. At a summer party the year before, to which 'spouses' and 'partners' had been invited, hadn't a drunk secretary hiked up her skirt and showed the dolphin marked on the outside of her thigh to a whole group of onlookers? Jack turned so that he was facing Wilma. Behind her, Victor leafed through a magazine.

'You should wait if you can't think of anything,' Wilma told him.

•

Fifteen minutes later, after smoking another joint in the street outside and drinking more vodka, Jack and Wilma were being led through a short passageway to a back room that looked like a barber's shop. Four swivel-chairs stood opposite four mirrors and Jack sat in one while Wilma sat across the aisle in another.

'Where are you going to have yours?' he asked.

'At the base of my back and a little bit to the left. About two inches long. Just a sentimental thing, you know?'

Victor walked in from washing his hands and pulled up a low stool beside Wilma. 'Only a small one today, huh?'

'Only a small one . . . *here!*' Wilma pointed to the space above her left buttock. 'About two inches long,' she repeated. Victor placed his finger and thumb on the area she'd pointed to.

'This big?'

Wilma nodded.

'Okay. I'll do a sketch in biro and you can check it.' Victor set the photocopied image of the juju doll on the counter beside him while Wilma got up, spun her chair round and then sat back down on it with her legs spread either side of the metal spine and her chest against the backrest. With both hands, she reached back and flipped up her skirt so that the skin was exposed, but also the two curves of her buttocks, the black delta of her underwear puckering up where her skin met the surface of the chair. At that moment Victor's brother took the nearest stool next to Jack and held out his hand.

'Hi!'

Jack shook it, tearing his eyes away from Wilma.

'Victor says you've chosen something.'

'A winged boot on my right arm. Do you know what I mean?'

'Like Mercury in Roman mythology?'

Jack nodded and Frank started to make a small sketch.

'Barefoot, a sandal or a boot?' he asked without emphasis.

'A boot. Definitely a boot.'

'With feather details or without?' Frank's hand continued moving above the paper.

'*With* . . . if you can fit them in,' Jack replied. 'I only want it small, about an inch across.'

Frank nodded. 'I think we can have a little detail.' The pen in Frank's hand dipped and scurried across the paper a few more times and then he passed it to Jack.

'Like this?'

Jack looked at Frank's drawing and nodded. A simple leather boot with elements of shading, the texture of the feathers suggested more than realised. Frank then guided Jack's chair to a position in front of the cubicle mirror and Jack took a last look at Wilma and the pale slope of her lower back which Victor was swabbing with alcohol before turning to face his own reflection. He looked pale and drunk. The whites of his eyes were fractured with red lines, his black stubble darkening every second (he'd shaved meticulously that morning yet there it was, rising through his skin), his broad nose greasy under the lights, the hint of a second chin sagging below his jawline. Jack looked for signs of nervousness in his eyes but found that he was staring back at himself almost without expression. In the mirror he saw Frank pull his stool closer and ask him to take off his jacket.

'First I am going to do a rough sketch on your arm with a pen so you can check the size and the proportions,' Frank told him and Jack nodded again. He shifted his weight in the chair so that his back was upright and tried to relax as Frank took hold of his arm and started to work on the surface of the skin with the tip of a biro. Immediately Jack felt himself tensing. Christ! The guy was just drawing on him and already his insides were squirming. Jack wondered what the needle would feel like, alternating this with trying to put the anticipation of pain out of his mind. All the people he'd ever spoken to on the subject of getting a tattoo talked about how painful it had been. They were almost reverent when it came to the pain (Jack felt the pen dig and probe the flesh of his arm) and used the same tone of voice as people who talked proudly of surviving broken arms, troublesome wisdom teeth, lengthy root-canal treatment and extracted tonsils. Jack hadn't broken anything, still possessed both his tonsils intact and had never been in the dentist's chair for more than twenty minutes of polite preventative inspection, so he still had no idea what to expect. And even Wilma had admitted that the pain had at times threatened to be unbearable.

'Take a look.' Frank had withdrawn his hand to reveal the outline of the image in blue biro. 'Like that?'

'Like that.'

'What colour do you want?'

'Black.'

'Okay. I'll get myself ready and then we'll start.' Frank now swabbed down the small counter to his right with a disinfectant spray and then laid out a sheet of paper he tore from a roll and taped down its edges. On this he set out the needle and the ink and then pulled on surgical gloves. It was at this point that Jack felt his bowels freeze and his heartbeat jolt upwards into a higher gear. Suddenly he was scared, a feeling that intensified as he felt Frank swab away at his arm, and as Jack looked away, there was the sound of the needles, a flanging whirr . . . and then the first *sensation*, like burning, on the skin of his arm.

'I'm going to do the general outline first. Okay?'

'Okay.'

Jack gritted his teeth and tried to centre his thoughts on the sensation of his molars grinding together. Frank was now talking to him in an easy-going tone, asking him questions about London, whether various clubs he'd frequented still existed, whether Jack had been to certain bars that he used to go to. Apparently Frank had lived there for a year when he was twenty.

'What were you doing in London?' Jack asked, steeling himself against the pain. It felt as if someone was taking a cheese-grater to his arm and grinding it mercilessly up and down against his skin.

'Nothing really,' Frank replied, 'I played keyboards in a band. I worked in a bar for a while, only for a short time. I designed the artwork for a record that a friend of mine made and drew a comic strip for a rock fanzine. I was really into graffiti back then so that took up a lot of my time.'

Jack, who had been the reluctant holder of many low-paid jobs in a variety of low-paying industries, had once spent a summer vacation working for Septex Services, a private company to whom other institutions (most notably London Transport and British Telecom) handed out cleaning contracts. Expecting to be a 'litter picker', Jack had been detailed to the 'graffiti squad' and had spent the summer wrapped in a protective plastic suit spraying detergent at the scrawled surfaces of buses and tubes, of bus stops and tube stations, the arches of flyovers and bridges, the scratched and pitted surfaces of phone kiosks and letterboxes. The shift lasted six hours, Jack clamping on his facemask at midnight and not taking it off again for six hours as his team scoured away the paint and ink down at the depot, or else outside on the streets of the sleeping city, the scribbles and doodles slowly fading in the acid foam that originated in the tanks strapped to his back. Jack initially decided against sharing this with Frank. Maybe graffiti artists hated the cleaners the same way gangsters hated the police? But feeling the relentless searing pain in his arm, Jack needed something to talk about. The conversation was like a relay race, a baton being handed from sentence to sentence. If one of them didn't keep talking then the baton would drop and Jack wouldn't have anything to say or anything to listen to and he'd be back to clenching his teeth against the pain. So he told Frank about his job and it turned out that Frank had been in London the same summer that Jack had worked for Septex.

'That's amazing,' Jack remarked. 'I hope I didn't destroy something you'd done.'

'Wouldn't matter to me if you had,' Frank replied. 'Some guys, they feel good when they see one of theirs up on a wall day after day. Me? The moment of satisfaction comes the second it's finished, when you stand back and see it for the first time, when you can still smell the fumes coming off the wet paint. Of course, the moment is only a moment and then you're running away in case you're about to get caught. Most of them I never saw again after that.'

'It sounds a bit like tattoos.'

'Very similar,' Frank agreed. 'Once a customer's left here I often never see the design again. Just a quick moment before I dress the skin and that's it. They pay and go.'

Now Frank started talking about other things he'd done in London. As Jack listened (he was concentrating and felt the beads of sweat collecting on his forehead), he forced himself to look into Frank's eyes, at the marbling of blues and greys in the wide rings of his irises, the miniature brown hairs that sprouted out between his eyebrows, the creases at the side of his mouth, the translucent yellow of his teeth, the tiny white swelling of pus at the base of a follicle under his lower lip.

'I even wrote a novel,' Frank was telling him and Jack sighed internally because at least he could talk about this and not think about the sharp *twangs* in his upper arm.

'What kind? I mean, what was it about?' Jack heard his voice tremble now, and thought that he felt the needle dig a little deeper into his arm, the bite of the agony finding a new edge as the metal probed deeper into his flesh.

'A science-fiction novel. You like science fiction?'

'Y-yes,' replied Jack, thinking that he only liked science-fiction *films*, that he'd never read a science-fiction *novel*.

'It's about . . .'

Now Jack could hardly control his thoughts. He heard Frank's voice sure enough, telling him of how the novel dealt with three 'timelines' – one in the present day, one in the Pleistocene era a million and a half years ago, the third occurring a hundred and fifty years into the future – but through his mind paraded a stream of images: Coco when she had said goodbye to him a few days before; Marie when he had first been introduced to her; Wilma flipping up her dress to reveal her buttocks and thighs minutes earlier; his parents; an old girlfriend whom he'd taken to Amsterdam the second time he'd visited (they'd split up, arguing on their second night in the city). How many people did Frank see in pain? Jack wondered to himself. How many widened eyes and crimped mouths and strange conversations – how much seeping blood?

'I-I-I'm writing a book t-t-too,' Jack heard himself stammer. The fingernails of his left hand were biting into the sweaty surface of his palm.

'Oh yeah? What about?'

'It's a-about a writer who m-meets this woman one day a year . . .' Jack warbled. His eyes were now locked on to Frank's and not leaving them, not for a moment, 'e-e-every year for eight years.'

'Is he single or married?' Frank asked.

'Married.'

'Happily?'

'H-h-he thinks so,' replied Jack, thinking that it was amazing to look into another person's eyes for so long and with such *need*. When did he ever look into Coco's eyes with as much longing? 'But then one day he meets this woman, a teenage sweetheart of his who h-h-he hasn't s-seen for ages . . .'

When did he ever look into Coco's eyes with as much longing? As they talked (and Frank seemed perfectly at ease returning his gaze every few seconds as he looked up from the point of the needle) Jack watched Frank's eyelids blink, watched his eyeballs twitch in their sockets.

'And what happens?'

'W-well they meet in a bar . . . b-by accident,' Jack heard himself say. His right arm now felt dead, saturated with pain. He was on the verge of screaming out that he wanted Frank to stop and getting up out of the chair and running through the streets outside. '– a-and they start talking . . .'

'Does he feel guilty?'

'When?'

'When he starts talking to his teenage sweetheart?'

'Err . . .' Just when Jack thought that things couldn't get any worse, he again felt the needle drive deeper into his arm, the pitch of the electric buzzing again modulating for a second, as if it were coming up against a greater resistance. For a second, Jack's mind saw his arm disappearing in a gush of blood and gristle.

'I g-g-guess so . . . I mean, *y-yes!*'

'And do they sleep with each other?'

Jack was straining for words and at the same time fighting for breath, fighting back tears and fighting to stay in the chair. Now his mouth moved and he heard words that sounded as if he was speaking them.

'Well . . . it's a c-case of . . .'

Now Jack couldn't speak. He felt himself giving in to the agony, surrendering to it. And yet he still heard his voice though he hardly sensed his mouth moving or his mind processing any information other than the fact that Frank was looking straight at him and that the needle felt as if it was probing *even deeper* . . . that he felt his eyes widen at a sudden stabbing . . . that he saw Frank's eyes widen almost imperceptibly in silent recognition of what he was feeling . . .

'That's it. Take a look.'

'It's finished?' Jack was suddenly aware that the whirring of the needle had stopped.

'All done,' Frank replied, sitting back in his stool.

Jack looked down at his arm and saw the black ink glistening on his arm. It looked like black oil, the shaded boot like a slick sitting on the surface of the skin rather than indelibly inserted into the meat of his arm through thousands of perforations, the outline of the feathers and the wings almost *dripping* as if they'd been drawn on with a fountain pen. Jack felt a smile slide across his face, a shit-eating grin that corresponded with the rush that surged through him.

'You like it?'

'I love it.'

Frank dressed Jack's arm and gave him a leaflet with information on how to let the skin heal. Wilma was going to be another fifteen minutes so Jack rolled himself a small joint and smoked it out on the street, almost wallowing in the sensation of his pumping adrenaline. When he went back inside, Wilma was standing with Victor and Frank by the front desk.

'How much do I owe you?' asked Jack.

'A hundred and twenty guilders,' Frank replied. Jack paid the money and shook their hands.

Then he and Wilma walked out into Warmoesstraat, the sun starting to sink behind the buildings on either side of the street. Jack checked his watch. It was half-past six. He was late whatever way he looked at it and he was in *trouble* whatever way he looked at it. *Fuck it!* he thought as he felt Wilma slide an arm round his.

'I need a drink and a smoke and another drink,' he told her. 'Shall we go back to Green Peace?'

'Can we go somewhere quieter?'

Jack searched her question for further intimacy (her hand had squeezed his forearm) but her tone was blank, preoccupied.

'Follow me,' she said with more energy and Jack felt her weight guide him through the crowds, past the bars that poured music out into air, along narrow streets where the neon lights

139

shimmered above doorways and the grim shapes of the waiting women. They turned a few corners and walked south down the Oudezijds Voorburgwal, past coffeeshops where drinkers crowded the pavements and the cycle paths and held up traffic. After a while they crossed Rokin and the Spui and reached a part of the city that was quieter, passing windows through which Jack saw families eating dinner, couples watching television, an old woman watering her plants. He wondered what Coco was doing and thought of how worried she must be, but also realised that thinking about her elicited no remorse, no desire to suddenly change direction and walk to wherever she was. After they'd walked a few more streets, Wilma and Jack stopped at a bar called Momentum where they drank Long Island Ice Teas in quick gulps, the filters crumpling in their fingers as they sucked the life out of their cigarettes. Then they moved on to The Zoo, a coffeeshop where Wilma again seemed to know the barman and again came away with a bottle of tequila without paying for it. Outside, they found a table overlooking the canal, sat down and passed the bottle between them. They'd hardly said a word to each other since leaving Victor's. Now Wilma spoke.

'How do you feel?'

'Amazing. I've never felt like I did when it was all over. A huge rush just crashing through me . . .' Jack stopped to sluice back more tequila. 'Better than coke, better than speed, better than anything. I felt *omnipotent*!'

'It's a real kick, isn't it,' Wilma agreed. She was sitting with her chair pulled up alongside his and Jack realised that his left arm had fallen loosely across her shoulders. 'How does *it* feel?' she asked.

'A little sore. You?'

'Sore. Gotta keep drinking,' she said as Jack pulled out his bag of Silver Haze and poured the rest of the contents into a rolling paper.

'I heard what you were saying to Frank. You never told me you were a writer?'

'You never asked. And anyway I'm still writing my first book so I don't know if I can call myself a writer quite yet.'

'I knew you were a writer. That's what I told myself when I saw you reading *The Long Goodbye*. You do anything else?'

'I used to but not any more. I live with my girlfriend and she more or less supports us.'

'What does she do?' Wilma asked.

'She's a corporate solicitor. I stay at home and write in the mornings. In the afternoons I clean the house, pick up her daughter Marie from school and do the laundry and the cooking and things like that.'

Wilma was silent. Jack was silent.

'Sounds like a good arrangement. Better than cleaning graffiti,' she said after a while. Jack didn't reply and instead lit the joint. He waited for Wilma to break the silence but she didn't say anything. He looked at his watch – it was now a quarter to nine.

'The thing is,' he started, handing her the joint, 'it doesn't feel like a good arrangement at the moment. I can't seem to write and I can't seem to explain to myself *why* – and I certainly can't explain it to her . . .'

'What's her name?'

'Coco. Really it's Chantal but everyone calls her Coco outside of work.'

'And does she put any pressure on you?'

'I used to think that she didn't. But these days . . . .'

'Jack. Can I ask you a question?'

'Sure.'

'How long have you been feeling like this?' Her voice was quiet and steady.

'About six months.'

'And have you spoken to her about it?'

'No. I guess I don't know what to say to her. I mean, what would I tell her? I keep thinking that at any moment my writing will come together and that I'll feel happier and get a clearer picture of how I feel about her.'

'You should talk to her.'

'And say *what*?' he asked. Wilma passed the joint back to Jack and he took in a deep lungful of smoke, the juices collecting on the surface of his tongue. 'Before I met her I lived in a bedsit and worked at shitty places doing shitty jobs and I never had enough energy to write. Or maybe I just couldn't write and living in a bedsit just made everything feel even worse, as if my whole life was moving towards a dead end. Now I live in a comfortable place where I don't have to share a bathroom with the mad postmen and winos who used to live in the same building as me. I don't have to worry about how I'm going to make the bills or the rent or whether my computer's about to get stolen. I'd feel pretty stupid telling her that I felt . . . *dissatisfied*.'

'That's a whole list of negatives and more about your living conditions than about her.'

They were silent again, smoking the joint until it was dead. Jack got up and went inside to buy a couple more grams and by the time he came out it was ten past nine.

'Okay,' he said, lifting their bottle to his lips, 'at ten o'clock I go and find her.'

'Where is she?'

'At Johanna's house. Johanna is Marie's grandmother. That's where I'm meant to be meeting Coco . . . where I *was* meant to be meeting Coco.'

'At what time?'

Now Jack laughed.

'At five.'

'Is she gonna be mad at you?' Wilma asked.

'She's going to be furious,' Jack replied. 'Too late now to do anything about it.' He started rolling another joint, hands moving instinctively. 'Let's drink. Christ! I haven't had a day like this for too long.'

'I got one more question.'

'What's that?'

'In your novel: does the guy sleep with his teenage sweet-heart, the woman he meets one day each year? You were about to tell Frank but you got interrupted.'

'He wants to when he first runs into her again – and at one point he thinks that he will. But they just have an amazing afternoon together, talking about their lives and explaining how they've changed since they were kids and what they want out of their futures.'

'And they decide to meet again, on that same day each year?'

'How did you know?'

'A lucky guess.'

'Well, you're right. They plan to meet for just one day the following year, and also the year after that, the central character never telling his wife about it – it's his secret.'

'What happens?' Wilma asked.

'Well, I've still got to write this bit, but one year she doesn't show up. The next year he goes back thinking that there's a small chance she'll be at their rendezvous. But again, she's not there. This time he tries to track her down, and when he finally manages to contact one of her parents, they tell him she died.'

143

•

A clock somewhere struck ten as Jack stood up and scrabbled through his pockets. The tequila was half empty, the second bag of Silver Haze empty save for a few green crumbs, and he swayed a little unsteadily on his feet as he searched for the piece of paper on which he had written Johanna's address.

'Where the fuck is it? If I've lost it I'm *really* in trouble.' It wasn't in any of his jacket pockets nor in his travel-bag. Eventually he found it folded up in a corner of his now empty wallet, where he'd put it before leaving the flat in Olympia so that he wouldn't lose it.

'Where the hell is this?' he said, squinting at his own handwriting. Wilma took the note from him.

'Hmmm . . . Prinsenstraat. It's about twenty minutes away. I'll take you there.'

Jack shouldered his bag and felt Wilma slide her arm round his. Again, he felt her weight guiding him through the streets and along the banks of the canals, the fluid reflections of the streetlights and the glow of the lit windows bobbing on the surface of the dark water. As they walked, they passed couples walking hand-in-hand and Jack imagined what it would be like to spend the night with Wilma, to walk with her through the streets cloaked in intimacy until they found themselves outside where she lived. They'd go upstairs and lie down on her bed and smoke a last joint and then roll towards each other's bodies. Later, they'd talk about *The Long Goodbye* and *The Big Sleep*, something he could never do with Coco.

'What about you?' Jack asked.

'What about me?'

'I don't know anything about you except that you had a tattoo done in LA, then one in San Francisco, another in New York and one in Amsterdam . . .'

'I had *two* done in San Francisco,' Wilma interrupted. 'And now I've had *two* done in Amsterdam. And you know that I went out with a college professor in LA who was obsessed with Raymond Chandler.'

'And I know *that*. What else?'

'What else?' She stopped for a second and Jack found that he was standing facing her, the tall houses looming up behind her.

'I guess it doesn't matter if I tell you,' she said, fumbling for a cigarette. As she lit it, Jack saw the flame trembling – maybe it was just the breeze? 'I have a habit of getting myself into bad relationships with bad guys. Like with the college professor in LA. He used to treat me like shit. You want to know more?' Jack nodded.

'The last few months I've been going with a guy in Amsterdam. Not a nice guy. Maybe you know the type? The sort that trades in drugs and prostitutes and likes to call them his "business interests". Well, I left him about a fortnight ago after he kicked me down the stairs one too many times and I asked an old boyfriend to lend me some money so I could get clear of him. Now I've spent the money so I've got to go back. At least for a while.'

Jack wanted to ask her why she didn't leave Amsterdam, fly back to America or somewhere else in the world, but he knew that she wouldn't have an answer. He even thought of looking in his wallet to see how much money he had to give her – but realised that of the three hundred guilders he'd arrived in Amsterdam with, he only had about fifteen left jangling around in his pocket.

'What's he going to do when you go back? Does he even want you back?'

'Oh he wants me back alright, if only for the sake of his

145

wounded ego. And he won't do anything to me, at least not physically, at least not straight away. Maybe this time I'll be able to work out a better plan.'

They walked on, arm-in-arm again, Jack again thinking about what it would be like to spend the night with her, to wake up with her and spend long leisurely mornings in Basjoe. No more having to hear about the latest developments at Scheider & Rex, no more school runs (though he would miss Marie terribly), no more ironing the 'family laundry' (what was he *doing* ironing the 'family laundry'?). By the time they reached the address on Prinsenstraat, it was half-past ten.

'This is it. You want that one there.' Wilma pointed at a house about twenty yards away. They turned towards each other and Jack looked at her face, the point of her nose, the crease where her lips met, the points where her eyelashes met her eyelids. The dark hairs (the same colour as her roots, Jack noticed) seemed stitched into the skin rather than growing out of it.

'Is she going to throw a fit?' Wilma asked.

Jack nodded. 'Probably.'

'Well I hope you come out the other side okay.'

'You too,' Jack replied.

'Me too.'

Jack kissed her on the cheek, feeling the dangling crosses of her earrings brush against his skin. 'Take care of yourself,' he said.

'Always do,' she replied. Already she was moving away from him and back towards the centre of the city. She rounded a corner, looking back at him for a second before she disappeared from view. And then Jack turned and started walking towards the house. All the lights seemed to be switched on and he felt his eyes twitch with every step. He took a deep breath a couple of feet from the door. Coco would be fine, he told himself. She'd be more relieved that he'd finally arrived rather than angry that he was so late. Jack took another deep breath and then reached towards the buzzer.

●

If Jack had spent the afternoon too drunk to realise that he was stoned and too stoned to realise that he was drunk, then he'd spent the last four hours too full of adrenaline and excitement to realise that he was both too drunk and too stoned. Now the adrenaline seemed to evaporate from his bloodstream, the ability to stand upright or focus his eyes or form words deserting him. He reached for the buzzer a second time. It kept moving but eventually his hand tracked it down and he leaned against it. Somewhere in his skull a buzzer sounded. Best to play it simple, he told himself, just apologise and try and be as charming as possible. It was only half-past ten so it wasn't like it was the middle of the night. The door was pulled open and Coco stood there, backlit by the lamps burning in the hallway.

'I'mshorryI'mlate.'

'Where have you been?'

'I . . .'

'Where have you been? Where have you been?' Coco's voice steadily rose in volume. Jack thought that she couldn't repeat herself again but he was wrong.

'Where have you been?'

'I . . . I . . .' Jack pushed past her into the hallway and put his bag down.

'Where have you been?' she asked again, now hissing quietly. 'I've been almost worried to death . . . Marie's been asking what the hell's going on . . . I would have called the police except that Johanna told me that they wouldn't do anything for a couple of days.'

'I'vebeenintown . . . aroundtown . . .'

'And you didn't think to call? We've been sitting here for over four hours wondering what's happened to you . . . I thought you'd been hit by a tram or something . . .' Coco's nose twitched. 'You've been drinking.'

'I . . . I . . .'

'You've been drinking. You're totally drunk.'

Now there was another presence in the hallway. A woman in her sixties appeared at a doorjamb, thin, petite, immaculately dressed. Johanna, thought Jack, remarking that she looked uncannily like Coco's mother. He held out his hand. 'Hi . . . pleeshedt'meetyou,' he heard himself say. The old woman paused before taking his hand with a tentative grasp and he noticed that she shared a look with Coco before disappearing back through the doorway.

'WhereshMarie . . . IwantoseeMarie . . . ishshestillawake?'

'She's asleep. Finally. Who have you been drinking with? On your own? You're totally drunk. How much have you had?'

'Whereshourbedroom . . . Ineedtoputmythingshaway . . .'

'*We* are going upstairs where you are going to tell me where you've been this afternoon. I think I deserve an explanation.'

Coco pushed past him and led the way up the steep flight of stairs. Jack followed, hands and feet working together as if he were climbing a rope ladder or a cliff-face. To make matters worse there was another flight of stairs to be negotiated after the first and another to crawl up after that. By the time he followed Coco into their bedroom Jack was gagging for breath, his t-shirt a wet rag.

'I'lljushthangupmyjacketandthenshayhellotoJohanna.'

Jack took his jacket off and threw it on the bed. The room seemed desperate to keel over on to one side so Jack let it, sprawling out on to the bed.

'What the hell are *these*?'

Her voice now seemed distant, metallic, impersonal, like a public-address system at an airport.

'I'llgetupinashecond . . .'

'Did you hear me? I asked what the hell are these doing on you jacket?' She was pulling at a long blonde hair that had meshed itself against the fabric.

'Idunno.'

'You don't . . .*you've hurt yourself!*'

'Wha?'

'You've hurt yourself?' Coco stared at the bandage on Jack's arm.

'Ishatattoo . . . itdushen'thurtshomushnow.'

'A tattoo, Jack! What the *fuck* have you done to yourself?'

Coco was finally silent for a moment and Jack closed his eyes. The ceiling was spinning and rolling and Jack felt himself gag. *I don't understand . . . I don't understand . . . I don't understand.* Jack slithered across the bed and reached for a metal wastepaper basket and felt the whiplash of his stomach muscles, acids on his tongue. There was a second and third set of convulsions before he could wipe his mouth on his sleeve and sigh, a cold sweat collecting around his neck, on his forehead, at the small of his back. At least now he could lie back and let it all go.

3

'What kind of girl loses one shoe?' Jack heard Coco say, but didn't pay her much attention as his eyes scanned the cobbles for the boot's partner. At the same time (and picturing the tattoo on his arm concealed by the stained dressing) he remembered the men standing outside the prostitutes' cubicles the afternoon before, men with faces like Rottweilers, with mouths like clenched fists and Wilma telling him how she'd been kicked down the stairs.

'Probably the sort of girl who wears shoes like that,' Coco said. 'Look! It's got little feathers *glued* to the sides. How *naff* . . .'

Suddenly Jack wanted to search the city for her, maybe ask the wrecked American at Green Peace where he might find her and check that she was okay, or else ask Victor or the guys at Basjoe. But he knew it was impossible. What could he say to Coco? How could he explain it? Jack looked at Marie stroking the cat and knew that he couldn't just get up and leave.

'Losing both shoes you could put down to carelessness or drunkenness – but to lose one? It makes me think something more *disturbed* has happened . . . I mean, who loses one shoe? Who would want to take off *just one*?'

In the deep-sea chamber of his suffering head Jack heard Coco's words echo and reverberate. Did she always talk this much? Now she was talking about how she'd lost her shoes at a law-school ball because she'd 'been so drunk'. *We were walking around Fulham Palace . . . me and this guy called Rollo Banbury.* She'd lost both shoes – but of course she'd never have lost *just one*. Coco carried on talking, going on and on and on. Did she ever stop? Would she ever stop? Something was growing inside Jack, an inner voice getting louder and louder. Why didn't she *ever* stop talking? Did he really want to know about Rollo Banbury and the law-school ball? And what kind of person used the word *naff* anyway? Soon this voice seemed to blank out everything else. Jack saw her mouth move but then glanced across the canal at the streets of Amsterdam and almost stood up from his chair, not hearing any voice other than his own telling him that if he didn't do something soon he'd explode.

OFF THE WRIST

The guilty catch themselves.

Anon

Adam realised that he was feeling a little drunk, and more than a little bewildered: how had they got on to the subject of sex?

He was sitting opposite Kate in the university bar. One moment they were talking about the seminar they'd just attended, the last class of the term on the German Democratic Republic; the next moment, Kate was comparing sex with music, chortling into her third pint of cider as she discussed genres, track listings and the 'difficult third album', taking the conceit to ridiculous extremes while Adam tried not to squirm too much in his seat. Initially, part of Adam had liked the fact that she was talking to him about sex as if he was one of the girls. But after a while, he wasn't so sure. The plus point was that while she was talking to him about sex, things seemed pretty sexy between them (and Adam did so desperately want to have sex with Kate). But every so often, this feeling would be sidelined in favour of another conclusion: what if she was talking to him like he was one of the girls because that was how she thought about him. Just one of the girls. The speccy dweeb who she sat next to in History. Adam could imagine her talking to her friends later on. *So, do you fancy him then?* they'd ask. *Him!* she'd scoff. *Of course I don't. I mean, he's a lovely guy and all that, of course he is, great for going for a pint with after class and for helping me when I haven't done the background reading or when I'm stuck on an essay. But I don't think of him like that, no way. I just don't. He's more like a friend, y'know, a mate, one of the . . .*

'Most guys wonder why they're just one-hit wonders,' Kate

sighed, slurring slightly as she rolled a cigarette. 'They should try making real music rather than three-minute pop songs.' She sounded throatily conspiratorial.

'So what's your favourite album then?' Adam asked, trying to sound salacious and innocent at the same time. Wasn't that how it was done, this flirting thing?

'I dunno, one of those prog-rock concept albums, you know, one of those records that goes on for hours and comes in four parts.' Kate broke down into laughter again before composing herself. 'No, seriously,' and now she looked Adam straight in the eyes, 'I reckon a girl wants variety. She doesn't just want one thing all the time. Sometimes she wants soul – deep, meditative and lingering; sometimes she wants rock – hard, uncompromising and unrelenting; on a Saturday night she might want something predatory, something hip-grinding and funky, something like *Saturday Night Fever*; but on a Sunday morning she'll want something totally different, something a little more blissed out, something like "Sunday Morning" by The Velvet Underground, d'you know it?'

Adam nodded his head, though her directness was definitely starting to make him feel uneasy, and in spite of the fact that he'd never heard any 'Velvet Underground'. He'd never listened to music whilst growing up, and still didn't really take much interest. When he was younger, he'd occasionally listened to whatever was on the radio, not because he liked it but simply because it was there, or else spent his time trying to avoid listening to the growling sounds his elder brother seemed addicted to locking himself away with, the curtains drawn, the patchouli joss-stick smoking away in the corner. His brother had been an obsessive goth ('*Goth*, Dad, not goth*ic*,' he'd whined incessantly throughout his adolescence), spending six years of his youth dressing in black clothes that had washed out to grey, not going outside and continually arguing with their mum as to whether she really did understand why he needed to crimp his hair before attending his grandmother's sixty-fifth birthday party.

Now his brother managed a call-centre up in Scotland and listened to whatever his wife listened to. And Adam had moved on to listening to whatever his flatmates listened to: house and garage – but also drum 'n' bass, hip hop and rap, R 'n' B. And there was always the radio.

'So anyway, are we going or what?' Kate asked briskly while she waved at someone she knew on the other side of the room.

'Where?'

'Out.'

'Oh right . . .' Adam hadn't been prepared for Kate to take the initiative.

'You were telling me before class that your flatmates knew some people who knew the guys who'd hired out the room above The Blushing Bride tomorrow night for a party. Shall we go?'

'Errr . . .'

Adam had been building up to asking Kate out in the classroom earlier on, while they'd been waiting for Professor Thornton to arrive, planning to casually insert his request into the conversation they were having about the last weekend of term. But he'd only got as far as mentioning the party, all the while preparing himself for the inevitable and imminent knockback, ('That's *sweet*,' she would tell him, 'but I've already got *plans* . . .') when 'Thumbscrews' Thornton had stumbled in, a fraying pile of belligerent tweed and corduroy, and the room had fallen into a fearful silence. Now, after class, Adam couldn't believe that he'd been spared the necessity of being persuasive.

'Errr . . . yeah . . . let's go,' he said. 'Yeah, let's. I mean . . . er . . . the party starts at ten so we could meet for dinner beforehand . . . if you like.' Adam felt as if dinner was something he should offer her.

'Well we could. But you know what I say . . .' Kate stopped to gulp at her pint. 'Eating is *cheating*. You get pissed more cheaply on an empty stomach,' she gulped again, 'and I'm skint right now. D'you know The Brazen Cow?'

Adam did. It was a tough-looking drinker out on the ring road, in reality called The Grazing Cow but renamed by the city's wittier students.

'They do pound-a-pint house lager there. We could get in early, get a few down us and then get to the party later on. If we're hungry we can stop by the chippy next to the cinema. See what happens, eh?'

Kate drained the rest of her pint and then shovelled her stuff from off the table and into her bag.

'So, shall I come round yours around seven?' she asked. 'You live on Stanley Street, don't you? That's nearer to the Cow than my place.'

'Yeah,' Adam nodded, 'it is. And seven would be good. Seven would be great. See you then.'

'What number?'

'Number forty-three.'

'Great, see you there, got to go, bye.'

Adam watched Kate walk off, her hips as they swung away from him, the back pockets of her jeans, the waistband of her pants visible above the faded blue denim, a strip of bare skin between this and her t-shirt. And Adam was still thinking about this strip of skin as he boarded the bus home twenty minutes later. He had kissed Janine, the last girl he'd been out with (they'd been out to the pub three times and got as far as stripping down to their underwear and fooling around on her mattress after the last of these excursions), on that exact spot, on the skin at the base of her spine, but he couldn't remember what it *felt* like. If Adam concentrated long enough on the memory of kissing Janine there, he was able to imagine kissing Kate there. But he still couldn't remember what it had *felt* like. Adam tried to remember what it had been like with Franny, the last girl he'd fooled around with before Janine, but that had been ages ago, a whole . . .

Adam's thoughts were interrupted by a guttural cough and he looked up to see a pensioner staring down at him. She was glaring. Glaring. For a second, Adam blushed, imagining that she was reading his mind, but then he realised that she merely wanted to sit down and was indignant that he hadn't yet given up his seat.

'Please,' he said, rising. He was getting off soon anyway.

•

The walk from the bus-stop took ten minutes and as Adam trudged through the dark streets, he observed the variety of Christmas decorations hanging in each lounge window that he passed, the gaudy tinsel and the neon Santas. When he arrived back home, Adam found that his flatmates were staying in for the evening. Elton was in the hallway as he came in through the front door, on the telephone to Samantha, his 'girl back home' in Peterborough.

'I know babes, I know,' he purred into the receiver, 'I find it hard too . . . no, I really do, but we've managed to be apart for ten weeks already and still stay together . . . yeah, I know the holiday's only a few weeks, but we'll have the whole summer to be with each other, won't we . . .'

Elton put his hand over the mouthpiece and winked at Adam.

'You alright, mate?'

'Yeah.'

'Yeah?'

'Yeah.'

'The others are in the lounge. I better get back to *this*.'

Elton rolled his eyes and then went back to murmuring at Samantha while Adam proceeded into the lounge to find Danny, Simon and Paulo on their hands and knees, the PlayStation flickering away in the corner.

'These friggin' carpets.' This from Danny as he rummaged through the plastic laundry basket that served as the lounge bin, somewhere to empty ashtrays and throw beer cans and pizza boxes. 'Small light-brown dots alternating with small dark-brown dots. How the fuck are we expected to find lost dope on this?'

'What about looking across the floor at ground level,' suggested Simon as he pressed the side of his head against the carpet and scanned the area in front of his face with a bicycle lamp. Paulo was picking up each cushion in turn and shaking it down as if it were a potentially armed suspect, at the same time asking Danny to visualise the last time he'd 'seen it' and suggesting that he 'retrace his steps'.

'If you tell me to retrace my steps one more fucking time, I'll . . .'

'You'll do what . . .'

'– I'll . . .'

'Found it!' Simon held the lost eighth aloft. 'It was down here, in this Chicken Basket box under the sofa. Someone get some beers from the fridge.'

Elton walked in at that point with an armful of cans so they all sat down.

'That Samantha on the phone?' Simon asked.

'Yeah.'

'She still giving you a hard time mate?'

'Yeah. A bit. But she still doesn't want to split up so I guess I'll get to shag her all through the holidays.'

'Who're you seeing tomorrow night?'

'Some Scottish bird. Lucy.'

'Shit football team, the Scottish,' offered Simon, picking up his bong.

'But I've also got to have lunch with that Diana girl again, tomorrow in the afternoon. She'd better not want to come to the party as well.'

'*Oh . . . Diana*,' chorused Andy, Paulo and Danny as they always did when her name was mentioned, to a tune that Adam had been reliably informed was Ultravox's 'Vienna'.

'Where're you going for lunch?'

'Her place,' smirked Elton.

'She got any flatmates?'

'Nah.' Elton smirked again, folding his arms behind his head, 'She lives on her own. Got a classy one-bedroom flat above that posh delicatessen on Potter Street.'

'What about you, Adam?' asked Danny. 'You asked that Kate out yet, the one you've been ogling all term?'

'Errr . . .'

'You *did!*'

'Errr . . .'

'I don't believe it,' scoffed Paulo, 'and she's coming to the party with you tomorrow?'

Adam nodded, deciding not to confuse the matter by admitting that it had been the other way around, that *she'd* asked *him* out. 'She wants to go to The Grazing Cow first.'

'The Brazen Cow! She wants to get tanked up, mate. You're *in there . . .*'

161

'Adam, you've fucking pulled, mate . . .'

'You'll be Clearing the Pipes like the rest of us tomorrow night . . .'

'Well I don't know about that . . .'

●

Clearing the Pipes. Adam shifted in his seat, sipped at his can of beer, stared at his knees, laughed nervously. Clearing the Pipes was something the other four regularly indulged in before a night out at the Campus Disco or one of the city's various nightclubs. There was always the same sequence of events: they'd each loiter in their own rooms with music blaring and get ready, splashing themselves with aftershave and pulling on clean clothes and polished shoes before they assembled in the lounge to wait for their mini-cab, a final joint passing from one hair-gelled head to the next. And then the cab would honk its horn outside and they'd all stand up to leave. *Everyone clear?* one of them would ask. *Clear!* the others would reply in turn, like a disciplined squadron of paratroopers preparing to jump into enemy territory, which would mean that they'd all had a wank earlier on. Adam sometimes went out with them (he didn't really like nightclubs – he hated dancing and he could never hear what anyone was saying). But he'd never joined in when it came to Clearing the Pipes. In the beginning, they'd asked him why not.

'You should give it a go,' Elton once told him. 'What if you pull tonight? You'll have a full tank, you'll be jumpy, you could . . . *misfire*. Why not whack one off before you go out? If you pull, then you'll really be able to knock the back end out of her.'

'You only get one chance to make a first impression,' Danny had advised.

'You don't want word going round all the girls that you

can't *deliver*,' Paulo told him, 'or you'll never score in this city again.'

Adam had told them that it just wasn't 'his thing', which was vague enough to have the others shrugging their shoulders and muttering things like 'Whatever, mate' and 'Up to you'. It was easier than trying to explain what he really felt, that their preparatory masturbation seemed somehow . . . *dishonest?* And after a while, the guys seemed to forget about it anyway, not bothering to address their comments to him as they headed for the front door the same way they'd grown used to not offering him joints or cigarettes when a packet was passed round (Adam was the only one among them who didn't smoke).

•

The banter continued for a little while and then gradually dissipated, finding other targets and other subjects. And then it faded away altogether as they became increasingly drunk and stoned and fixated on their computer game.

Around midnight, Adam stood up and said that he was going to bed. He'd thought that he was tired enough to fall asleep straight away – but up in his room, he found himself lying there in his boxer shorts and t-shirt, staring at the ceiling and thinking about Kate. Danny had been right, Adam thought to himself, he *had* been ogling Kate all term. Right from the very first seminar, Adam had found his eyes continually flicking across the classroom and coming to rest on her. Did she sense him staring at her? he'd wondered each time, feeling guilty but also unable to stop himself. Kate dressed simply, jeans and woollen v-necked sweaters that seemed demure but also seemed to plunge towards the crease of her cleavage. There was that charcoal polo neck she often wore, made out of a fabric that moulded itself to her arms and breasts.

One time, Adam had peered over the rim of his copy of

Anatomy of a Dictatorship and secretly watched her yawn, right from the moment her eyelids had started to lower themselves languorously towards her cheeks and her lungs began to draw in air, through the moment she gathered her arms up behind her head (her breasts now seemed to be moving *towards* him at an incredible rate), to the moment her lips parted and the hem of her jumper lifted away from her belt buckle and revealed the soft skin of her belly.

Lying there in bed, thinking about the silver ring that pierced her navel, Adam felt the muscles between his legs bunch and flex, the tension gently rising in unison with the restlessness in his fingertips. Beneath the ring, the waistband of Kate's jeans pouted at him and he imagined unzipping her. Somewhere among the thoughts flying around his head, Adam heard the voices of the others downstairs. *What if you pull . . . you don't want word going around* . . . Adam thought of Kate lying back on his bed as he approached her (he wanted her to suffocate with pleasure; he wanted her to look at him *afterwards* with damp eyes, her breath redolent with satisfied desires), and found that he had a palm wrapped around the solid trunk of his erection. For a second, Adam considered ignoring it, considered rolling over, shutting his eyes and falling asleep, considered allowing the following day to come flying towards him with its fresh potential. But then his hand started moving, kneading and rolling the skin. She would be there in his bed, stretching back in her white underwear. During the moment itself (tomorrow night? *Tomorrow night!*), Kate would run her hands through his hair, trace out shapes over the back of his neck and ears. Adam would cup her breast, his body repeatedly dipping towards her, and Kate would moan, as if surprised at some new sensation, her arms clawing uselessly at the sheets, her heels grinding into his buttocks . . . Adam felt his body convulse and then freeze for a single, breathless pulse. Seconds later, every cell of his body was sinking back into the mattress, his lungs quickening to compensate for that lost heartbeat of oxygen.

And then nothing. Adam was back in his bedroom staring at the shadows on the ceiling but also looking down on himself as he lay there in his bed, his cock damp in his hand and the duvet already sticking to his stomach.

●

Adam awoke the next morning before any of the others. Standing in the lounge amongst the ash and grease of the night before with a cup of coffee, he shuddered at the thought of Kate arriving at the house later and having to sit among all the mess. But as he sipped at his mug, Adam reasoned that it didn't matter. He and Kate could go to the pub straight away. And as the others had pointed out to him, and as he himself realised with decreasing scepticism (and more than a few tremors of confusion), he had indeed *pulled*. Adam tried to be logical. He had fancied Kate Williams for the whole term. And now she'd asked him out, to the Cow to get drunk, and then to a party. *See what happens, eh?* A logical analysis of the situation so far pointed to . . . Adam swallowed, and then drained his coffee before picking up his jacket and heading off to catch the bus.

The city centre was busy: raincoated women cloyed the damp aisles of the market with their trolleys and prams and bags of shopping; spruced couples, arms linked, drifted over the cobblestones on their way to buy appliances and new clothes; children ran from shop to shop spending their pocket-money on sweets and comics. After another coffee and a croissant in a bakery, Adam felt more resolute about the evening ahead of him, perhaps even started to look forward to it. At the local music store, he pulled a copy of *Saturday Night Fever* from the rack, John Travolta poised on the cover, The Bee Gees grinning above him (were they considered bad or good? Adam could never work out what other people thought) but he had needed to ask a shop assistant about The Velvet Underground.

'Excuse me,' he asked, 'have you got "Sunday Morning" by The Velvet Underground?'

The shop assistant grunted and Adam wondered if he knew that he was buying a CD he'd never heard and probably wouldn't like (or, more mysteriously, wouldn't *understand*) just because he might be sleeping with a girl in his class later on that day unless she had a sudden change of heart in which case he'd be stuck with it . . .

'"Sunday Morning" is a *track* on a Velvet Underground *album*,' the shop assistant sighed. 'Do you want it?'

'Errr . . . yes?'

'Follow me.'

The shop assistant led Adam across the shop without a word, automatically stopping by a rack and wearily pulling the CD out from amongst hundreds of others as if its location was hardwired into his brain.

'Ah, the one with the banana on the cover,' said Adam cheerily. For some reason, the image was familiar to him. The shop assistant grunted again and then led him all the way back to the counter.

'That'll be £9.99.'

Adam paid and left, a smile fixed to his face. Outside the shop, he was so pleased with himself that he couldn't help but take the CD out for another look.

There it was: 'Sunday Morning', track one.

•

Adam had lunch in Chicken Basket and then took the bus back home where he found Simon and Danny slouched in the living room in their dressing gowns, smoking a joint as they watched the French Open, transfixed at that moment by a slow-motion replay of Marie Pierce winning the last point.

'Would you take a look at that,' Simon was saying, 'would you take a look at *that!* Muscle tone, aggression . . . she's beautiful, a fucking goddess.' Danny, head and mouth bent down to a mound of Frosties, stared at the screen over the edge of his bowl. He wasn't really listening, but then Simon wasn't really talking to him anyway.

'You can forget about frigging Anna Kournikova . . . will you look at *that* . . . Kournikova's a fucking child compared to *that*.' Simon waved the burning point of the joint towards the screen. 'Look at that cross-court top-spin forehand . . . fucking perfect . . . at least Pierce can fucking play . . . breasts *and* talent . . . a gifted hitter of the ball, a fucking natural, each shot just coming off the wrist . . . alright Adam? You alright, mate?'

'Yeah.'

'Yeah?'

'Yeah.'

Adam stayed and watched for a while, and then sloped upstairs to his room. Sitting on the bed, he decided that he would tidy up. Adam tried to picture the way he would lead Kate in through the front door and up the stairs later on when they came back from the party, tried to picture what she would see when she first walked in. Adam wanted it to be perfect, and put on his new Velvet Underground CD while he paced around the room stuffing dirty clothes into cupboards, changing his bedclothes (Adam grimaced when he thought of the night before), organising his books into neater piles and opening the window. Soon he was finished, the room arranged so as to look unarranged, the carpet clear of the debris, the condoms he had dutifully bought months earlier lined up inside the top drawer of his bedside table. Adam had bought them from a machine in a pub toilet because he'd been unable to face the girls behind the counters in any of the local chemists. He had been sure that they would imagine him with an erection and shuddered at the thought. Now Adam imagined himself with an erection, but this time with Kate's fingers running up and down its length. Adam sat back down on his bed and pictured the two of them together and again heard the advice of the others from the night before. Should he try Clearing the Pipes this one time? What did he have to lose? Was it really so *dishonest?* Adam scratched at the skin behind his ear. He should try it, he told himself, surely it was harmless?

But then there was the question of how soon to try it before the date? Should he try before he and Kate left for the pub, or later? Adam realised that there wouldn't be time after they'd left the house. He couldn't imagine slipping away into the pub toilets later on and giving it a go while everyone else outside the cubicle was chatting and taking pills and smoking joints. No, he thought, he would definitely have to do it before leaving the house. The next question Adam asked himself was how long should he wait. Right until the last possible minute? Or should he get it over and done with? Looking down at his straining crotch, Adam paused for a second. *He could do it straight away*, he told himself, *at least then it would be done*. He looked at his watch. It was coming up to four o'clock. Was there any point in waiting? How much difference could a few hours make? Surprised at his own decisiveness, Adam cleared his mind and reached towards his flies only for Simon to burst into his room.

'Wha?'

'Only me – you alright, mate?'

168

'Yeah.' Adam hoped he wasn't blushing as he tried surreptitiously to twist his body away from Simon.

'I just wanted to ask if I could borrow a t-shirt. You got
any clean ones?'

'Yeah – in that drawer over there.' Adam pointed and Simon
took one out. 'This one okay?'

Adam nodded.

'Thanks, mate.'

Once Simon had shut the door behind him, Adam took in
a deep breath. There was no way he could have a wank in
his bedroom while the others were in the house. As Simon
had just proved, someone could walk in at any minute. Adam
thought about locking himself in the toilet and paced across the
landing. Shutting himself inside and quickly lowering the seat,
Adam was about to unroll some toilet paper when he gagged.
Someone had stunk the place out! Adam tried to ignore the
stench but the smell was even worse than in the public toilets
in town (he would only dare enter *them* for an accelerated piss,
and then only when he was desperate). Staring back at the poster
of the tennis player scratching her bum Blu-tacked to the inside
of the door above a picture of the England squad, Adam tried
one more time to overcome the desire to flee, tried to cajole
himself into an erection, to wheedle his cock into action, but
it was no good. The air in there was swampy with warmth
and odour, almost solid, almost *fibrous*, and Adam was forced
to emerge and return to his bedroom.

Back on his bed, Adam suddenly felt lost and slumped back
on his pillows wondering what to do. He lay there in silence
for a while, a cold throb of panic insinuating itself into
his breathing and across the back of his neck, and he caught
himself imagining him and Kate in bed together again. But
this time she wasn't moaning nor running her hands along his

spine nor grinding her body against him as she surrendered to the freefall of pleasure. No, Adam was imagining Kate turning away from him as he shamefully pulled himself out of her, unable to stifle a quiet sigh of disappointment as she resigned herself to getting more sleep than she'd intended, her thought that it had hardly been worth putting the condom on in the first place almost audible in the darkness . . . Adam snapped himself upright. Sod it! he muttered, and trudged back across the landing towards the loo. It's just a smell, he told himself, it would all be over in moments and then he could get on with preparing for the evening ahead, start looking forward to it again, go out and have a good . . . Adam turned the handle to the door to find that it was locked.

'Who's that?' Paulo's voice.

'Sorry . . . er . . . it's Adam.'

'You alright, mate?'

'Yeah.'

'Look, mate, I think I might be a while. You desperate?' Adam heard the pages of a magazine being turned over, a turgid cough, a whiff of cigarette smoke.

'No, it's okay, don't worry about it,' he replied.

Once more back in his bedroom, and by now feeling the panic starting to take hold of him, by the roots of his hair, by the throat, Adam buried his face in his hands. It was going to be a disaster, he told himself, it was going to be a catastrophe unless he . . . Adam gritted his teeth and told himself in the most authoritative tones he possessed that there was nothing else he could do but get it over and done with right there and right then. No one was going to come in, he told himself. How long could it take anyway? What was the mathematical probability of being interrupted? The others seemed to manage it, no problem, so why shouldn't he? Adam's fingers closed around his zip and . . .

'Oi, mate!' Elton burst into his room and Adam almost burst into tears. 'Oi, mate, you got any shower gel I can borrow?' Adam stammered. His mouth couldn't form words for a second, not that it seemed to matter to Elton. 'I'd get some myself but the corner shop's run out.' Elton paused to leer. 'I ended up shagging Diana all afternoon, mate. Better get cleaned up before I go out with Lucy, if you know what I mean.'

It took all of Adam's self-control not to simper when really he felt like curling into a ball and sobbing. 'It's over there,' he pointed to the shelf where he kept his toiletries, 'help yourself.'

'Cheers, mate. You've saved my life.'

Elton helped himself and Adam got up off the bed and slouched downstairs into the lounge. Simon and Danny were sitting on the sofa watching a *South Park* video, sniggering every so often and bending their heads for a series of hits from the bong.

'Alright, mate – what you been up to?' Danny asked.

'Nothing,' Adam replied, almost too quickly.

'Cool,' said Danny.

Adam sat down and stared at the screen, not really taking in the cartoon, instead looking at his watch repeatedly and wondering what he could do. It was well past five o'clock. Kate would be arriving in two hours, he told himself. Where could he go? Adam briefly considered a wider range of options, desperate plans that had previously seemed ridiculous. *The end of the garden behind the rotting structure their landlord laughably called a shed?* No good – it was raining, and he'd be spotted by the neighbours in any case. *The phone-box on the corner?* He'd get himself arrested. *He could do it in the toilets in the betting shop across the street, or else he could hide under his bed or shut himself in his wardrobe or* . . . Adam told himself to stop being stupid. He would just have to wait until the toilet or the bathroom were free. Simple as that.

He sank back into the sofa and tried to relax. But it soon became impossible: neither room looked destined to be free ever again. Elton seemed to have *installed* himself in the bathroom, Adam was able to hear him humming as he splashed away under the shower on all three occasions that he went up to check. And Paulo remained locked in the toilet, still smoking cigarettes and still flipping through the pages of his magazine. Around six o'clock, Paulo suddenly appeared in the lounge. But before Adam could move, Danny was up out of his seat and walking out the door muttering that he 'had to take a crap'. Adam couldn't believe it. He almost felt like lashing out at something, at somebody (he even thought about trying to run up the stairs and beat Danny to it). But in the end he resigned himself to defeat. *This* was his destiny, he told himself, *this* was all he deserved: a night doomed with sexual failure.

•

Adam was still cursing himself a quarter of an hour later, and simultaneously half-believing that he was cursed, when the phone rang in the hall. Simon got up to answer it (it was his turn) and after a while came back into the lounge with the news.

'That was Jezza and Farid. They say there's been a big session going on at their house all afternoon. They've had some girls over from the art college and they want us to go round and help them out. I said we'd be over by half-past for a drink and that we can try and take them all out to the party later. Sound good?'

Suddenly the house was a flurry of activity, doors slamming, music being turned up, insults being hurled back and forth from bedroom to bedroom. Within ten minutes, Adam watched as all four of them assembled back in the lounge in fresh clothes, the air sharp with the scent of their aftershaves.

'We ready, boys?' Elton asked. He'd called Lucy and told her to meet him later at The Blushing Bride.

'Have a good one tonight, Adam. See you at the party later on, mate.'

'Yeah . . . and good luck,' offered Danny. 'Not that it sounds like you're going to need it.' They trooped out into the hall where Adam heard Simon ask them all in the hallway if they were clear.

'Clear.'

'Clear.'

'Clear.'

And then they were gone.

It was like a miracle, Adam thought to himself, switching off the video and basking in the silence. *It was like a fucking miracle!* He looked at his watch – it was six-thirty, which gave him a whole half-hour to . . . Adam got up and stretched, let his muscles relax along the length of his arms and back. He would stroll upstairs, he would take his time, things had worked out perfectly. He would be clear, he would be clear, he would be *clear*!

Adam walked up and into his room. Should he turn on some music? What was the point! Lying down in his bed, Adam was almost casual about undoing his trousers. Why not try and *enjoy* it? he asked himself, his mind almost racing on ahead into the evening to the moment when Kate would grab hold of him and *whimper*. Soon, his right hand was clamped around his erection, a wad of tissue paper in his left. *No hurry,* he told himself, *no hurry at all – he had all the time in the . . .* Adam froze suddenly.

There it was again, the sound of the front doorbell.

There was a pause. And then it rang a third time, Kate's voice sounding out in the street below. 'Adam? Adam? Are you there?'

She was early. She was *early!* Gulping, Adam thought about ignoring her voice (how long could it take – she wouldn't have to wait more than a few moments, would she?) but when he gazed down at the wilting flesh in his hand (so weak and limp compared with the hard knot of excitement that had built up right in the base of his pelvis where it would lurk until the time came), he knew that it would be futile. Outside in the street, Kate's voice sounded out once more.

WHITE WEDDING

Fighting games allow players to battle each other's characters . . .
Do you want to be a blonde, sandal-wearing Greek woman in a
miniskirt, or a supernatural pirate with two enormous broadswords?
A Croatian behemoth or a Hawaiian Sumo wrestler? Bruce Lee in
a gold-lamé leotard . . . ?

Steven Poole, *Trigger Happy: The Inner Life of Videogames*

1

Out behind the hotel, I'd just finished reading the printout of Clarity's email when I caught sight of Jimmy bumbling through the glass doors and out into the Vegas heat. *Is that what I look like?* I asked myself, as if it had never occurred to me before. Jimmy spotted me almost immediately, but then it wasn't as if it was hard: like him, I was eighteen stone of lard gently sweating in the sun.

Jimmy was dressed in one of his four Leeds United shirts and a pair of Bermudas and I watched his rudderless approach through the aisles of loungers. Even from a distance, I could see how hungover he was: the bulky cocktail in his right hand trailing beside him like a medicinal drip; the red mottling smeared across the pallid surface of his face; the wayward stumble.

'Morning, mate.'

'Morning, Jimmy.'

He paused to catch his breath, his damp cheeks puffing in and out, the polyester of his shirt already transparent against the doughy flesh of his arms and his back.

'You were up early.'

'Jimmy, there's some . . .'

I tried to tell him about Clarity's email, but he interrupted me with a wave of a his fat fingers.

'Enjoying your last morning of freedom, mate? I understand, say no more.'

His head twisted above his chins and he caught the eye of one of the cocktail girls who roamed the scorched concrete in white bikinis and synthetic 'grass' skirts that barely fringed the tops of their thighs. One of them clicked her way over to us and Jimmy slurped at his Mai Tai as he ordered another.

'Thanks luv.' His sunglasses tracked the swish of her green tassels and stacked calves as she sashayed off towards the bar. And then he manoeuvred his body down on to the lounger next to mine and lay back with a sigh, a seam of sweat already built up along the folds of his forehead and on the sausagemeat of his cheeks.

'Great night last night, eh?'

'Jimmy . . .'

'I felt *fooked* when I woke up this morning. Didn't recover until I'd had breakfast.'

Jimmy slapped his belly with a contented smile and I watched it wobble.

'Jimmy, there's something I've . . .'

Now some of the others appeared across the pool – Robbie and Jules, who worked at the arcade with Jimmy and me, Mandy and Damon who I knew from College – all of them with hands wrapped around colourful drinks. Jimmy stood up and waved his Mai Tai like a flag, sounding out an 'Oi oi' in greeting and soon they were all thrusting their hands towards me.

'Morning, Boomer . . .'

'Congratulations, mate . . .'

'You've made it to your big day . . .'

'Are you nervous . . . ?'

'Have we got time for a few drinks before we go to the chapel?'

Only Jimmy and I had been to Las Vegas before and the voices of the others buzzed with excitement.

'Have you seen the buffet breakfast here? All you can eat for five ninety-nine . . .'

178

'You should have seen the girl selling cigarettes down by the blackjack tables this morning. She was checking me out . . .'

'They're prostitutes, Robbie . . .'

'No they're not . . .'

'They might as well be . . .'

'I tell you: *she was checking me out* . . .'

'They've got Hitler's car up there,' said Jules. Obviously, he'd made it to the Classic Auto Show up on the sixth floor. 'A bullet-proof 1939 Mercedes 770K. And an Alfa that belonged to Mussolini *and* a Packard that belonged to Emperor Hirohito. It's like a fascist car rally up there.'

'Was Hirohito a fascist?' Mandy asked. 'I thought he was a god until 1946 when he was forced to renounce his deified status by the Allies. After that, wasn't he just an impotent symbol?'

Jimmy offered round Regals which only Robbie accepted. Then Al and Ian strolled out through the glass doors and on to the concrete, Kris and Charmain following hand-in-hand a little way behind. There were more handshakes, more congratulations, more excited voices.

'We've just been to the Luxor . . .'

'Tomorrow we're going to have a "Round Table Breakfast" at the Excalibur . . .'

'You sit there and have breakfast with these people dressed up as medieval Lords and Ladies who say "Forsooth" a lot and "By my troth, good sir" and so on while you drink foaming tankards of orange juice and eat your pancakes with skillets . . .'

'Great night last night . . .'

A three-way argument broke out between Ian, Jules and Al as to whether a *skillet* was a leather shirt, a piece of medieval cutlery or a type of frying-pan. On the other side of the group, Kris pointed out that Arthurian mythology predated medieval history by at least five hundred years ('depending on how you look at it'), a period of time your average American could only possibly hope to understand in Disney dimensions.

'No wonder they turn historical figures into cartoon animals. Foxes, lions, ducks, chickens, bears. History's about as intelligible a proposition as Mickey Mouse to this lot.'

I looked down at the printout I was holding. Between my thick fingers I could feel the paper soaking up the dirty film of grease that had been building up on my hands, imagined the paper clamped between my thumb and tensed index finger turning the same colour as the insoles of my trainers. *Should I tell them all about Clarity's email?* They'd be disappointed for me, and they'd all be very good about feeling sorry for the fat boy whose fiancée has just . . . *I should tell them about Clarity's email!* Now the others talked about the wedding anyway. The girls talked about what they were going to wear while the boys talked about what they were going to drink, pulling open a newspaper to catch up with the football scores back home. *Did Jimmy have his speech ready? Did Robbie have time to play roulette before the limousines arrived to take us to the chapel?*

'What are you wearing, Boomer?' Damon asked

'Are you nervous?' Mandy asked. 'I can't wait to see what Clarity's wearing. I bet she looks stunning.'

It was then that Jimmy proposed a toast. 'Hey everyone, don't . . .' I started, but Jimmy told me not to be shy.

'To the bride and groom.'

Everybody drained their glasses (in the general excitement, nobody noticed me ignore mine and spread myself back on my lounger. How could I tell them?) and Jimmy signalled to the waitress.

'So what are we all drinking?'

'I'll have a 57 T-Bird . . .'

'A Kamikaze . . .'

'Sunburn . . .'

'I'll have a beer . . .'

'A Caipiriñha for me please . . .'

'A Strawberry Daquiri . . .'

'A Banana Daquiri . . .'

'A Down Under Dreamsickle . . .'

'What the *fook* is that?' spluttered Jimmy.

'Irish Cream, Orange Juice and a splash of soda,' replied Mandy. Jimmy shrugged his thick shoulders.

'Whatever . . . and another Mai Tai for me. What about you, Boomer?'

I held up my Bloody Mary – I'd barely touched it.

'You not drinking today?' he asked. A round of jeers about 'last-minute nerves' circled the group. *Get 'em down you!*

'Where're we having a drink afterwards again?' Robbie asked.

'For the millionth fucking time – Caesar's.'

'I only fucking asked.'

'So, Boomer, married life *awaits*. You ready to get hitched, mate?'

I sat up, picked up my drink and stared into it. Bubbles of lime juice swirled amongst the grains of pepper and pools of sherry while little powdery islands of celery salt floated across its surface.

'I . . . er . . . erm . . . *Yes*. I mean, *I'm* ready anyhow.'

'You don't sound it, mate.' Jimmy punched me on the shoulder. 'Stop poncing about and have a *real* fucking drink.'

'No, I'm serious, listen. *I'm* ready. I just don't think that Clarity is.'

'What do you mean . . . ?'

'What's happened . . . ?'

'Has she rung you?'

'No,' I replied, vaguely aware of the ring of worried faces looking back at me. 'She sent me this email.'

I finally held up the piece of paper for all to see.

'I tried to ring her room in Caesar's Palace earlier this morning. They say she never checked in.'

'What about Anita and Lottie?'

I put the email down on the lounger in front of me.

'They haven't shown up either. So I went and checked my email and I found this waiting for me.' I stared at the folded printout as did everyone else.

'What does it say?'

'Well, I'll put it this way: we've got a spare ring.'

2

Dear Jason . . .

•

I try to ring you from my bed. A receptionist comes on the line, introduces himself as Randy and asks me how I am, asks how he can help me.

'Hi. My name's Jason Boomer. Could you put me through to Clarity McClellan?' I ask. 'I don't know what room she's checked into, but she would have arrived yesterday morning.'

Randy puts me on hold, Dean Martin singing 'That's *Amore*' cutting across the background sound of the lobby. A few seconds later there's a click and I expect to hear you come on the line, your voice husky with sleep. But it's Randy again.

'I'm sorry, Mr Boomer, Miss McClellan hasn't honoured her reservation at this time.' I ask about Lottie and Anita who were booked to share a room and I get the same response.

Where are you?

I put the phone down, tell myself that you must have tried to ring when we were all out last night and that there'll be a message waiting for me at reception, a call saying that there's been a problem with the connecting flight, with bad weather or lost luggage, a family crisis maybe, or a hostage situation on the tarmac that can't be avoided.

•

It seems criminally clichéd to tell you this isn't an easy 'letter' to write. When you get to the end of it, I hope you get your own sense of how difficult it's been for me.

•

Down in the lobby thirteen floors below, the phalanx of slot machines juddering away behind me, I ask a receptionist whether a message has been left for me, trying not to let my voice crack.

'No,' she replies, scanning through a card index. 'Nothing at this time, sir.' *At this time! At this time!* I ask if there's a terminal where I can check my email and she gives me directions to the Business Services Center.

'Walk back the way you came, toward the rear of the hotel, past the roulette and craps tables on your right, past the dollar slots on your left and down through the mini-mall until you get to elevator bank G. There, you take the elevator up to the third floor, then come out and . . .'

I find it eventually, log into my account and find a message waiting for me.

Sender: C McClellan. Subject: [none].

'Dear Jason,' you start and the first thing that strikes me is that you've called me 'Jason'. *Jason?* Haven't I always been 'Boomer' to you? From our first night together until . . .

•

By now you'll know I'm not in Vegas. The fact is I'm not coming.
I don't want us to get married.

183

*There. I've said it. I hurts me to write it and it hurts me to think of
you in Vegas without me. Do you remember when we were last there?
I almost can't believe how quickly it all happened. The four days we
spent there were like a dream. I thought I might explode from how I
felt about you. Every second with you felt, and has felt, like something
special. And this is the way it was right from the start, right from when
we first met. Was it only 6 months ago?*

●

You're right. Things happen quickly.

I remember Jimmy shaking me in our hotel room on the final
day of the *Blipz Magazine* Videogames Tournament last July.

'Time to wake up, mate,' he says quietly. I don't tell him
I've been lying there for hours, wondering about the Final.

'How are you feeling?' he asks. 'You nervous?'

'I . . . I . . .' I notice a little muscle tension in my fingers and
wrists as I rub my eyes.

'You need some breakfast, mate,' he says, slapping me on the
back. 'Room service? Or shall we go downstairs?'

I ask Jimmy to order something from downstairs while I
shower and by the time I'm dressed, a waiter's brought up a
tray of food: a two-litre bottle of Coke; two blueberry waffles,
each one the size of a frisbee and smeared with whipped cream;
a pot of coffee; a couple of Snickers. Jimmy and I quietly munch
our way through it all, Jimmy flipping through the latest copy of
Power Up while I scan a new issue of *Batman: Legend of the Dark
Night*. When we're finished, Jimmy picks up his magazine and
walks out on to the balcony to smoke a cigarette while I turn
on the console that we've plugged into the hotel TV.

'So who's this "Clarity McClellan" you're fighting?' he asks,
pixelated by the mesh of the flyscreen.

'I dunno.' You were just a name on board to me then. 'She's
unknown, English . . .'

I never try to know about an opponent before I play them. That way, all it boils down to is what happens out there on the screen.

'Who'd she beat in her semi-final?' Jimmy asks.

'She beat Hans Andersen yesterday in two straight fights. Andersen was fighting as Yoshimitsu.'

'*She beat Andersen?*'

'Two fights . . . so I'm told.'

'And what are *you* doing?' Jimmy's now inside the room, staring at the controller in my hand.

'I thought I'd get a little practice in before we go over to the Hilton.'

'But you *never* practise on the day of a fight!'

I shrug. But Jimmy's right. I never practise on the day of a fight. Everyone has a different way of preparing for a competition, I guess. Some players get stoned while others go swimming. Some research their opponents while others believe that the key to success is to drift out into the most anonymous arcade they can find, the grassroots of the game where the loners lurk with their customised special moves and left-field technique. There are some players who spend hours reciting memorised input codes for ten-string hit manoeuvres as if they were re-learning their times-tables, as if they were trying to train their mind to operate to the rhythm of *Tekken*. And there are those who practise like maniacs right up until the last minute, getting up early on the day of a tournament fight to spar all morning. Usually, like yesterday when I was waiting to play the semi-final, I just sit and flick through comics all morning to take my mind off the game ahead. But *this* morning I feel too tense to read.

I don't feel any better when Jimmy and I arrive at the Hilton just before noon. In the cab, Jimmy chuckles as he's paying the driver. He can't believe that I've made it to the Final and I tell him that I can't believe it either and by the time we reach the *Tekken* arena my head is buzzing. There's already a strong crowd milling around the spectator galleries, a few famous faces from the past (Jeff Pass who won the final two years ago; Ricky Simmons who was a *Streetfighter* World Champion three seasons in a row), a handful of groupies, gangs of pale skateboarders in ripped jeans, metal fans and petrolheads, software executives in suits whispering earnestly into each other's ears, journalists, photographers. I formally announce my arrival to the referee and he tells me that the other finalist hasn't arrived yet.

Now Shaun Warren, one of the *Blipz* editors, approaches with a tape recorder and asks me how I feel, tells me that I fought 'one helluva battle' yesterday in the semi-final. Somewhere, a flashbulb explodes, a camera, a live webcast.

'We thought it was going to be a massacre after we saw the first fight,' he says.

'So did I,' I say.

I'd fought as Jin Kazama while this season's top seed, Kim Chang-ho, had fought as Hwoarang. Last year, I'd faced him in the quarter-finals and he'd wiped me out, dispensing *overdamage* with an array of devastating kick attacks that were dispatched in unblockable sequences. A year later, all I was concentrating on was not letting the same thing happen again, an attempt that had immediately looked futile.

'He chewed you up early on in the first fight,' Shaun says, 'then spat you out with a ten-string hit combination and it looked as is if he was going to do it to you again in the second. When he suckered you into that Neck Snapper and pushed your damage up to eighty percent, the word in the stands was that you were *dead*.'

Again I nod.

'What was going through your mind?' he asks.

I tell Shaun it was a matter of not giving up and of *thinking* one's way to victory.

'Hwoarang players are always the most susceptible to vanity,' I say. 'Hwoarang's programmed with the ability to execute the most spectacular kinds of extended kick sequences. As a result, some Hwoarang players get distracted by the possibility of pulling off glamour kills.'

'Are you saying that the top seed from Korea was overconfident?'

'I think he got sloppy at the point where he could have won the fight.'

'Well you sure made him pay. From that point on, you were *ruthless.*'

'I hit a rhythm,' I shrug. 'Maybe I was lucky?'

What else can I say? In the third fight, I just waded in and put Hwoarang down in a matter of seconds, Jin always in a position where Hwoarang couldn't really touch him, each move arriving at my fingertips before he could duck, dodge or block. When he tried to counter-attack, I just sidestepped and punished him. When he tried to throw, I reversed him and counter-attacked myself. Sometimes it's like that.

'And now you're the favourite,' Shaun continues. 'Does it make it harder when you know that you're three rounds away from ten thousand dollars and a sponsorship deal?'

It's then that I see *you* for the first time.

Suddenly I'm stuttering.

'Err . . . I-I-I . . .'

I tell Shaun that I don't really know how I feel to be so close to the first prize, that I've never been in a final before, and I watch over his shoulder as you introduce yourself to a steward.

Then you're both walking towards me. You tap the referee

on the shoulder. 'Hi,' you say. 'I'm here for the final?' you say, as if you need to ask permission.

Shaun and the guy with the camera back away for a group shot, the referee hesitating slightly before shaking your hand, and it's then I realise I'm staring at you. You can't be more than a couple of inches over five feet, in a yellow summer dress the colour of pale butter, daisies printed on the cotton, hazel brown eyes and hair like a scrambled ball of dry straw shooting out of your head.

You extend your hand and I realise I'm *still* staring at you as I shake it, your fingers like matchsticks between the fleshy curves of my fat paw.

'Hi. Clarity McClellan.'

You smile, and I stutter.

'J-Jason Boomer,' I reply.

'Nice to meet you.'

You tell me that you were watching in the gallery yesterday.

'That was gutsy,' you say. 'But I knew you'd win. Do you remember that moment in the second fight when he pulled off that Neck Snapper? Everyone around me in the stand thought you were *out*. But I knew you'd win.'

You smile again, your thin lips (slightly dry, I notice, and almost cracking) parting to reveal tiny teeth.

'I hoped you'd win,' you say.

●

And this now brings me to the heart of things – why have I changed my mind? How could I suddenly turn my back on the person who has felt like a part of me from the moment I first knew he existed?

●

More journalists appear, each with questions. A writer from *wayofthewarrior.com* asks if I think the fact that both finalists are British heralds a new era of European dominance in beat-'em- up gaming – and there's even a woman from the *Sunday Times Magazine* asking me how I feel about 'fighting a girl'.

'It doesn't really enter my mind *who* I'm fighting,' I tell her as I look across to see you signing an autograph for a young skatepunk in the audience. 'Up there on the screen, it's one character against the other.'

Then we're asked to stand together to have our photograph taken (*am I blushing?*), a ridiculous pair staring into the flashbulbs, you with your scarecrow hair and your wispy arms and your sandals, me like a giant doughnut in a Megadeth t-shirt towering above you. The photographer asks us to move closer together so he can get a tighter shot. Does your hand brush against mine?

We're each given five minutes to prepare ourselves.

'So *that's* the mysterious Clarity McClellan,' says Jimmy. 'Well, she doesn't look like any *Tekken* player I've ever seen. She looks like one of the girls from *The Little House on the Prairie*. Anyway big man, you can take her.' He slaps me on the back. 'Good luck. Just *relax* . . .'

The referee comes over and says it's time to start and I walk over to the machine and join you at the controls as the computer flashes into the Character Selection Screen.

'Right . . . who's gonna call?' the referee asks, standing behind us.

I nod in your direction and he spins a quarter up into the air.

'Heads.'

The coin lands heads up.

'You choose first,' you say, looking me in the eye.

'OK, you heard the young lady. I'm gonna stand back now and let you guys get down to it. You know the rules . . . first to win two fights . . . good luck to both of you.'

The lights dim, two beams picking us out in the darkness,

the ranks of spectators going silent. As always, I slide my cursor across to Jin Kazama and hit the left punch button. Now I wait for you to choose your character. Who were you going to be? Julia Chang? Nina Williams (her counter-attack would be her best weapon against Jin Kazama)? Or were you going to be one of the guys? Heihachi Mishima with his ferocious Tile-Breaker Punch . . . Lei Wulong with his Tornado Kicks, his Dragon Blast and his Drunken Master special moves? Your cursor flicks negligently across the screen in front of us, and also on the giant screen suspended from the ceiling above us, until it comes to land on the face of Ling Xiaoyu and the crowd behind us gives out a sigh of anticipation. It's going to be a battle of conflicting styles, Jin's raw power pitched against Ling Xiaoyu's hustling agility and her capability for lightning-quick counter-strikes. I take a deep breath, tense and relax my hands, spread my fingers out beside the control-stick and buttons and I'm staring up at the screen, mentally preparing an opening attack sequence, when I feel you tap me on the shoulder.

'Good luck,' you say, and suddenly I'm looking into your eyes, wondering whether you're just trying to break my concentration and telling myself that *no one* wishes anyone else 'good luck' in *Tekken*, that the game's about the ruthless desire to beat the other player into a lifeless mess. But I'm looking into your eyes and I'm saying 'You too' as if it's the most natural thing in the world, as if I've met you before. And then we're both looking at the screen in front of us, Ling Xiaoyu in her schoolgirl's uniform, Jin stripped down to his waist, pulling his studded gloves tight around his fists, a giant tongue of flame leaping up his right trouser leg, streaks of black lightning branded on to his rippling bicep. This is it, I tell myself, this is it . . .

Round 1 . . . FIGHT!

Suddenly I'm closing in on you. I've got a prepared sequence in my head and I let my fingers fly at the buttons. I want to get the drop on you right from the start. I want control of the battlefield. I want to deliver maximum damage. The only way you can hurt me is if I stand back and let you.

And if I come in close . . . ? A Backhand Punch, a Spin Kick to the head that picks up the momentum of the first punch and doubles it, a crunching *Majinken* punch to your ribcage that twists you sideways. I don't hesitate and follow up with a throw, grabbing your arm, burying my elbow in your neck and catapulting you down on to the floor. As you roll back to your feet (your damage meter creeping towards the halfway mark), I'm already asking myself how long you're going to take to recover. Now you try a two-punch Bayonet – a simple move that I block easily – followed by a Backstep 'n' Roundhouse that I almost see too late, dodging only split-seconds before you make contact. Still, it leaves me open for a second and you duly connect with a series of Windmill Slaps, your slender arms scything through the air across my face and taking you down into a Phoenix Crouch. You then try for a Splits Sweep but I read this early, jump over your scissoring legs and deliver a Twin Lancer combination and an unstoppable horizontal *Donuki* punch that blasts you back across the screen on to the ground. I charge immediately. Just as I thought, you've lost your rhythm and you panic, crouching too early (expecting the obvious sliding kick) and making it all too simple for me to leap into the air instead and twirl through a sequence of Phantom Kicks . . .

K-O!

The computer growls and there's a round of applause and a few wolf-whistles from behind us as it runs through a replay. Up above, the action is repeated on the massive screen: two towering figures, six feet high, playing out the last attack. I try to stare at my hands, but there's this temptation to look across

191

at you. Usually I'd prepare myself for the next fight, try not to get too confident, try to ignore the braying from the stands and just *focus* on the glowing screen. But I need to look across at you. Are you humiliated? I've just taken you down with a near perfect score in the first fight of a World Championship Final . . . *how does that feel?* Will you dismiss it and spit back a response in the next fight? Or are you broken, unnerved, lost? I turn my head to see you staring up at the giant screen as it replays the final torrent of kicks, your eyes tracking each foot as it connects in slow-motion, your lips slightly parted, the corners of your mouth twitching (into a smile – *into a smile?*), the tiny saw-edged tips of your teeth glistening in the same flickering light that strobes through your eyelashes. Your nose twitches (I can't take my eyes off you. Even with everyone watching, I can't take my eyes off you . . .) You move a hand to your hair, pull a strand back behind your ear, your skin, a swatch of freckles across your nose.

Jin Kazama . . . WINS!

My eyes snap back to the screen out in front of us.

Round 2 . . .

Here we go again. There's the split-second pause. I feel both of us tense beside each other, both of us breathing in slowly, waiting for . . .

FIGHT!

I decide to attack straight away again, not wanting to surrender initiative. Maybe I'm only seconds away from victory, I think, *just a few well-executed moves . . .* I close in on you with a simpler opening, a double *Majinken* punch combo and another horizontal *Donuki* punch, a 'Body Piercer' that takes your damage meter up to forty per cent. *If I could just connect another . . .* I pause for a beat before inputting the second attack (I want to time it *just right*, I tell myself) and then try to Shoot The Works just as you're getting up, all four limbs striking in rotation. But you're up faster than I expected and parry all four blows before skipping backwards out of range. There are purple sparks as I lunge towards you hoping for a grapple (I plan a couple of Cyclone 'Bitch' Kicks followed up by a Can-Can Kick and a juggle attack) but you jump back leaving us standing facing each other.

Nothing happens for a second. Who's going to move first? I crouch so that I can rise up into two *Tsunami* Kicks but you anticipate and thrash me out of the air with a sweeping Cloud Kick. While I'm recovering, you move through a Phoenix Crouch into a double forearm smash and as I'm stunned backwards I'm already thinking that my moves are getting too predictable. You pause for a second – *why should I wait?* I move in: ten-hit combos with variations. *Left foot to the stomach, a right jab that hurls me into two kicks that . . .* you block my first attempt so I repeat the attack, but this time pull out of the manoeuvre early and reverse my body back into a *Kasumigeri*. Again, you block each strike. Now we both start throwing a few simpler punches amid a flurry of feints and sidesteps . . . suddenly you cut across me, two jabs to the face . . . a reverse flip that has you flying through the air and landing on my shoulders, your thighs straddling my face. You slam your fist down on to my crown and I crumple. When I finally stagger to my feet, you jab again, this time throwing in a Reverse Punt that has me floating high in the air and gives you all the time in the world to charge in and finish me off with a Sky-Scraper Kick when I finally fall back towards the ground.

K-O!

There's a haze of flashbulbs from behind us and I can feel the anticipation in the crowd rising as the third fight becomes a sudden-death decider. During the slow-motion replay, I ask myself how the hell I lost the last round but there doesn't seem to be a definite moment where I threw the fight away. One moment I was a couple of moves away from victory. The next you were anticipating my attacks as if they were your idea in the first place. And then I tell myself that it doesn't matter what happened, that we're fighting the best-of-three which means I'm still only one round away from victory. *Make or break, Boomer*, I tell myself, *make or break . . .*

Ling Xiaoyu wins . . .

There's a split-second before the deciding round starts and I tell myself to do nothing else but prepare to jump back and take up a defensive stance. What are you doing?

Round 3 . . .

A deep breath, I twist my head so that you're a faint blur at the edge of my vision . . .

FIGHT!

Okay, I think, let's *end* this. I try to launch into a *Majinken* followed by a Demon Killer (it should give me the chance to juggle you up into the air and follow up with a series of *okizeme* attacks) but you swat the first punch away. That shouldn't be a problem in itself, I think, the Demon Killer should still connect . . . *but you drop down into Phoenix Stance and roll to one side before closing in for a throw.* Because you catch me on my blindspot, you inflict extra damage. What will your follow-up attack be? As I'm rolling back up on to my feet, you're already circling me before unleashing a Phoenix Strike, both hands flying towards me, both hands crackling with energy and flinging me back across the screen. *How the hell did you create the time for that?* I glance at the damage meters – you've taken me up to fifty per cent while I've yet to land a punch.

Suddenly the spectre of being taken down with a perfect score becomes frighteningly possible. I roll back to my feet and come straight back at you with a jab that connects and a sidestepping Thunder Strike. I'm looking to *juggle 'n' float* but you back away, swat away my next punch with a left-handed Knife Chop and then go down into a Phoenix Crouch. *Okay*, I think, *I learned my lesson from the last time* . . . I immediately try a Can–Can Kick – something to scoop you off the ground and up into the air where I can pile in with some heavy punches – but you're suddenly back-flipping out of range like a gymnast. I press forward, looking to connect with a double uppercut, but you cartwheel to one side. I sidestep, knowing that you're a blink away from landing a Reverse Punt, and swing a gloved fist towards your head only to swipe at empty space as you leap up over my head and land behind me. Again, you could land a two-punch combination before blasting me up into the air but you simply land a backslap for minimal damage before backing away.

One more attack, I tell myself, and I'm finished. What should I try and do? I try a few simple moves, two- and three-punch combinations, a series of Phantom Kicks, a Gut Punch, a double uppercut rising out of a defensive crouch. You swat and block, dancing out of the way as I vainly lob myself at you. Suddenly Jin Kazama feels slow. Suddenly *I* feel slow. I attempt another assault but you block each move almost before it's even started and just as I see a chance to land a kick, you've moved through a combination and I'm lying on the floor unable to get up . . .

Ling Xiaoyu . . . *WINS!*

It's over.

You turn to look at me . . .

•

What can I say? I got scared. I woke up a week ago and I realised I was frightened to death. I thought about spending the rest of my life with you, about what that meant and why I was even thinking of such a thing, and

I suddenly had a feeling that somehow our getting married wasn't MY choice any more, that in some way it was a decision that was being made for me.

•

Behind us, there are cheers. I don't need to look up and watch the slow-motion replay. If I want to, I can replay the perfection of your final attack on the insides of my eyelids, the double slap and the Belly Chop forcing me backwards, the electricity gathering between your fingertips as you draw your arms up and round through the air, a ball of light, your Palm Strike driving me twenty feet back across the floor to the sound of a thousand whips cracking (I see stars, I see stars), your body holding its final position like a gymnast at the end of a tumble.

Now we're both turning away from the control panels and a crowd rushes towards you with a trophy and a blown-up cheque that almost threatens to hide you completely. I can hardly bear to look at you. You reach across and offer your hand – I take it for a moment, hold it among my fat knuckles – and then you're swept away by the referee and the guys in suits. The crowd are on their feet, their applause swelling as you're handed the trophy, the flashbulbs flaring across your face. At some point, someone takes my photo and I mumble something about the better player winning.

•

Can you believe this: I got ANGRY about the fact that you are who you are and that this person slotted into my life so perfectly. It made me feel predictable, out-of-control, frightened. I tried to talk myself out of it – but couldn't. Anita tried to talk me out of it – but couldn't (when I said to you last week that I was helping her get over her split with Michael, I was white-lying, it was the other way around. She was trying to talk me out of . . . THIS).

So I've changed my mind. Maybe I need to grow up. Maybe we both need to get a little older, I don't know . . . But one thing's for sure: if I'd gone through with things, I'd be lying to both of us because once I'd started doubting us, I couldn't stop.

•

Later, back at the Imperial Palace, Jimmy and I stare at the pool, drinking beers and watching the reflection of the sky as the temperature finally starts to drop. My 2nd prize cheque for two thousand dollars lies on the table between us, next to Jimmy's which is made out for a thousand dollars (he finished fourth in the Driving Sim Challenge). Jimmy asks me if I'm okay for the thousandth time.

'I'm fine.'

'You . . .'

'I'm sure.'

'I've never seen anyone fight the way she did in that third round. Poise, timing, variation, three-dimensional sense . . .'

I don't say anything. Jimmy tells me that he's arranged for us to meet some guys from Special Intelligence, the electronics company where his brother works, and that we're all going have a few cocktails together before going on to the end-of-tournament party at the Hilton. I tell him I'm not going.

'You're not coming?'

'I'm not coming. I think I'm just going to eat a buffet-dinner, wander around the casino and get an early night.'

Jimmy offers to have dinner with me and then go on to the Hilton later but I tell him not to change his plans.

'And you'll be okay?' he asks.

'I'll be fine. I just didn't expect to lose today,' I say, forcing a laugh, 'I'll be over it by tomorrow.'

Later, I push the food around my plate in one of the restaurants and then amble my way back along the aisles of cranking droids to the bar where I maintain a neat stack of dollar bills by my beermat and watch the towers of the candy-striped chips rise and fall at the nearby roulette table.

It's then that I notice that you're sitting at another bar across the casino floor from me, a crowd of blackjack tables between us. You're alone, a mystified look on your face as if you're puzzling over something, sipping from a green drink that matches the colour of the dress you've changed into. I wonder if I should I walk over to you, whether you'd be pleased to see me. Are you already waiting for someone? A friend? *A boyfriend?* Will you look at me and flinch like everyone else?

Before I know it, I'm rolling my way through the tangle of tables towards you.

'Hi.'

'Hi.' You stare back at me.

'You're staying here too?'

'It's the cheapest place I could find on the Strip.'

'Me too. Anyway, I just wanted to say congratulations. We didn't get a chance to talk earlier.'

'Thanks.'

'I've never seen anyone fight the way you did in the third round . . .'

'Thanks . . .'

'I mean, to be totally honest, it was . . . er . . . the best I've . . .'

'Boomer, you'd better stop before you make me blush.'

I stop.

'How do you know to call me "Boomer" and not "Jason"?'

'I heard your friend call you "Boomer" earlier.' You laugh. 'I like it, it's funny. Have people called you that your whole life?'

'Pretty much. What about "Clarity"?'

'Born with it and stuck with it. I don't really like it, it's like

198

being part of a bad hippie joke. And I've tried to shorten it –
but what would I shorten it to? *Cla? Clarry?* There's "Claire",
but that seems like a different name altogether.'

You don't seem to be hurrying to get away from me so I sit
down on a barstool and offer to buy you another drink. You ask
for a Midori Sour and I ask you why you're not at the party at the
Hilton. You say that you don't really go to parties, dipping your
lips to the straw, the liquid in your glass rising like mercury.

'What about you?' you ask.

'What about me?'

'Why aren't you at the Hilton?'

I don't say anything, stare down at my Mai Tai. The umbrella
hooked over the rim of the glass has hula girls printed on to its
paper panels.

'Boomer,' you say, 'are you angry with me for winning this
afternoon? Do you want to talk to me about it?'

'No, I'm fine, I really am,' I say, taking a deep breath and
twisting on my seat to look at you. 'I mean, I'm *disappointed* . . .'
I start, but then realise that I couldn't care less about the Final
when I see you looking back at me, pulling your shawl round
you a little more tightly.

'Have you looked around Vegas yet?' I ask.

You shake your head, say that you've hardly left your room
over the last three days.

'Me neither. Do you want to go for a walk along the Strip?'

You nod and we head towards the door, leaving our drinks
barely touched on the bar. Outside, the air is hot and dry
and you unwrap your shawl, draping it over an arm as we
slip into the steady stream of the other couples already out
on the street.

'Can I say something to you?' I ask.

'Sure.'

'This year was your first *Tekken* finals, right? I mean, I haven't seen you here before.'

You nod.

'I just think it's amazing that you've won in your first year. You must have beaten Tony Santos and Marek Jozwiak.'

'Tony Santos in the second round, Marek Jozwiak in the quarter-finals,' you say.

'So where the hell did you learn to play *Tekken*?'

You've always been into computer games, you tell me as we cross the street in front of Caesar's Palace. You grew up by the coast in South Devon, Torbay, a little place called Goodrington, nothing more than a cluster of holiday homes, caravan parks, chip shops and ice-cream parlours. By the time you were eight, you were telling your mother that you were reading on the beach and really sneaking into the beach-front video arcades for long hot summers of *Robotron* and *Galaxian*.

'It lasted until I was eleven,' you tell me. 'Three blissful years. And then I got caught by my mum. She freaked, told me that the arcades weren't for girls like me, that they were "drug dens", that I was never to go back. So I promised that I wouldn't. But I did, almost straight away, and got away with it for another three years until I got caught again.'

You laugh, say that it wasn't as if you were up to anything *bad*. You were still top of your class, you tell me, and always would be, though you make it sound as average an achievement as doing your laundry.

'So why all the hassle?' you ask me.

We stop inside New York, New York for coffee-cake and you tell me that it soon didn't matter. By the time you were sixteen, your parents had given up trying to stop you. And a year later, you'd been offered a place by Somerville College, Oxford to study History and your parents pretty soon stopped

200

minding about anything. You got the A levels you needed, a degree three years later, and you've just finished a masters degree on the American Revolution.

'An academic genius *and* the *Tekken* World Champion,' I joke.

'I'm not really World Champion,' you say, 'unless I can successfully defend my title in Stockholm in November. And anyway, I don't do much else besides play computer games and read books. It's not like I'm much good at anything else.'

•

Maybe that helps explain things a little better, maybe it doesn't. I know I can't tell you to forget me. And if I feel guilty telling you that I'll be thinking of you every second of every day, it's because I know it can't help you understand my decision any more clearly. But you know I believe in the truth, and that's the way it will be . . . me thinking of you, thinking of you and knowing that I might have made a terrible, terrible mistake. If it is, then I guess we'll have to live with it. I hope you can. I hope I can.

•

Now we wander further up the strip, to the Excalibur and to the Luxor where we drink more cocktails. You ask me questions and I tell you all about being one of the security guards at the Trocadero Centre along with Jimmy.

'The Trocadero – where's that?'

'Piccadilly Circus. Surely you know where that is?'

You shake your head, say that you've never really been anywhere outside of the West Country except Oxford, and suddenly I'm telling you all about it, the six floors of arcade games, the crowds of kids each weekend, the bored staff in colour-coded shellsuits, the gangs of waiters drifting in from nearby Chinatown during the afternoons to gamble their tips on the fruit machines and play a few rounds of *Tekken*.

You ask me what happens next. Do I want promotion or a different job and I tell you about the programming course I've been doing, two years of learning Visual C++.

'If I can't make it as a professional gamer, at least I can get a new job coding games.'

Finally our glasses are empty (our fourth drinks? our fifth?) and neither of us makes a move to order more.

'Shall we walk back to the Imperial Palace?' you ask.

Outside the Luxor, we cross the Strip and walk back along the other side. I'm speechless when I feel you slip an arm through mine and you don't talk either for the whole twenty minutes that it takes to get back to the hotel. *What are you thinking?* Do you want me to kiss you – or are you merely being friendly? Do I even know *how* to kiss you (I can't remember the last time a girl put her arm through mine, let alone the last time anything more happened)?

And then we're back at the Imperial Palace, walking through the mayhem of porters and waiting cabs and into the hotel lobby. From where we're standing, we're equidistant from both the bar and a bank of elevators.

Another pause.

'I . . .'

'So . . .'

The both of us stop and laugh a little nervously.

'You first . . .'

'No. *You* first!'

You tell me that you were thinking of going upstairs to your room.

'Me too. What floor are you on?' I ask, staring at your face but unable to read what you're thinking.

'Fourteenth. You?'

I laugh. 'The fourteenth too.'

Feeling a little foolish, we walk over to the elevators and step inside where I press the button and the door closes. Again, you slip your arm through mine and I wonder whether I should kiss you. But I imagine the pitying expression you'll have on your face when you have to tell me gently that it 'wasn't what you had in mind at all' and don't make a move towards you. Then we reach the fourteenth floor and the doors slide apart.

'What room are you in?' you ask.

'Er . . . me and Jimmy are sharing 1414.'

'I'm in 1427 – I think that might be across the corridor from you. Isn't that a funny coincidence!'

I laugh nervously and we duly stroll along the corridor towards our rooms. I notice that we walk apart now and tell myself that I was right, that you were just being friendly the way some women are, that nothing could fill you with more horror than the idea of me making my clumsy pass at you.

Then we're standing outside room 1414, directly opposite 1427.

'I was right,' you say.

'You were.'

Through the thin door to my room, I can hear the sounds of laughter and drinking, the sounds of a computer game squawking away. Jimmy must have brought some people back for a few drinks.

'Well, I've had a lovely evening,' you say.

'Me too. And congratulations on winning today.'

'Thanks,' you say. Now you're trying to stretch up and kiss me on the cheek, but you can't reach, even on tip-toe, and before we know it we're in each other's arms and trying to kiss and trying to get your door key out of your purse and let ourselves into your room all at the same time.

●

Don't try to reply. I won't be on this address any more. I'm going travelling, Japan first to do some playtesting for a software company, then through Asia, checking out the Arcades and learning a few new games. PLEASE don't try to follow me.

•

Later, as the rising sun comes up over the desert horizon, we're lying in your bed and it's my turn to tell you about how I grew up playing computer games. Perhaps it all started when my mum left suddenly (my mum had gone . . . *where?*) and I would have to stay in our neighbour Jackie's front room after school. That was the first time I remember playing a computer game. Usually I would sit there watching cartoons until Dad got back from the site. But one day, when I was about nine, Jackie's husband Ken (short for Kenzo – he was the first Japanese guy my father could remember living in Bromley) had just returned from a business trip with a primitive computer console and a game called *Pong*. You say you remember *Pong*, two vertical lines, one on ether side of the screen, each batting a dot of light across to the other as if it were a tennis ball. *As for me?* I remember the feeling of never wanting the first time I played it to end. It felt good, swatting the dot back across the screen and beating the machine, and Dad had needed to drag me away when he finally arrived back from the building-site.

After that, I played *Pong* each day before tea until I was ten and Dad said I was old enough to come home from school on my own. After that, I would go to the chip shop round the corner from our house where I would play *Scramble*, or to the petrol station where they had an *Asteroids* machine and I soon learnt to *two-tap* and *lurk* so that my ten pee would last for an hour.

Was it healthy to take so much pride in having logged the ten all-time highest scores on the machine?

1.	BOO	501,280
2.	BOO	450,420
3.	BOO	385,320
4.	BOO	360,280
5.	BOO	360,200
6.	BOO	258,260
7.	BOO	100,120
8.	BOO	90,360
9.	BOO	88,380
10.	BOO	88,220

If I walked in after school to find that some PEA or JIZ or FUK or TIT had come in during the day and grabbed the eighth or ninth spot on the ladder, I would play until I'd knocked his initials off the screen. Sometimes it would take three hours and other kids would often hang about waiting for me to finish so that they could have a go. When they realised how long I was likely to be *with just one credit*, they'd try to put me off by taunting me about my weight. But I'd learnt to ignore such insults by then, learnt to shut them out (I'd already ballooned up to around thirteen stone and suffered enough abuse at school to have acclimatised to it) and just played on regardless.

After that? Soon they opened an arcade in Bromley High Street. It was mainly filled with fruit machines, but there were a few video-games and I'd go there as soon as my last lesson was over, grab a couple of Mars Bars, a pack of Golden Wonder and a can of Coke for lunch, and then settle down to a few hours of *Space Invaders* and *Defender*. And by the time I was thirteen, the first home computers and consoles were coming out and I just played at home.

You ask me how I ended up working at the Trocadero. I tell you that I left school at sixteen and started working with my dad. I was seventeen stone and six feet tall – humping bricks up and down ladders came pretty easily – and four years of being a builder earned me more than enough to buy a PC and more games. And then two years ago Jimmy's dad who worked with us told me that Jimmy was starting a programming course while he worked part-time as a security guard 'up in town'.

'You could do that,' he told me and he was right. There was another job going at the Trocadero. As for the course? Enrolling was only a matter of paying the fee and pretty soon I was moving my stuff into the spare room at Jimmy's new flat in Kentish Town.

•

No one else knows exactly where I'm going to be, not my parents, not Lottie, not Anita – you could waste too much time looking for me.

•

Jimmy asks me where I spent the night when I see him the next day and he can't believe it when I tell him.

'And you're going to stay in Las Vegas another three days?' he asks.

I nod.

'With *her?*'

'Why not? I won two thousand dollars yesterday. The plane ticket and expenses so far only add up to about half of that so I'm going to blow the rest on staying here with Clarity. Obviously, she's got ten thousand to play with.'

Jimmy's silent for a while. And then he laughs.

'*Yer dark fookin' horse!*'

And then it's just you and me in Las Vegas for three nights. We keep your room at the Imperial Palace but eat in Caesar's across the road. We take blackjack lessons in the Aladdin but lose two hundred dollars in the Mirage. We spend the nights making love (and with you curled up in my arms) and in the mornings I watch you swim ('fifty lengths at least three times a week', you tell me, 'but preferably every day'). I never want it to end.

On our last night in America, I want to ask you what you think will happen to us when we get back to England but I'm too afraid to say anything and you don't say anything either, not even over dinner which we eat in almost total silence. Later, we take a cab up to Fremont Street and walk past Winner's Wall and the Golden Nugget towards the outskirts of town where we find a bar with an old *Gorf* game that's still only a quarter a play before returning to our room an hour or so later. You still don't say much and I feel too awkward to bring up the subject of what happens next and pour myself a drink from the mini-bar instead to give myself something to do.

It's then that you turn on the console that's plugged into the hotel room TV.

'What are you doing?' I ask.

'I thought about playing some *Tekken*. I haven't played since the final, not for three days. It feels kind of strange not to have played for so long.'

You're right: neither of us have played *Tekken* since the final.

'Want to play?'

You nod towards the spare controller and I stare down at it but don't pick it up. The last thing I want to do is get thrashed by you with near perfect score after near perfect score.

'Play me!' you say again, the sound of the game loading up in the background, 'I loved that chickened reversal you pulled off against Kim Chang-ho in the semi. You were too busy concentrating but you should have seen him! His whole body froze the moment he realised that you suckered him.'

'He never expected it . . .'

'It scared him shitless! But that's Hwoarang players for you, all fur coat and no knickers . . . and *so arrogant!* They all believe that they're invincible . . .'

'It's not even a hard move to pull off if you see it coming – you just have to think one stage ahead . . .'

Suddenly I'm sitting next to you on the thick carpet (like my mum's slippers, I think to myself – her slippers are one of the few things I remember about her), the flashing lights streaming across our faces as I load up Jin Kazama in his leather jacket and leap across the dojo towards you, fist flying. I take the first fight, you take the second. I take the third but you take the fourth.

'You're not going easy on me now you're the World Champion and I'm a humble runner-up?' I say, connecting a White Heron with Arching Roundhouse manoeuvre.

'I told you Boomer: I don't consider myself to be World Champion until I've defended my title in Stockholm in November. Mind you, if you play like this, it shouldn't be too hard . . .'

When you call me Boomer, my body throbs with electricity (on screen, you're Firedancing towards me and I counter with an Electric Guard before lashing you with a set of Twin Lancer punches). When you execute a two-punch combination with backslaps and a Reverse Punt, you tell me that the most beautiful thing about *Tekken* is the fact that Ling Xiaoyu players call the Reverse Punt move 'Mistrust'.

'Mistrust,' you say, 'that's beautiful.'

After twenty fights, we're tied at ten each. I take the twenty-first, you take the twenty-second and twenty-third but I put you down with a buffered Headbutt in the twenty-fourth to tie us at twelve victories each. Twenty more fights (and an hour later), we're tied with twenty-two victories each, all the time talking about what we're doing, thinking out loud, swapping strategies and moves.

'Ling's left jab – timed at eight frames,' you tell me as you jab with your left, 'the equal fastest move in the game.'

'Her right kick's timed at ten frames.'

You try a Sunrise Fan attack but miss and I deliver the appropriate punishment.

'Now you're definitely going easy on me,' I tell you. 'The recovery time for that one is monstrous, eighteen frames or something achingly slow like that.'

'Maybe I don't want to put you off,' you say, rolling to your feet and cartwheeling away.

'Put me off what?' I ask, powering up and coming at you with a Corpse Splitter.

'Me.'

'You?'

'Me. What's going to happen to us, Boomer? Maybe you don't know, but I *need* to talk about it.'

On the screen, you close in for a Slam throw (with forearm chop) but I backstep before dancing in close to wrap my arms around your body and force you to the floor, straddling both legs across your breasts and driving in a series of punches. Twenty-three twenty-two to me.

'I don't think there's anything you could do to put me off you,' I say. 'And I can't imagine not being with you. I could visit you – in Oxford or in Devon. If you like.'

'I was thinking . . .' You pause to open the next fight with a one-two and Lotus Twist before backing away. 'I was hoping for something closer.'

By the time we're tied at forty fights each, we can't play any more, and we both lie back on the floor and watch the lights from the Strip outside play across the ceiling. You've told me that you want to move to London now that you've finished with Cambridge and I tell you that you can stay with me if you need a place to stay while you look for your own place and it's then you ask me why you would need your own place.

The next day we fly back to England and you sleep in my lap. I just stare down at you for the whole journey and stroke your hair. If I've been wondering for three days when all of this is going to end and asking myself what I've done to deserve you, I'm also telling myself that whatever I've done, I've done it *right* and that this is *never* going to end. It's never going to end.

At Gatwick we almost can't bear to say goodbye to each other. But after two weeks you move into the flat in Kentish Town and we both start practising for the Stockholm Tekken Challenge where we'll both go on to lose our respective semi-finals.

•

If we do ever run into each other, then I'll walk on over and say 'Hi', I promise, and maybe we'll go for a beer and see where we are in our lives. It's not that I'm leaving things open to chance (and I don't expect you necessarily to greet me with a smile) – more that if fate does ever find us in the same place again . . .

•

Which one of us first suggested the idea of getting married? I remember the night clearly. I get back from a late shift. I find you in bed playing *Wipeout*. I wash. I climb into bed next to you and while we race in split-screen mode you tell me how happy you are, that playing *Wipeout* in bed with me makes you the 'happiest person alive'. Things go blurred at that point. One minute we're racing around some secret courses. The next we're planning which hotel to stay in when we go back to Las Vegas to get married.

'Jimmy can be my best man.'

'Lottie and Anita can be my bridesmaids.'

'My dad will come.'

'My parents won't, I don't think: they can't even handle the fact that I'm a gamer so I can't see them flying to Las Vegas to see me get married. But I think they'd ultimately be happy for me.'

'Would you rather get married here?'

You shake your head. 'I would love to get married in Vegas. We could travel separately and not see each other for the first night. You could stay in the Imperial Palace and I could stay at Caesar's.'

'I didn't know you were so old-fashioned,' I say.

'It'll be more romantic. And then we could meet the next day at the chapel – and then we'd be married. It would be so beautiful, Boomer, it would be so beautiful . . .'

•

Look after yourself. And always believe in yourself, even if it seems I haven't been able to.

Clarity.

3

'So she's postponed it?'

'I don't think so,' I said, staring at the water in the pool and remembering watching Clarity diving into it six months earlier.

'What's she said?' asked Jimmy

I told them all that Clarity never arrived in Las Vegas, that she didn't want to go through with the wedding.

'It's just last-minute nerves . . .'

'We can call her, can't we . . . and get her back?'

I shook my head. And then I shot up out of my lounger and started stumbling towards the shadowy interior of the hotel.

'*Boomer!*'

Somehow I managed to get to away before anyone could

stop me. Maybe everyone was too shocked to react quickly enough. Maybe they realised that I needed to be alone for a while. Maybe I ran, a dumb bumbling blob grunting my way through the Imperial Palace and out on to the Strip. I stopped for breath on the edge of the sidewalk, drawing stares from the people passing by, and for a moment I remembered how once I'd had to run away from a couple of glue-sniffing skinheads who were throwing stones at me as they chased me across the local rec ground. I'd burst into the nearby café that time for shelter, stumbling and crying, only to be laughed at the by the road workers camped around the plastic tables with mugs of tea. And then I saw Caesar's Palace across the road and I marched across. Inside the lobby, I almost stormed up to the reception desk and demanded to see Clarity, as if she was sitting in her room suffering from an attack of last-minute nerves. But of course she wasn't there. She wasn't there.

Where could I go?

I drifted through the gaming tables and into a shopping mall styled like a Roman forum, white stucco pillars, fountains in the middle of cobbled piazzas, a fake blue sky overhead with cotton-candy clouds painted on it. Clothes shops. Souvenirs. Ice-cream parlours. A gallery with a cylindrical aquarium around which corkscrewed a rainbow of tropical fish. Eventually I found a bar and drank down a few beers and remembered meeting Clarity here the summer before and how we'd planned the whole trip three months later.

We'd announced our plan to get married a week after first talking about it. As it turned out, my dad hadn't wanted to come (he couldn't handle the flight, he'd said, but wished me the best of luck and hugged me and Clarity with his broad, tattooed forearms) and Clarity had been right about her parents – they hadn't wanted to come to America but invited us to stay with them in Devon when we returned. Would our friends be able to come? We weren't sure, but after telling a whole crowd of them, enough people committed themselves to make it worthwhile and we went ahead with buying plane tickets and putting down a deposit for hotel rooms and a slot at the Little Chapel of Flowers.

At the bar, I thought about reading Clarity's email again, but realised that I'd left it on the table by the pool in the Imperial Palace. Maybe the others were reading it. It was then that Jimmy found me.

'Boomer. Are you alright, mate?'

I asked him how he knew where to look for me and he shrugged, saying that he hadn't, that everyone had been out looking for me. He held out the printout.

'Here you are. None of us read it,' he added. I didn't take it so he put it down on the bar and pulled up a stool.

'I'm sorry, Boomer . . .'

'It's not your fault.'

'I know but . . .' Jimmy asked me if I'd tried calling England to see if I could get hold of her or her parents? Anita or Lottie? I shook my head.

'I've read it and I know Clarity well enough to know that if she says she can't be contacted then she's out of reach.'

We were silent for a moment.

'How are the others?' I asked. 'Everyone's come all this way. I can't believe I've let everybody down.'

'It's not like it's your fault,' Jimmy said.

'It feels as if it is.'

'They'll be okay. They are worried about you, though. *I'm* worried about you.'

'I . . . I . . .'

Jimmy put a hand on my shoulder. 'Tell me?'

213

'I feel as if it's my fault because I should have known better. This is how things *should* turn out for me. This is how things *always* turn out for me. I feel as if I've had my six months of happiness and now it's back to being fat and lonely for another twenty-five years. I knew it was all too good to be true.'

Jimmy looked at me.

'Did Clarity ever *once* make a comment about your *weight*?' he asked.

I shook my head.

'Not once?'

'Not once.'

'And are you saying that you didn't feel fat once while you and Clarity were together?'

I shook my head again. 'No,' I said, 'I felt happy.'

Jimmy sighed. 'Mate, you may have felt happy – but you were fat as well. *Happy* fat.'

He lit a Regal.

'Now you're *sad* fat.' He puffed on his cigarette. 'Look, mate, you may feel like shit, and I admit that I haven't read her letter to you. But I don't think Clarity left you because of anything like that.'

We sat in silence for a little while. Jimmy asked me if I wanted another drink and I shook my head.

'You're right, Jimmy: I feel like shit.'

'I don't think you're going to feel any different for a while,' he said. 'I'm not going to lie to you and I can't put it any other way. But let's go back to the hotel and take it from there. We'll let the others know that you're okay and call the chapel and tell them what's happened. After that we can decide whether we go back to England straight away or in a few days. We'll do whatever you want – that's one thing I can promise you.'

I looked around me at the crowds of sun-tanned people filing past. For a moment, all I wanted to do was be sitting on my own with a computer game, any kind of game (it didn't matter) as long as it was an electronic world with fixed objectives and where the only issue at stake was how *good* I was and how many special moves I knew.

'Let's go,' Jimmy said again, gently, and I nodded. For a second I thought of leaving Clarity's email on the bar. I wondered if I could even bring myself to touch it. But then I thought of her and folded it into my pocket.

'Let's go,' I said, 'let's just go.'

Now we walked back out of the mall with its Roman Temples and its statues of gods and gladiators, past the bars and cafés and shops selling golfing gear and tuxedos and wedding dresses. On the other side of the gaming rooms, we found a travelator that would take us back out on to the Strip.

'You ready?'

I nodded, and as we both stepped on to the moving walkway we allowed ourselves to be carried towards the midday sun.

THE PROJECT

In an infinite universe there can exist an infinite number of
extraterrestrial human beings, and in fact an infinite number of
beings identical to myself.

Paul Davies, *Are We Alone?*

Sometimes I wonder
Why I spend the lonely nights
Dreaming of a song
The melody haunts my reverie
And I am once again with you

 Nice work, Ray, you tell yourself as you haul the cab out of
the dark funnel of an underpass and through the static glare
of another intersection, an old song blaring at you through the
radio speakers, *real nice*. Not content with losing Tess, you've
made your best friend mad, you've gotten yourself thrown out
of Wizard's for brawling and now you're driving drunk. The
way thing's are going, surely it's only a matter of time before
you get pulled over and the shit really hits the fan.

When our love was new
And each kiss an inspiration
But that was long ago
And now my consolation
Is in the stardust of a song

 Could you screw things up any worse? For a moment you
don't know where you are and when you look out through
the windshield, you suddenly realize that in your drunken
confusion you've driven back to the block where you and
Tess used to live. A reflex? The only thing you could do
now to make things worse is ditch the cab, walk up to your

old front door and start banging on it, start screaming at the
top your voice the way you did more than a few times just
after Tess threw you out.

> Beside a garden wall
> When stars are bright
> You are in my arms
> The nightingale tells his fairy tale
> Of paradise where roses grew

You remember the last of these occasions. You were lonely.
You were hysterical. You looked like a haggard tramp (you still
hadn't found a new place to live and were sleeping in the back
of the cab at the time). The door had suddenly swung inwards
and your heartbeat had quickened as you thought: *at least she
opened the door this time, at least she opened the door!* It was then
you realized that you were staring at a stranger, an elderly man
in a vest leaning heavily on his walking stick, shapes moving
nervously in the hallway behind him. He told you that the
last tenants had moved on (no, they hadn't left a forwarding
address) and it was at that point you knew it was over.

> 'though I dream in vain
> In my heart it will remain
> My stardust melody
> The memory of love's refrain

Now you switch through the channels wanting to listen
to anything but old love songs. On another station there's a
discussion about the death toll from last year's monsoons and
what people can do to avoid disaster this year. On the next

there's pop music, the kind of stuff that kids listen to, moronic monkey chatter over a backbeat of clashing gears. On another channel the sports results are coming through . . . *the Stars beat the Meteors . . . the Comets beat the Fireballs . . . the Satellites beat the Novas* . . . suddenly you can't decide whether you're sick of the disembodied voices rattling around the inside of the cab or whether silence would be worse. You turn the radio off. You turn it back on. You turn it off again. After a few moments, you boot up the engine and pull back out into the traffic and head east for the couple of four-by-fours you call your new home.

It was all going fine, you reason, as you fly through the near-empty streets. Earlier on, you'd just dropped a couple off in the South Parallels (thirty credits with a five credit tip) when the light on the com-link on your dash flickered from green to red. It was Jeff and he was calling to see if you wanted to clock off early and drink a few beers. Sure you did, you said, and you both agreed to meet at Wizard's even though you never met anywhere else. It took ten minutes to get there. Jeff was already waiting for you with a pitcher and a couple of glasses and he came over and gave you a hug when he saw you, slapped you on the back with the gigantic wedges of his hands and the two of you shot a few frames of pool. While you were playing, you swapped stories about some of the freaks and crazies you've had in the back of your cabs the last few days, the usual hacker monologues of jumped fares, bad traffic and foul-mouthed lunatics. And after a few drinks, you were pouring out another pitcher when you looked at Jeff and considered how he's been dutifully meeting you at least two nights a week ever since Tess left, never letting on that he's worried about you and always making sure you're not on your own for too many nights in a row. And you think: *Typical Jeff,* your heart glowing, *a bear-sized guy with a bear-sized heart.* In return, you don't let on that you know he's just looking out for you and that Betsy probably doesn't need her husband spending half his free time babysitting some guy who cheated on his girlfriend the same way she doesn't really need you coming over for a home-cooked dinner every Sunday. And then, catching yourself smiling, you thought that maybe you were starting to feel better about things, that maybe you were starting to *recover.* So you told him, nothing dramatic, just one guy talking to another guy.

'Jeff,' you said, draining your glass and refilling it (spilling a bit, but not too much), 'I think I'm starting to feel better. I think I'm really starting to be myself again.'

'Yeah? That's real good, Ray,' he replied, 'I'm glad. I don't know what I'd do if Betsy ever left me, I don't know how I'd cope.'

'Well,' you said, bending down to take a shot, 'I'm starting to *cope.*'

Of course it was then that you saw Georgia Jones walk in through the steel doors, watched as she stalked up to the bar in her heels and skirt. Jeff must have noticed you tense up because you immediately felt his heavy hand come to rest on your shoulder, heard his voice in your ear.

'Easy, buddy! Best just let it go, huh?' you heard him whisper and you heard yourself tell him that you were fine as you refilled your glass and drained it and refilled it again. You remember Jeff's hand lingered on your shoulder a few seconds longer. And then he was stooping into the bright light to take his shot and you were looking over towards the bar again. There she was. You watched her wait to order a drink, your grip on your cue tightening as you saw her turn and laugh at something one of the guys sitting nearby had said. Her teeth glistened in the damp light, you noticed, as she pushed a thick stripe of black hair behind an ear and laughed again, and you wondered what dumb line the chump on the barstool had grunted at her.

And then you watched as she allowed him to buy her drink for her, watched the way she twisted her body on to the vacant stool next to him, legs crossing and the hem of her skirt riding a little higher up her thigh. *Who was he?* You thought you recognized him as one of the bruisers who worked down in Mechanics & Maintenance at the depot. And Georgia's eyes, you noticed, glanced in your direction, metallic buttons that fixed themselves on to yours for a moment before triumphantly turning away . . . suddenly you were upending the last of the beer into your mouth and walking over towards her, Jeff's voice somewhere behind you, Georgia not turning to face you until you were shouting at her across the space of a couple of meters, the chump standing and moving himself between the two of you with his hands raised. You were shouting, you remember, but what you were saying seems to have been deleted from your memory. At some point you felt Jeff's hand trying to pull you back and you remember shaking yourself free of his restraining grip. At some point the chump slammed both hands against your chest and knocked you back a couple of steps, his body lunging across the gap and his face looming into yours, the flattened trowel of his nose and the scuffed humps of his cheeks bristling against your face, his breath mingling with yours. At some point you brandished your cue at him and it was then that several pairs of hands reached out towards you and pulled you backwards. As you were dragged away, slurring and screaming, you looked back at Georgia to see her calmly meeting your gaze, her face receding into the distance as you were hurled out into the steaming night, and you couldn't help but remember those same eyes closing and the murmur of expectation that had slipped out from between her parted lips when your faces had merged outside her apartment door.

Outside Wizard's it was Jeff's turn to shout into your face: *what the hell were you thinking? Was this what you called 'coping'?* By then you were crying and almost unable to breathe. You were thinking about Tess and the way you'd both eaten that last meal in silence, the way she'd suddenly put her knife and fork down on her plate and pushed it away, her food barely disturbed. Her face had turned pale (how quickly her face had voided itself of colour, you thought, your body suddenly tingling with alarm) and you saw her throat tremble as if there was a small creature trapped inside it and you asked her what was wrong.

'What's the matter, honey . . . ?'

'Some of the girls at work have been gossiping,' she'd interrupted. 'Th-th-there's a rumor going around that . . .'

For the millionth time, you can't believe that you were so stupid. The girls in the dispatch rooms have nothing to talk about all day. Jeff and you were always laughing about it. Jeez . . . *Tess* and you were always laughing about it. Why had you ever been foolish enough to believe that you'd be able to keep the whole thing from her?

And now you think back to the parking lot outside the back of Wizard's: why did you pick up a trash can and hurl it at Jeff's cab before driving away? Is any of this *his* fault?

You focus on the road ahead, glance into the rearview expecting to see the blinding glare of a Trooper's patrol lights bearing down on you at any moment. But the air is empty behind you and soon you pull out on to the Mariposa Skyway where the traffic is heavier, climbing up into the express lanes and jinking the cab in and out of the hulking transporters speeding their way out to The Circuit and the freight yards over on East Point. Up above, you can see the squat shapes of the off-world mining rigs as they come in to land, giant lumbering shadows amongst the swarms of Guide Pods that weave around them like fireflies, the huge surging bellow of their anti-thrust audible above the cab engine as they slowly lower themselves towards the ground. Beyond them, the skyline burns blue and yellow and orange above the city, the massed clouds writhing and bristling in the sky like giant beasts, like mutant sea monsters wrestling with each other through the depths of an incendiary sea.

•

The following day you wake up to the sound of the terminal in the next room flicking on and blaring the news in through the doorway: economic fluctuation, a collapsed block over in the Ten-Forties, the latest in the election race, satellite footage of the radiation storms sweeping across the Arctic tundra, the first reports of an industrial explosion on the moon. You lie there for a few seconds, letting the sound wash over you before you sit up in bed and it's then that you realize that you're still in yesterday's clothes. For a moment you wonder if you put them on the day before. And then you drag yourself out of bed and undress and throw it all on to the pile that's already festering in the corner of the room and wonder how you ever managed to become such a slob. *Wasn't it Tess who was always the untidy one out of the two of you?* You limp through the squalid undergrowth of your apartment and slump down on to the floor of the shower stall, tell yourself that you've got to pull yourself together or . . . *or what?* All you can see lying in wait for you is another day behind the wheel of the cab, another day drifting through the maze of city blocks and yet another fitful night of regret and self-loathing spent drowning in the meaningless blue light of the terminal screen. *How can you kill this feeling? How do you kill it? How can you kill this feeling of dumb uselessness?* Without Tess, you just feel part of the city's grinding machinery. Eating to shit, only to feel hungry again. Drinking only to feel hungover and to crave more drink. Washing yourself only to get dirty again. And there was work: mindless, repetitive, anonymous. Whole days spent in the cab processing the banked tiers of traffic on the city's streets, the fares, the credits, the aliens and spooks who climbed into the backseat twenty times a day.

Now you think about Tess and you remember the first time you met her. Earlier that morning you'd headed out to pick up a fare on Battery Drive when an empty school bus ploughed into your right fender and crumpled the front corner of the hood. After an argument with the driver (you still remember him now, a guy with a face like ploughed concrete who denied all responsibility even though you'd been stationary and he'd more or less impaled your cab on the front of his bus), you'd ditched the cab at the side of the road and caught the sub back to the depot. There were forms to be filled in – insurance, disclaimers, 3rd party verification, replacement vehicle rental – and you walked up to the office only to round a corner and run straight into a woman. It was as if she appeared out of nowhere only to smack straight into you, the mound of papers she'd been carrying scattering over the floor around your feet. Quickly, you bent down to gather them back together – but so did she and your heads clashed.

'Ouch!'

'Ouch!'

'Hey, I'm real sorry,' you said.

'That's okay,' she replied, two long fingers massaging her forehead.

'Would you believe this is the second collision I've had

today,' you said with a smile. 'Some idiot just totaled the front of my cab. You don't happen to know if you've got any IF110s and a VR303 amongst all this?'

They were just dispatch-clerk rosters, she told you, and you realised that you hadn't seen her before.

'You new?' you asked.

'Just started,' she replied, 'it's my first day.'

The next thing you noticed was how tan she was, the white dress she was wearing only emphasizing the honeyed color of her skin. You asked her if she'd been on holiday and she told you that she'd just been on a two-week trip to one of the resorts along Pleasure Beach. She wasn't wearing a wedding ring and you wondered if she had a boyfriend.

'Have a good time?' you asked. She nodded but told you that she'd been lonely now and then.

'I went on my own. I guess I expected to meet people, but it was mainly couples and families. Still, the rest did me a lot of good: cleaner air, lots of sleep, leisurely meals, lots of evenings watching the sun set slowly over the sea.'

You held out your hand and told her your name was Ray. She said that she was called Tess and you managed to stop yourself from asking her out then and there. And then a week later you loitered outside the depot canteen in a pressed check shirt and red sports jacket until you saw her walk in for her lunch-break and then you duly slipped into line behind her. You started talking. *How was her first week? Were the others being friendly to her?* You told her that the girls in the dispatch center could be ruthless with newcomers but someone nice like her shouldn't have any problems making friends.

Then the two of you got talking about sports. Did she want to go to watch the Novas with you? They were playing the Asteroids the following Friday night at the Novadome and a friend of yours who worked a security shift at the stadium could get you a pair of good tickets. It turned out that Tess *did* want to go see the Novas. And it turned out that Tess wanted to go to the pictures the following Friday and eat baloney rolls with you at the Lonely Island fair afterwards. And it turned out that Tess wanted to drink Margaritas and dance to jazz and salsa at The Fuego after that and it turned out that Tess wanted to drive out to Griffiths Point after that and park the cab and watch the fiery tails of the rockets taking off from Armstrong on the horizon along with all the other couples. And then a few months later it turned out that Tess wanted you both to live together. So did you and you both gave up your apartments for a larger one in Lower Sunset.

Now you ask yourself: what was life with Tess like? *Come on, Ray, what was it like?* It was paradise. Between the two of you, you had little money to spare. But life in the apartment seemed to *throb* with contentment and the city outside seemed like a magical toy for the two of you to play with together. Looking back, you can hardly believe that you're the same person as the man you remember back then, the guy who woke up with Tess each morning, the guy who drove her to the depot at the start of each day and the guy who brought her home each evening, the guy who took her to bed each night. But you can hardly believe that you're living in the same city as you did back then. *Back then?* Was it only a couple of months ago? You remember your life together reaching some kind of peak and the two of you suddenly lying in your bed having just made love and one of you suddenly talking about starting a family. You can't remember which one out of the two of you mentioned it first but suddenly you were both excited, the two of you almost daring the other to come right out and say it: you wanted to have a child. Neither of you cared if it was a boy or a girl but both of you knew that you'd have to start saving. So you both started taking on more overtime. You started driving sixteen-hour shifts and Tess started working a few nights. You saw each other less and less, your only contact for days sometimes being the brief moments you passed each other in the hallway of the apartment or in a corridor at the depot, the two of you pausing for a weary kiss before going your separate ways.

And then Georgia Jones showed up. You remember walking into the office and seeing her there. You couldn't take your eyes off her breasts, the dark hair, the immaculate lips. The two of you started talking (a matter of basic courtesy surely?) and when she said that she'd 'see you around', her teeth lined up in a smile, you couldn't help but reply: *yeah, see you around*. And you *did* see her around. While Tess was sleeping off another double shift at the apartment, you seemed to be finding more and more reasons to stop by the depot and you'd see her *everywhere*. In the canteen. In the office. In the diner across the street. At Wizard's – but also at other hacker bars, at Travis's in The Loop and at Easy Andy's over on Palantine Hill. And then one time you passed her on the steps up to the depot's entrance lobby. You both stopped to say 'hi' (you were going in, she was coming out) and when she asked you for a ride back to her apartment you nodded with a quick look over both your shoulders.

And then a fortnight later you were eating dinner with Tess when she told you that *she knew*.

Sitting there in the shower stall, you let your head bang back on to the tiles, let the water sluice through the opening of your slack mouth. Telling yourself that it's all your fault doesn't seem to make things feel any better and as the water splashes down, you imagine a universe where you could gather your will and force the water to travel in a different direction, to flow upwards from off the top of your head and back into the shower head. In such a universe you'd be able to unravel the tangle of mistakes that you've made and you'd eventually find yourself back at that day two months ago when you walked into the dispatch room to query your payslip. Only then would you let time start moving forwards again only this time you wouldn't take any notice of the new girl in the tube dress who stared at you from behind her screen with matted eyelashes. No, you'd be polite (you'd still say hello, introduce yourself and welcome her to the firm with a standard smile) but you'd think of Tess and remember to be grateful for everything you had.

Now you get up and step out of the shower stall to dry yourself (realizing, given the stink coming off the damp towel, that you're probably only making yourself dirty again) and it's then that you hear the terminal beep. You have a message waiting. *Maybe it's Tess*, you think to yourself immediately, and then groan at yourself for being so stupid. The other thought is that it might be Jeff and you wince at the memory of the trash can bouncing off the hood of his cab the night before. But when you check, you see that the message waiting for you has been sent from 'THE DEPARTMENT OF SOCIAL EVOLUTION'. The Department of Social Evolution? What the hell is that – a charity? You read the contents of the message, and then read it again, just to make sure you understand it:

We are pleased to inform you that you have been selected as a potential contributor to an exciting scientific program that is currently being initiated by the Department along with the full support of the Government at an Executive level.

To this end, the Department would like to invite you to attend a consultative meeting with one of our Directors in order that you might learn more about this exceptional opportunity. You are under no obligation to respond to our request. But we would like to take this opportunity to emphasize the unique nature of our proposition.

We have contacted your employers and notified them of our intentions, arranging for you to be away from your place of work should you wish to accept our offer. Furthermore, we would credit you with a modest sum as a sign of our commitment to you should you attend such an introductory meeting . . .

What could the government possibly want with you? You check the message for evidence of a hidden agenda but there doesn't seem to be any. Confused, you decide to call the number at the end of the message to try to find out some more and almost immediately there's an efficient female voice on the other end of the line.

'Department of Social Evolution. Can I help you?'

'Hi,' you say. 'My name is Ray Straychek. I've just received a message from your department and I was wondering if you could tell me what it was all about?'

There's a pause while she brings your data up on her screen.

'Yes . . . Mr. Straychek . . . apartment 33089, Westside Towers. Can you tell me what you would like clarified for you?'

'Well,' you say, 'the message tells me that I've been selected to be part of a government experiment. Can you tell me more about it in advance?'

'Everybody's asked that,' she replies, 'but I'm afraid I'm not qualified to tell you any more than you already know. What I *can* say is that you've been scheduled for a meeting with Professor Zowber should you wish to take up our invitation and that he really is the best person to explain it all to you.'

You pause for a second, and then tell the woman that you'll be in later. *What the hell!* you think (noting the address at the end of the message), *at least it would be time away from the cab*. And immediately you feel your spirits lift at the thought of doing something different.

•

You pull the cab out on to the street and up into the traffic, the crowds on the steeped sidewalks moving like sleepwalkers, drained faces staring wearily into the screens of their communicators while the sky churns above them, waves of gray and white and black waiting to unload themselves on to the city below. *What would Tess make of all this*, you ask yourself, *what would she make of you being part of a 'government experiment'?* But then you're always wondering what Tess is thinking and always wondering what she's doing. When it came to thinking and doing things, you remember, she always seemed to be the same as you. Maybe that's changed now? Who knows.

It takes you half an hour to arrive at the address you have for the Department of Social Evolution and when you get there you're surprised. You expected it to be situated in the wing of some larger administrative block but find that it has a building all to itself, a towering structure disappearing upwards towards a vanishing point miles above. Walking across the wide plaza and through one of ten revolving doors into a marbled lobby, you stride up to the reception desk and introduce yourself to one of the several brightly uniformed women sitting in a line.

'I received a message this morning asking me to attend an introductory meeting,' you tell her and she asks you for your name.

'Ray Straychek.'

She taps this into her terminal. 'Ray Straychek.'

You nod. 'That's me.'

She asks you to verify your identity on a palmscanner and then consults her terminal again.

'Welcome to the Department of Social Evolution, Mr. Straychek,' she says, 'and thank you for responding so promptly to our invitation. You've been scheduled to meet with Professor Zowber. He's currently in the middle of another meeting but should be available for you shortly. Would you mind waiting? He really shouldn't be very long.'

You shake your head and are directed to a bank of padded chairs on the other side of the lobby where you take a seat and glance at the other people around you who are also waiting. You hope to see some distinguishing feature that you all share, a clue as to the reason why you've all been summoned, but none presents itself. None of you seem to have anything in common except that you're *there*.

Then, after maybe fifteen minutes, a uniformed woman comes over to you and tells you that the Professor is ready and you follow her across the lobby to an elevator. Inside, she punches a code into the console mounted on the wall and there's the distant sound of momentum, if not the sensation itself. Are you being lifted into the sky or lowered into the bowels of the building? You can't tell. Moments later the steelplex doors slide apart and you find yourself being led along a dark, windowless corridor with a row of doors on your right-hand side. You count them as you pass each one and eventually the woman stops by the twenty-fourth.

'Here we are,' she says and knocks. The door opens and a man appears.

'Mr. Straychek?' he asks her. She nods. 'Please,' he says, now turning to you and gesturing towards the room beyond, 'come in.'

You walk in and find yourself in a rectangular room. The far wall is entirely transparent, a floor-to-ceiling window, and as you look through it, you realize that you must be hundreds of storeys up in the air. You think of the grimy porthole back at your apartment. When you looked out of it, you saw . . . you saw a thousand other dark portholes staring right back at you, pale faces appearing here and there like dim lights. *But here?* From this height, the city grid lost its symmetry and took on a more organic form, the channels and grooves of the city streets and skyways more like the tubes of some miniature organism viewed through a microscope.

'Would you like a drink?' The man's voice from behind you.

'Er . . . yes please.'

You turn and look at the guy again. He's tall and thin and though he must be at least a decade older than you he has smoother skin and pampered sandy hair and for a second you think he's some public-relations hotshot, some kind of corporate charmer the Department have sent to schmooze you before the Professor shows up (will it be bad news, whatever it is they have to say to you?).

And then you realize: he's the Professor.

'I'm Max Zowber. Pleased to meet you,' he says as if he's been waiting for you to make the connection yourself. 'Some water?'

You nod, eyeing the tall pitcher on the desk, the only piece of furniture in the polished room besides two easy chairs that sit facing each other by the window.

'Take a seat,' he says, pointing with a manicured finger as he pours out a glass. 'It's a terrible time of year, isn't it, everyone waiting for the monsoons.' He hands you the glass and sits down opposite you. 'Though I expect it must mean a busy time for cab drivers?'

'Why?' you ask, noticing that your voice has become brittle with expectation.

'I imagine that the demand for cabs increases when the weather breaks. Day after day of heavy rainfall, no one wanting to use public transport . . .'

'It's actually the worst time of year for us,' you say, taking a sip. The water in the glass tastes like water but doesn't feel like any water that you've ever come across. It feels like something heavier, like honey or milk. 'When the rain finally falls people just hole up in their homes. No one wants to go anywhere. Things go pretty dead.'

Zowber looks at you, his eyeballs freezing for a second as if he's making an internal calculation. 'I guess you're right. I've never thought of it that way.' He eases back in his chair but continues to look directly at you. 'Anyway,' he says, 'you must be pretty confused as to why you've been invited to come here.'

You nod. 'So, where do we start?' you ask.

Zowber undoes the buttons on his suit jacket, a suit that looks as if it cost a fortnight's wages, and then folds his hands together.

'I guess we start with you telling me how much you know about the history of recent space travel.'

You pause for a second. This wasn't what you expected.

'What everyone else knows, I guess.'

'Which is?'

You cough, take another sip of water as your memory gropes its way back to the history lessons you sat doodling through when you were a kid. 'Well, as far as I know, until about a hundred years ago man couldn't realistically explore space much further than the moon. The main problem, as I remember it, was that they couldn't produce rocket engines with enough power to drive a ship fast enough to make the journey worthwhile. I mean, if it takes eight months to travel to the next nearest planet, what's the point?'

You stop. Zowber doesn't say anything so you continue.

'After that, they developed . . . what are they called . . . *fusion engines?*'

'"Fusion engines" is the layman's term for them, yes.'

'And the way I understand it, these fusion engines meant that ships could travel at far greater speeds. After that, scientists developed a way of shielding astronauts from the intense gravitational forces produced by traveling at such speeds. And now we can make it to the edge of the solar system, but not much further. Is that right? That's all I know.'

'More or less,' Zowber replies, 'and that's more than most people know in fact.' He stops for a second before continuing. 'For the last ninety-seven years, man has managed to travel safely at increased speeds, thanks largely to the technological advances made possible by the Richard–Felix experiments at the end of the last century. Thanks to them, and also to significant advances in the field of biophysical stasis, it became possible for mankind to travel to the edge of our system in a little under two weeks. A remarkable achievement in its own way. But one has to ask oneself: what exactly have we gained from such a possibility? Perhaps very little.'

'I thought we were able to mine the nearby planets for resources,' you say, painfully aware of how naïve you must sound. 'That's what we were taught in school anyway.'

'And you're right,' Professor Zowber replies patiently. 'The kinds of advances we've been talking about have reaped certain *material* rewards. But in broader terms, we have still gained very little. The kind of distances we're talking about are still less than infinitesimal when compared with those presented by stellar geography at even just a localized galactic level. Such distances give us no hope of meaningfully traveling much further beyond the edge of our solar system, let alone the possibility of the human race exploring far enough into space to reach another planet fit for colonization or give us even the remotest chance of contacting intelligent lifeforms whose existence so far remains only philosophically probable.

'Of course, if we could travel at the speed of light or faster, this would become possible but unfortunately the last two hundred years of space exploration have been limited by a problem that is, paradigmatically, extremely twentieth-century.'

Zowber sees that he's starting to lose you and explains himself.

'In order to cover the distances required to reach even the nearest star system that looks as if it could support human life, we would have to travel at the speed of light for four and half years. Given that our current technology only allows us to travel at one percent of one percent of that speed, reaching that star system is, for all intents and purposes, impossible. Until now, that is.'

You feel the hairs on the back of your neck stir.

'What? You've developed . . . *warp* engines?' you ask, now wondering more than ever before why the hell you've been summoned to this meeting. Zowber chuckles.

'No, not quite.' He leans forwards in his chair. 'Putting fiction aside for one moment, scientists are still experimenting with various possibilities for superluminal speed travel . . .'

'Superluminal?'

'Faster-than-light.'

'Oh, I see.'

'Various government departments, as well as several corporate concerns with obvious vested interests, have been testing the theoretical envelope that scientists proposed over two hundred years ago: will man ever be able to travel faster than the speed of light?

237

'We've tried to cover every angle,' he continues. 'We've reconsidered every one of our assumptions with regards space-time relations, reinvestigated our understanding of Absolute Time and *simultaneity*. We've explored Alternative Gravity theories, electromagnetism. We've experimented with various types of fuels and propellants, with exotic matter that produces negative energy densities in space, with . . .'

Zowber stops mid-sentence.

'I'm sorry,' he says to you, 'maybe I should put it to you a different way.'

He gets up, walks over to the desk and returns to his seat with a single sheet of paper taken from a hidden drawer. This he holds up in front of your eyes by two opposing corners.

'You see this piece of paper, right?'

You nod.

'Now imagine that this piece of paper is space and we are at *this* corner.' He inclines his head towards his left hand. 'Now imagine that the diagonally opposite corner represents our intended destination, a place we want to get to, a planet four and a half light years away, for instance. What I've been saying so far is that for the last two hundred years, we haven't had the technology to travel from one corner to the other quickly enough for the journey to take less than the length of several thousand human lifetimes. Scientists have been trying to come up with ways of traveling more quickly across the gap between the two corners, or else investigating our understanding of the gap in case it turns out that the gap wasn't what we thought it was . . .'

'And now you're going to tell me that you can jump across the gap in a second,' you interrupt. 'Or something like that.'

Zowber lowers his hands and looks at you. 'Not quite,' he says, 'it's more a case that the gap sometimes isn't as large as

238

we thought it was.' He raises the piece of paper again and holds it in front of your eyes. 'For centuries, almost everyone believed that space was a fixed environment. However, for the last two hundred or so years scientists have understood that space is always expanding, that if this piece of paper represents a portion of space then this piece of paper is gradually getting larger and larger.

'Now here's the exciting part. In the last decade or so, scientists have realized that the fabric of space itself is subject to another effect. It moves. In a word: it *ripples.*'

'Ripples!'

'Like a wave.'

Both of you stare at the piece of paper he's holding up between your faces. Slowly, he begins to manipulate it between his fingers so that it starts to curve and undulate between his hands and you realize that you are holding your breath.

'How . . . you mean . . . why does it do that?'

'So far,' Zowber replies, 'we don't really know. Scientists have long suspected that gravity could effect the topology of space-time but not to the massive scale that our instruments have been revealing over the last few years. The forces that seem to be causing these . . . ripples . . . appear to be one level up in the hierarchy of cosmic processes so the scientific community have labeled them as *metagravitational.*

'Now look,' he snaps your attention back to the piece of paper, 'remember our two points in space, the one representing where we are now and the one representing the point where we would like to travel to but can't.'

Your eyes follow as he simulates a ripple through the piece of paper that's large enough to bring his fingers together.

'If one of these ripples was big enough,' you say, suddenly excited that you seem to be finally understanding something, 'then it would essentially mean that the distance between the two points was shorter – short enough for a rocket to cover the distance within a human lifetime.'

'*Exactly*. Of course, it's only possible if we know how to cross the gap between the two points rather than have to go the long way around, the route represented by the surface of the piece of paper.' Zowber suddenly smiles at you. 'But I'm glad to say that we do.'

You stare at his fingers and at the space between them. So far, what he's told you makes sense. Just. But what is it he wants from you?

'So you have your two points in space,' you say, 'and you have your rocket. And you even have your wormhole or tunnel through space that saves you having to go the long way around . . .'

'We prefer to call it a *window* rather than a *wormhole*.'

'A "window" then.'

'Yes.'

You pause for a moment. 'I'm not exactly astronaut material,' you say. Zowber chuckles again.

'No, you aren't. Not exactly.'

'So why am I here?'

'Ten years ago we started being able to predict these metagravitational ripples,' he says to you and you get the feeling that there's a whole lot more to know. You're not wrong. In the same kind of language as before (though now you feel that when he uses the word 'we' he seems to be referring more specifically to himself or to some team of scientists that he belongs to rather than the scientific community in general), Zowber explains to you how a research group discovered a star system containing a planet that looked as if it could sustain human life but could never be reached using conventional

240

methods. It wasn't four and half light years away: *it was four thousand five hundred light years away.*

'Once we knew that a metagravitational ripple would essentially bring this planet into reach, we examined it intensely by way of long-range telescopes. It was then we realized that the planet could sustain human life . . .'

'Y-y-you want me to travel to this planet?' you ask.

'Not exactly.' Zowber notices your alarm and his voice softens. 'Please don't worry,' he says. 'There's nothing sinister about what I am going to tell you . . .'

'You'd better tell me then.'

Zowber puts the piece of paper down. 'To put it as simply as possible, the window to the destination planet has been open for about seven years and will be for about another seven. Initially, we sent a probe through the window. We didn't know what the result of this first experiment would be. But, sure enough, it seemed to survive the journey intact and sent back clear communications signals from its new location. The slight time delay on these signals encouragingly suggested that although the probe had initially traveled through the window, the return message traveled across what we might call conventional or linear space.'

'The surface of the piece of paper.'

'That's right, the surface of the piece of paper. Then we sent several reconnaissance probes through to verify our assumptions as to the nature of the target planet, the composition of its soil and atmosphere and so on. After that, we sent yet another probe – though this time we programmed it with flight instructions to return back through the window. That worked too. After that, the logical next step was to send through a team of astronauts.'

Zowber sighs.

'They didn't come back. Monitoring devices on board the probe suggested that they didn't even *materialize* on the other side even though the probe did. We're still investigating what this means, but it seems clear so far that organic material doesn't survive the journey for some reason that we still don't know about.'

'And what was the next step?' you ask coldly.

'We didn't know for a while. Everyone was pretty dismayed by what happened to the first team of explorers. A lot of people called for the cessation of all further research activity and everyone involved was certain that any further loss of life was unacceptable. Research was suspended for a while. And then someone came up with an idea that seemed feasible. What if there was a way to transmit the blueprint for an organic object through the window rather than the organic object itself? We looked at medical technology and principally the technology used to synthesize the organic tissue that medical science currently uses to replace damaged or dysfunctional organs. Then we developed that technology so that it could theoretically synthesize a complete body . . .'

'A cloning machine?'

'If you like.'

'Aren't those illegal?'

'Of course. Obviously we had to make certain legal guarantees – but the unique nature of how we're applying the technology seemed to satisfy almost all the moral opponents to this next stage of the plan.'

'What happened next?'

'We launched a ship carrying the cloning machines through the window. This emerged near to the destination planet and positioned itself in orbit around it. Then we transmitted data containing a sample genetic matrix out to the ship across conventional space. To begin with, we opted for limited trials and were successful. We transmitted the code for a human liver and sure enough the cloning machine generated a fully functioning human liver. After that, we tried other human organs – the spinal column, the renal system, the heart and so on – and were successful each time. The next step was to attempt to send across the complete gene map for an entire human body. We calculated this using averages derived from statistical information and duly transmitted the data except this time the machines failed to successfully generate a cloned organism. We tweaked the figures, tried again and failed again.'

You ask what went wrong and Zowber tells you that it's complicated but it seems as if an artificially constructed gene map results in a cloned organism that is physiologically too unstable to survive. *Inviable* is the word he uses.

'Which is why you're here,' he tells you. 'It appears that the machines need an already functioning and naturally generated gene map in order to replicate an organism successfully. Therefore the Department of Social Evolution is asking thousands of citizens to decide whether they would agree to volunteer their genetic information so that it can be transmitted across to the target planet. In short, we're hoping to build a race of colonists generated from the genetic templates of citizens living right here and right now.'

You're speechless.

'That's probably quite a lot of information for you to take in all at once. Is there anything you want me to clarify?' he asks quietly.

'Let me get this straight: you want to make a copy of me and then beam that copy of me out to the other side of the galaxy. Is that right?'

'Well, approximately *half* way across *our* galaxy.'

'I don't know what to say . . .'

'Some people we've spoken to want to run out the room and forget they heard any of it.'

'Part of me does too.'

After a moment's thinking, you ask Zowber why you've been selected as one of the candidates for cloning and he tells you that the process has been more or less carried out at random. The scientists have only two broad criteria affecting their selection process: they're looking for as wide and varied a cross-section of genetic templates as possible and they obviously want to exclude as much pathological data as they can from the outset.

'Look,' Zowber says to you, walking over to the desk and refilling your glass, 'it's not surprising that the whole proposition makes you feel pretty strange. It can still feel unreal at times, even to me, and I'm a trained scientist who's been working with these kind of ideas for twenty-five years. What I suggest is that you go away and think about all the things I've told you. You're under no obligation, though the Department certainly feels obliged to give you the chance to consider what we've been saying before you either dismiss or accept our proposal.'

You sit there.

'Why don't you spend some time thinking about it?' Zowber says. 'Come back in a few days and tell me how you feel. You could ask any questions you might have thought of and I could try and answer them.'

•

You're led back to the elevator by the same uniformed woman as before and as you pass by the twenty-four doors on your left, you wonder how many interviews are taking place at that exact moment throughout the gigantic building.

And then you're out on the street, eventually climbing into the battered leather seat of your cab and drifting out into the gray city. You don't even think about logging in with the dispatch center to say that you're available for any work. It hardly seems worthwhile compared with absorbing everything you've just been told. All you can think about is the idea of being transmitted across the galaxy. *What would it feel like?* you ask yourself, but then realize you have no idea. The last thing you asked Zowber before leaving his office was what the whole colonization program was called. Perhaps you weren't asking out of simple curiosity, perhaps you were just trying to get a handle on things?

'A few people were inclined towards calling it something like "The Exodus Plan" or "The Adam Experiment",' he told you, 'but thankfully it's not the sixties any more and we do things a little less dramatically. So we call it "The Project". Nothing more, nothing less.'

You then asked him why there was a need for The Project. Why try and colonize another planet in the first place? What was the ultimate point behind the whole exercise? What was the scientists' motivation? You immediately wondered if there were some impending catastrophe threatening the planet that Zowber wasn't telling you about, a gigantic asteroid on a collision course or some massive and imminent breakdown in the planet's atmosphere. But Zowber put your mind at ease. There wasn't an apocalypse waiting out there in space and the planet was going to continue toiling along just as it had for thousands of years: the thinking behind The Project was apparently 'scientific and humanitarian', an entirely benign first attempt to explore and colonize deep space.

Sitting behind the wheel of your cab, you breathe a sigh of relief. But it still doesn't help you get any sense of what it will feel like to be transmitted across the galaxy and by the time you reach your block you've failed to make any more sense of what might happen to you.

Back in your apartment, you slump into a chair. What would it feel like? *What would it feel like?* For a while, all you can think about is *The Cosmic Drifter*, a comic strip you used to read when you were a kid that featured a superhero who traveled through space by simply willing it to happen. He would concentrate for a moment, his body tensing before it collapsed into a single beam of energy that sped out into the darkness, his atoms imploding in a race to get to the other side of the galaxy.

But then you tell yourself that this isn't what will happen to you at all. This is not what Zowber explained to you. They were simply going to make a copy of you, an exact physical replica, and now you can't help but wonder how it would feel to know that there were two of you.

Automatically, you now raise yourself out of the seat and start to clear the scattered dregs of your possessions that lie around the floor of the apartment, anything to give you something to do while you consider The Project. The task takes a few hours and soon the place looks almost fit for human inhabitation. You even manage to scrub down the shower stall and spend an hour at your terminal clearing your backed-up correspondence. There's a message from Jeff waiting to be answered and typically there's no mention of your stupidity the night before, just a note saying that he tried to call you over the radio earlier in the day to see if you were okay. You think about telling him about The Project but in the end just call him in his cab to apologize. Down the line, Jeff tells you that he was worried about you when he couldn't get hold of you out on the road and you tell him that you're sorry about hurling the trash can at his cab, that you want to pay for any damage. But he dismisses your offer, telling you that you both know that his cab 'always looks like a piece of shit' and you agree to meet up in a few nights' time.

After you've spoken to Jeff, you slump back into your chair and flick on the terminal only to turn it off again. The news. Gameshows. Pornoflicks. More footage of the radiation storms. A public-information documentary about the monsoons. None of it seems to matter to you for now. None of it helps you get a grip on the idea of existing in two places at once. The realization that your double might exist, not in some parallel universe, not in some other dimension, but simply a great distance from where you are now causes you to shudder with . . . with *fear?* Eventually you get up, your head spinning with possibilities and questions that you can't seem to answer, and you walk into your bedroom, taking off your clothes and hanging them in the closet before climbing into bed. *What if you ever met yourself?* you wonder. *And what chance would your clone have of surviving on the new world?* The last thing you think before you finally fall asleep is that you haven't thought about Tess for hours, not once since you walked into the Department of Social Evolution. And then you're not thinking of anything.

●

'I didn't expect to see you so soon,' Zowber tells you. 'Most people we've spoken to have taken at least a few days before they've given us an answer.'

'Really? I thought about what we discussed all yesterday and all last night. There didn't seem to be much point in waiting any longer to get back to you with my questions.' You're talking to him in the same room as before, sitting in the same chairs and drinking the same heavy water.

'And what are they?' Zowber asks.

'Well, obviously I've been pretty confused. I guess the idea of being cloned makes me feel . . . *afraid*.'

Zowber nods, and replies that you've reacted normally.

'The idea of being cloned obviously violates the sense you've had of yourself as an individual,' he tells you. 'A sense that you've had of yourself all your conscious life. Also, maybe the fear is a result of misunderstanding something that we've discussed.'

'I thought that too,' you reply. 'The first thing that worried me was the chance that I . . . that I might meet myself. Is that dumb?'

'Not really.'

'Every time I think about that, I feel . . .'

You hesitate. You don't know what to say.

'Perhaps we should split your question into two parts and consider two appropriate answers,' he says. 'First of all, I want to suggest to you that to describe the human being cloned from your genetic template as "yourself" is to overstate the truth of the matter.'

'What do you mean?'

'The clone, for want of a term, is only a *physical* replica of you. It will look like you but it won't necessarily think exactly like you or act exactly like you. Far from it in fact. And you will have no sense of its consciousness either. After all, it will be living in a totally different environment to any you've encountered. To put it another way, you'll be two discrete organisms in two very separate locations.

'As for the chance of you meeting this cloned replica of yourself, I would say that there is no chance of this. Sure, it's not as if in some real sense the clone will be living in a separate dimension to you – the target planet exists in the same galaxy as we do, the same plane of existence if you like.

But it is theoretically *impossible* for you to reach that part of the galaxy. Organic matter doesn't survive passage through the window. And if you were to attempt to travel to the target planet through conventional space, it would take you a minimum of one and a quarter million years traveling at the top speeds currently available to mankind.'

'One and a quarter million years?'

'A long time. A long way,' Zowber tells you. 'So unless we work out a way of traveling at superluminal speeds in your lifetime, it seems safe to assume that it is extremely unlikely that you could ever travel to meet your clone, or vice versa.'

'And you say the window's only open for another seven years?'

'Give or take a few hours.'

You're silent for a while, trying to understand the distances being described, the quantities of time. It's almost impossible.

'I don't know if this sounds stupid,' you say.

'Try me.'

'Well, it's just that I feel ... *protective* of this other "me". I hate the idea of a copy of myself going somewhere that I don't know, somewhere that might be dangerous.'

'That's not stupid at all. Nor is it really that surprising.'

'Will I ever be able to have a chance of monitoring my clone on the other planet, check that I'm still alive?' you ask. Zowber shakes his head.

'The logistics of offering such a facility are too complex,' he says.

'Can I at least know what the other planet is like?'

Zowber smiles. 'Of course you can.'

He takes a small console from out of a jacket pocket and presses a button that causes a panel in the far wall to slide back and reveal a screen.

'There it is,' he says as an animated diagram of a star system glitters into view, 'the third most central planet out of nine, orbiting its star at an average distance of about a hundred and fifty million kilometers.'

The animation zooms in towards a blue planet and its solitary gray moon.

'It's a beautiful place really,' Zowber tells you, almost sighing. 'Like a mirror-image of our own, but untouched and unspoiled. What else can I tell you? It has a stable meteorological environment with an acceptable yearly range of average surface temperatures for sustaining human life. Eighty-five percent of its surface is covered in water, not the polluted sludge we've ended up with on this planet, but oceans of clean water rich in biodiversity and minerals. The land formations, such as they are, have reached a stage of stability in terms of their tectonic maturity and present potential colonists with vast landscapes rich in fauna and flora.'

'It sounds like paradise,' you say.

'Is that a scientific term?'

You look at Zowber and see that he's joking.

'No, you're right,' he continues, clearing his throat. 'Like you said, it really is a beautiful place.'

'How are the clones going to live? Are you just going to . . .' You wave your hands in the air. 'Are you just going to dump them on the planet's surface and see if they survive?'

'A good question. First of all I have to say that what I'm about to tell you is a little outside of my specialist field. Essentially it's anthropological in nature. But I can offer you a reasonable account of what we intend that will make sense.'

You shrug.

'Okay,' Zowber says. 'What we've planned is this. Once we have the cloned population assembled, we intend to organize them into tribal groups and place them in their own territories within the most habitable parts of each continent. We're not sure exactly what will happen but we're aiming to simulate the conditions that the human race experienced about forty thousand years ago here on our planet.'

'Why forty thousand years?'

'That was the last time our species evolved genetically. After that, we hope that the colonists will develop along similar cultural lines to how the human race developed here.'

'But how will they know what to do?' you ask, imagining yourself for a moment in a desert, naked and alone and dying of hunger. 'How will they know how to eat and hunt and cook and defend themselves from predators? How will they know how to do *anything*?'

'Our primary method will be to educate them, principally by way of rudimentary symbol systems which we hope they will interpret as the work of primitive ancestors.'

Zowber presses another button on his console as he turns to face you and the diagram on the screen is replaced by images of stick men and childish images of various animals daubed on to rocks.

'Cave paintings?'

'Cave paintings, sculpture, carved tablets, elementary scrolls. It's amazing really,' he says. 'We know that as a species we used these media successively to communicate back to ourselves our sense of ourselves – and also to communicate this information to other members of our developing society. Given this, we're going to fabricate a whole primitive cultural system on the target planet, a simulation of ancient culture as it existed on *this* planet between forty and twenty-five thousand years ago. What we hope is that the cave paintings and other primitive artefacts will serve as a kind of "instruction manual" for the colonists, that they will assume these proto-information-systems are the work of pre-existing generations and insert themselves into the evolutionary timeline accordingly. If everything goes to plan, they'll see the cave paintings depicting scenes of hunting and cooking and other social processes such as child-rearing and food-sharing and eventually start imitating them, believing the diagrams to have been painted on to the walls by their ancestors. Natural evolutionary processes should then also start to have an effect, which is to say that those colonists who learn to take our cues will stand more chance of surviving. Instinct will also undoubtedly play a role too, especially in matters of language development and so on.'

'What if the clones don't catch on?'

'We've designed a series of more interventionist strategies that we can employ during an initial incubation period of the colonization. For instance, we've established a plan whereby we'll artificially synthesize various primitive tools and then distribute them around the colonists' habitats: axe-heads and hunting weapons, flints and other fire-making tools, simple clothing and cooking implements. Again, we assume the colonists will believe that the objects have been made by forebears or innovative contemporaries. And again, we hope our artificially constructed "instruction manual" will play a massive role here, helping the colonists to work out what these objects are so that they can use and copy them. In a similar way, we'll have fabricated rudimentary shelters for them to live in rather than leaving them to fend for themselves.'

You tell Zowber that it sounds as if a lot of the clones are going to die and he agrees. But he tells you that a lot of them are going to survive as well.

'It's not as if they're going to suddenly wake up on a barren planet surface in the middle of nowhere and have to work everything out for themselves,' he says. 'They're going to find themselves in a lush savannah environment subtly moderated to help them survive, an environment artificially contrived to give them the best possible chance of thriving and developing. In many ways, they've got a better chance than our prehistoric forebears ever had because we'll be watching them every step of the way. We've even arranged for camouflaged machines to operate on the planet surface, remote-controlled machines that will deposit food and materials in nearby locations should the colonists initially need assistance, though obviously we want to be as withdrawn as possible.'

Zowber stops and then asks you if any of what he's said makes you feel more comfortable. You nod, in as much as you understand that the scientists are essentially attempting to replicate what happened *here* on this planet and that your clone is going to be a 'caveman copy' of you. The idea's almost comical.

'Will you guys ever try and contact them?' you ask Zowber.

'We debated that one for a while,' he replies. 'A lot of people couldn't see the point of committing so much time and energy unless we were going to maintain contact right from the start. But there were some of us who thought that this was a unique opportunity to see what would happen if the human race were given another chance. How would they develop? What could they come up with that we haven't been able to? In the end both sides reached a compromise.'

'How did you do that?'

'Well, we first agreed that we weren't going to make direct contact with the colonist population. Such contact would inevitably place the colonist population under our control, something no one in the Department wanted. To put it

253

simply: it goes against the grain of the ethos out of which The Project was inspired. But it was also agreed that along with the tools and shelter and cave paintings, we'd also plant certain other types of objects in the colonists' immediate environment, artefacts that had no practical use but could be interpreted as what we might call religious symbols. The colonists' need for a moral and spiritual framework should ultimately attach itself to these points of focus and start to develop. To put it another way, we're going to give them "gods".'

'Why do you want to do that?'

'We hope that by coding certain kinds of information into the meaning of these "religious artefacts" we could eventually direct the colonists to start thinking about the existence of intelligent life elsewhere in the galaxy and to start looking for it, that if we can coax early generations of colonists into believing that there are higher cosmic entities at work in their universe, then it's only a matter of time before they start wondering if there are more tangible entities out there waiting to be discovered. Yet again, we hope that such a process runs in a similar fashion to what has happened here on this planet. And obviously such an activity lies *extremely* far off in the colonists' future, tens of thousands of years. But it's worth getting these things established right from the start.'

'Are you saying you're going to give them a religion that will make them come looking for us?'

'Well, our very distant successors anyway. They may never take the hint. But then again, they might.'

Neither of you say anything for a while.

Then you say that you'll do it.

Zowber is slightly surprised and asks you if you want to tell him your reasons and you say that you don't often get the chance to have a caveman double. More seriously, you say that it's too extraordinary an opportunity to pass up. 'It's not like there's a catch,' you tell him.

'Well, we do anticipate some lingering emotional disorientation amongst some of our volunteers, something similar to the sorts of reservations you showed earlier. So we will be offering a counseling facility to all our volunteers. But we hope that after a while it will ultimately feel like a dream to you all: slightly familiar, slightly unreal. Does that make sense?'

•

Later, down in the lobby, Zowber gives you the details of this counseling facility in case you need it and shakes your hand.

'I'm glad you chose to volunteer, Ray. Thank you very much.'

'That's okay, Professor,' you reply. 'To be honest, the whole experience has made me feel strange – but it's also made me feel kind of special.'

'That's because you've undertaken an involvement that *is* special. You're amongst the very first human beings ever to be offered an opportunity such as this.'

Then Zowber lets go of your hand and walks back towards the elevators while you turn and walk towards the revolving doors, taking a moment to glance over at the people in the lobby waiting for their interviews.

Outside the Department building, you stretch and blink. After telling Zowber you wanted to go ahead and be part of The Project, he buzzed an assistant who took you to another office where you signed several forms. After that you were taken to a preparation suite, an almost bare white room where you showered and changed into a hospital gown before being led by a nurse into another small room where you were left alone. A voice from a hidden speaker asked you to strip and lie on a metal panel. It felt strange initially. But then the panel retracted into the wall, feeding you into the dark interior of a tube that was warm with whispering circuitry, and you were surprised that you felt no panic. *Look straight ahead*, a female voice breathed, *look straight ahead* . . . a pair of visors descended onto your eyes and suddenly everything except the edge of your vision was blacked out. For a moment, you strained inside. For a moment you saw some kind of green ignition flare at the rims of your eyeballs and your muscles started to tense . . .

You felt stiff immediately afterwards, contracted, as if your entire body had minutely recoiled from something, and Zowber explained in the recovery room that you were only unconscious for a second, just enough time for the computer to take a sample of all the relevant tissue. Zowber called it a *momentary aphasia*: the process stunned your brain with a blast of light at a certain frequency that disconnected your consciousness from the relevant pain receptors. He also told you that a scan of your gene map already revealed that it was free from 'any problems' and that your data would be transmitted out to the target planet along with that of other successful applicants the following week. You said that you couldn't believe that it would be so soon and Zowber replied that there was little reason for a delay.

Now you stretch one more time, feel the bones in your spine and shoulders clicking, and then turn to start walking back towards the block where your cab is parked. It's then that you see a figure hurrying away from you, a woman who's just come out of the Department building.

Tess?

It couldn't be her, you think.

Tess?

'Tess!' you shout out. Is it your imagination or does the woman bunch her shoulders and accelerate away at the sound of your voice. Suddenly you're running after her, zig-zagging through the crowd, and finally catch up with her further down the street.

'Tess? *Tess!*'

Tess turns to face you and you can't believe that you're looking at her again. You never thought you would get the chance. But there she is. You want to grab hold of her but don't in case you scare her and you feel your hands flapping uselessly at your sides.

'What do you want?' she asks, now moving towards you.

'I . . . I . . . err . . . how are you?'

'I'm good. Now what do you want?'

She doesn't sound angry, more like she's in a hurry to get away from you.

'I wanted to . . . I don't know what I wanted. You've moved.'

'Well, you were banging on the door every night. What did you expect me to do?'

'Don't you want to stop and talk?'

'If I wanted to stop and talk, I'd have called you, wouldn't I?' Tess stares you in the eye. 'Look, I gotta . . .'

'You came out of the Department building,' you say, desperate not to let the conversation falter. If you can just keep her talking . . .

'You've been asked to volunteer for The Project, haven't you?' you say.

Tess doesn't say anything, but looks at her feet for a second.

'You *have*! Me too!'

'So what?'

'*So what!* Are you going to do it?'

'I've already done it. We're getting beamed out next . . .'

We?

'What's his name?' you splutter. 'Who is he?' And then you realize what she means.

'Boy or girl?' you ask. Slowly.

'Girl.' Tess now looks at you defiantly. 'And yes: it's yours.'

'Mine?'

'Who else's? It wasn't me that was screwing around.'

Your head's spinning. 'How long? How long have you been pregnant?'

'Two months. I knew the day I found out about you and that slut. I knew the day before in fact and was going to tell you. And then I found out about . . .'

She lets her voice drop.

'But now you're pregnant,' you say, your stomach quaking, your hands trembling. 'Surely we can . . .'

'I'm going now,' she interrupts.

'You can't,' you sob. 'Surely I've got . . .'

'You've got *nothing*, Ray. Nothing.'

'But . . .'

'The Department has taken our genetic reading, mine and the baby's. Once they've called me to confirm that we've been beamed out, I'm terminating . . .'

'You *can't!*' You grab hold of her shoulder but she swats your hand away, tells you that you relinquished your responsibilities *way back*. You're about to grab her shoulder again, looking to do anything to get her to stop for a second and make her talk to you when you're suddenly aware of a presence looming up behind you.

Stand back . . .

The growl of a Trooper's amplified voice.

Stand back . . .

You turn to face the Trooper, hands raised in innocence, and your eyes take in several things all at once: the visor, the studded gloves, the steelplex kneepads, the gigantic speeder parked up behind him and the massive weapon dangling from his belt. But you also keep half an eye on Tess, afraid she'll disappear into the crowds while you explain yourself.

Are you okay, ma'am . . . ?

Tess nods. 'It's fine, officer. We're just old friends who've fallen out.'

There's a pause while the Trooper checks that the situation is what he thinks it is and you think you can see his eyes move on the other side of his visor, a throb of tension moving along gunmetal points of his knuckles.

I suggest that you move along home, ma'am . . .

Suddenly she's gone. She's gone. Then the Trooper's helmet turns to face you again and you wonder if he'll haul you in just for the sake of it, haul you in and throw you in the tank just to scare the shit out of you . . .

Citizen, you . . .

Suddenly an alarm sounds off somewhere. For a moment you wonder what else you've done wrong. And then you realize that the sound you're hearing is the sound of the Monsoon Sirens starting up all around you. The Trooper's helmet appears to freeze for a second, dipping slightly towards one shoulder as he seems to be receiving a message on his radio . . .

You'd best hurry to your vehicle or nearest public transportation facility . . .

You nod, daring to glance over your shoulder for only a second at the direction that Tess ran off in with your child inside of her. Everywhere around you, people are running for cover, bright spots of color scattering in different directions. Already the sky is starting to pulse, as if the clouds are flexing their muscles. And when you finally duck your head down to get into your cab, you feel the first globs of sticky rain hitting the back of your neck.

Then you're in your cab, pounding your fist against the dash, pounding away until your hands ache. You hit yourself (who else is there?) on the chest, on the head, and you slam a fist against the frame of the door again and again until you draw blood. And then you just sit there crying, the rain hammering down on to the roof of the cab, an endless roaring drum-roll, thunder thrashing through the sky above you. Should you drive home? What would you do then? And what would you do tomorrow? Or the day after? For a moment you think about calling Jeff – but what could he say to you that would make any difference?

Now you boot up the engine and tear the cab through the streets. Before long, you're out on the Eight-Eighty-Eight, nosing the hood through the flaming mist of red tail-lights and scorching headlamps, the flicker of the passing lane-beacons strobing over your face. The rain rolls off the windshield, the wipers toiling their way through the thick sludge of dirt and oil and burnt gas thrown up by the passing juggernauts plunging west and out of the city. Soon you've left civilization behind. Maybe you can make one of the cities lying out there in the gloom in twenty hours – maybe you'll just keep driving. Outside, you get faint glimpses of the toxic earth, blasted rock formations, a cursed landscape under a bruised sky, your eyes focused on the glittering backwash in front of you. All you can imagine is the three of you – Tess, yourself, and the child – strolling through a sun-drenched valley humming with life, the kind of valley you've only read about in history books and fairy tales.

Sunlight. Sweet-tasting air. Running streams.

Space.

For a moment, you see the three of you all together, holding hands as you pick your way over the lush ground. And though you know that there's no reason to believe that the three of you will live together far away on the other side of the galaxy, you can't help but think that you might.

THE TRAIL

What ravishes me is an outline of a body . . .

Roland Barthes, *Fragments of a Lover's Discourse*

This is how it happened. I still don't know if it makes sense yet, but this is how it happened.

Last Tuesday, I sold another painting, a twenty-by-eighty *interpretation* of Wile E. Coyote from the *Roadrunner* cartoons as a Broken Wino. It was my third sale in as many months.

'If it keeps on like this, it's going to be a good year for me,' I thought, as Henrietta (my agent) dropped off the cheque and drove away in her blue Saab. And that night I duly went out with the Boys to celebrate. We started off drinking Caipiriñhas in The Back Bar on Dean Street before moving on to The Chase on Wardour Street for dinner where we drank a couple of bottles of wine each and flirted furiously with the waitresses. After that, we all went back to Jake's place in Bloomsbury where we continued to get drunk and at some point I crashed out in the spare room only to find myself awake again just before six the next morning with a rabid headache and a bladder like a timebomb. Why does indulging in the merest drop of alcohol over my ten-unit limit mean that I *always* wake up preposterously early? Jake can drink for a solid eight hours and sleep like a baby till five the next day while I'm doomed to waking up spaced and drained not too long after the birds have started their infernal singing outside.

I got up, had a piss and then drank as much water as I could while writing a short note for Jake. Then I stepped out into the pearly dawn light and took my first deep breaths of the day. 'Breakfast,' I thought. 'Now there's an idea!' *If I can just fill my stomach and get home to Shepherd's Bush . . . maybe I could have a snooze* . . . I sauntered down towards Soho, down Tottenham Court Road and Charing Cross Road before taking a right along Old Compton Street and ending up at a little Italian café I know on Winnett Street where they serve up the best panini west of Genoa. A cappuccino and some Parma ham and rocket on toasted ciabatta did a lot to help me feel human again. After that, I drank another cappuccino while I read for three-quarters of an hour (I've been re-reading *Children and Television* by Robert Hodge and David Tripp) and then settled the bill before walking up to Oxford Circus. 'Thank God it hasn't got too busy,' I thought, as I entered the tube station, bought a ticket and stepped on to the escalator going down to the Central Line platforms. I always feel cheated when I'm on the underground during the rush hour. After all, isn't that one of the reasons why I do what I do: to *never* be in the underground during the rush hour?

It was then that I saw her.

She was standing on the 'up' escalator on the other side of the metal divide. And she was *beautiful*: tawny corkscrews of hair spiralling out of her head in random directions, each one like a delicately twisted filament; eyes like two swirls of dark cocoa. I couldn't take my eyes off her and I thought she would notice me staring at her as the escalators drew us level. But she didn't (she was engrossed in a book that I couldn't see the title of). And then we glided past each other and I suddenly wondered if I could sprint down the rest of the way and race back up the other side and try to talk to her. *Surely I was destined to talk to her?* I had one of those feelings I sometimes get when I see a beautiful or intriguing stranger: the feeling that if I don't somehow talk to them right then and right there, then my life has lost something for ever.

I didn't go up to her of course. How could I? I was in London. Once, when I spent an Australian summer in

Perth, I couldn't believe how friendly everyone was. Starting a conversation with *anyone*, male or female, was as easy as saying 'G'day' and 'How're you doing?' But in good ol' tight-lipped London? She'd think I was hassling her, another sleazy bloke with dark intentions.

And in any case, I'm useless at random encounters and can never make the first move. I never know what to say and everything sounds like a terrible chat-up line. If I can get into conversation with a woman by way of some other agent or by some unexpected *force majeure*, by way of introduction through a mutual friend, for instance, or by sitting next to someone at a dinner party or by having to share a taxi or if the woman herself deigns to make the first move (and of course there was that one time I got trapped in a lift with a Didi from Mornington Crescent that led to ten days of student gigs and snakebite-fuelled sex) . . . well, then I'm okay. I can more than hold my own in terms of conversation, can be intermittently witty and am occasionally even considered highly desirable.

Jill, a platonic girlfriend of mine (she said I was too much like her brother for her ever to be interested in me, but that she could see what other women liked about me) once said that she thought this was true too and put it down to the fact that I was chronically shy but that when I settle into conversation with a woman, I have the ability to make her feel as if she's the 'only woman in the world' while I'm talking to her. Jill said that this aspect of me was – what was it she said? – *powerfully seductive!* Well, maybe that's true. Maybe it isn't. Whatever, I know that when I really fall for a woman, I *really* fall for them regardless of whether I've known them ten minutes, ten days, ten weeks or (on two occasions so far) ten months. I want to know all about them. I don't want them to fit into a conceived notion of what I think a woman should be like (I haven't got one) and I'm a good listener. What can I say? I can't help being interested in what someone thinks or wants or feels.

Anyway, I digress. By the time I'd tossed the ideas back and forth in my mind, I'd reached the bottom of my escalator while the woman with the corkscrew hair had reached the top of hers and disappeared from view. She was gone and it was beyond debate: whether I was good at talking to women or not couldn't change the fact that the chances of seeing her again in a city of ten million people were only a whiff greater than none at all.

•

Then it happened again.

I laid up in bed for the whole of Wednesday, watching the Cartoon Network, *Teletubbies* DVDs and re-runs of *Sesame Street* while I recovered from my hangover. And then I spent each of the following days taking it easy, but nonetheless managing to put in a few hours on my next piece, a ninety-by-ninety painting that *re-presented* the cartoon birds from *Roobarb and Custard* as an Existential Chorus of Judgement. I didn't throw myself at it and was more than happy to splash away with my paints for a few hours as soon as I got up and let the rest of the day dissolve into a twilight of lethargic contemplation. On Sunday, I even let myself take the day off, woke up around ten and watched TV until two before strolling out to a nearby restaurant for some brunch.

It was there that I saw her.

I'd almost gone somewhere else, to either Chez Marcelle, a Lebanese place in Olympia, or to the pub for a roast (when it comes to meat and potatoes, I'm very *meat 'n' potatoes*). But as I walked past one of my favourite cafés, Antonio's on Goldhawk Road, I saw that my favourite table by the window was free.

'Great,' I thought and I walked in. Antonio makes a superb Eggs Florentine and I ordered some and a machiatto and opened up my copy of *Children and Television*, savouring the prospect of at least an hour's unadulterated satisfaction of both mind and stomach. It was then that I heard an agitated female voice at the table opposite mine break the silence.

'Eddie? It's Charlotte . . .'

'A mobile-phone user,' I thought to myself, 'how *nineties*.'

'I'm just ringing to say that I can't make it to the cinema today . . . yes, I know it's last minute, but something's come up, something that I can't put off . . . well I'm *sorry* but I can't . . .'

Her voice stopped suddenly and I guessed that Eddie had hung up on her. Quickly I peered over the edge of my book to see what Charlotte looked like and found myself staring at a woman in her late twenties in grey trousers and a cropped jumper. Once I started staring at her, it became difficult to stop. She had butter-blonde hair and pale milky cheeks, the uppermost curves of which were slightly reddened, a light dusting of inflammation across the skin that spoke of cigarettes and drink and late nights. Her eyes were the colour of frosted zaffer, her lips a naked pink, a cigarette gripped tightly between bitten nails (no wedding ring, I noticed).

She put her mobile-phone back in a leather satchel that rested against the leg of the table and then stared out of the window, smoked, her fingers twirling a silver fountain pen above an open notebook and a half-drunk espresso. Was she a writer? Or a poet? She was just staring out the window, smoking, her eyes looking down occasionally to consider what she'd already written before . . . suddenly Charlotte scribbled something in her notebook, a number and a squiggled bit of writing that I couldn't read. Then she stuffed it into her bag along with her pen and bolted her coffee before getting up and pulling on a blue duffel-coat. '*What was that*,' I wondered, '*inspiration?*' I watched as she flipped some coins on to her table, easily more than enough to cover her bill, and then purposefully strode out of the glass door on to the pavement. I twisted in my seat. Which way was she was heading? She crossed to the far side of the street and then walked up the Goldhawk Road towards the station and before I knew it, I was wiping my mouth, dropping a tenner on the table and walking out after her.

'*Now what the hell are you doing?*' I asked myself. '*You've definitely crossed a line!*' I told myself to turn back, that if I stopped straight away then I could dismiss the whole thing as a stupid moment of self-indulgence and walk away guilt-free. *But there she was!* Twenty metres in front of me and I was still trailing her. Shit! I realised that I'd left my book on the table. I could still go back and get it – *but then Charlotte would be gone* . . .

'Turn back!' I urged myself more gently, trying the Art of Gentle Persuasion. 'Go back and get your book from the restaurant and then go home and have an aspirin or something . . .' *But what if this was love?* I quickly realised that this was ridiculous and that I could only compare what I was doing with the kind of romance one saw in cheesy adverts. But hadn't *everything* about her face seemed immediately familiar to me from the moment I first saw her? Surely that meant something? *It wasn't as if I was doing anything to hurt her* . . . Charlotte now jumped on a 94 bus that pulled up at a stop a few yards ahead of her. Should I jump on? Or should I let it go?

I realised, as I leapt on to the running-board, that if I'd accused myself of 'crossing a line' earlier, then that line was now a point receding quickly into the distance and into the past along with the bus-stop. *But it was all so exciting too!* I'd immediately seen that Charlotte had climbed the stairs to the upper deck of the bus and I quickly slipped myself on to one of the bench seats on the lower deck, pretending to read a discarded newspaper. 'Good thinking,' I told myself. *What kind of ticket did I want?* Think quickly! I bought one that could take me all the way to Oxford Circus and I reasoned that I could wait until I saw Charlotte get off the bus and then just pick up the trail again. More great reasoning! And when she got off the bus, I could harmlessly engineer some randomly harmless moment in which I could engage her in harmless conversation and see what harmlessly developed from there.

Now I wondered about Charlotte's phone call in the café. 'Something had come up that she couldn't put off' – that was what she had said to Eddie before he hung up on her. What had she meant by that? I realised, my heart fluttering, that I couldn't possibly live without finding out. *Okay then*, I said, making a pact with myself, *you find out what it is she's got to do that she can't put off, that means she can't go to the cinema with Eddie (whoever he is!). And then you call it quits. After that, you go home and you never do this again.*

A few more minutes passed, the bus stopping at the bottom of Ladbroke Grove and then once more at the top of the hill. Then it pulled over on Notting Hill Gate and Charlotte came down the stairs from the upper deck and stepped off on to the pavement.

I was ready.

I waited until she'd started walking (I peered round the side of my newspaper and tracked her progress) and then I got up out of my seat and jumped out on to the pavement just as the bus started to pull away, giving myself a twenty-yard gap

271

as she walked away towards the corner of Pembridge Road where she turned left. A few yards further on, she paused by the zebra crossing and I hung back and watched as she walked into the Italian restaurant on the other side of the mini-roundabout. Where could I go? I looked around and saw a cappuccino bar across the road.

And I laughed because a minute later we seemed to be moving in parallel. Charlotte took off her duffel-coat and hung it over the back of her chair. I took off my jacket and hung it over the back of mine. She ordered a latté. So did I. Then Charlotte took out her notebook and pen, lit a cigarette and started staring out of the window again. *What was she thinking?* 'She must be a writer,' I thought to myself as I poured sugar into my coffee and stirred it. 'Was her writing the thing that she hadn't been able to put off?' If so, I liked it. I was the same. As an artist, one sometimes has to sacrifice relationships in the real world to allow the space and time for one's inner world to flourish. Some people didn't understand that. But I did.

Now I focused on the expression on her face. Her eyes seemed strangely still, as if she was actually picturing something internally, as if she was always concentrating, and this fascinated me. It was almost as if I could track the rhythm of her thoughts by watching each twitch of her eyelids and nose, each itch she scratched, the way her breathing rose and fell.

She sat there for an hour and I never took my eyes off her.

Then she got up (she'd done little more than sit there gazing at the street before writing down a couple of lines of her poem or story into her notebook) and walked back to the main road, crossing to the other side and waiting for a bus going back to the Goldhawk Road. I duly followed her and was pleased that

272

two 94s came at once. I got on the second and followed her
as far as far as Shepherd's Bush Green where she got off and
started walking up the Uxbridge Road before turning down
Devonport Road. Where was she going? And what was the
thing that she couldn't put off? Had it already happened? I
let her get a full forty yards ahead of me and watched as she
got her keys out of her bag and let herself into number 27, a
typical West London two-up-two-down. *Now what did I do?*
It was getting dark, I told myself, I couldn't possibly stand
there all night and I'd fulfilled my earlier contract with myself.
Or had I?

●

After ten minutes of standing there looking at the house, I
suddenly felt foolish. Why the hell was I standing there? My
fingers where starting to ache with cold and I badly wanted
a coffee and to wrap up in a blanket in front of my TV. So
I walked home and cooked Crab Cioppino and drank half a
bottle of wine in the living-room before collapsing into bed
at around nine-thirty. *Maybe I didn't want to face up to what
I'd done earlier in the day . . . maybe I was just spending too
much time on my own in the studio . . .* whatever, I woke up
around three the next morning and then lay there in a daze,
I seemed to alternate between praying for sleep to arrive again
and dreaming that I was awake and restless. Neither satisfied.
My bed felt large and cold and when the birds started singing
in the street outside and the room was swimming with damp
half-light, I knew (as I often do) that my chances of drifting
back into a deep, nourishing slumber were getting slimmer
with every second. Also, I couldn't get Charlotte out of my
mind. Was the house I'd seen her walk into hers (she'd had
keys and she'd let herself in with an identifiable familiarity)?
It could have been Eddie's, or a place she shared with another

273

lover. Maybe she was having an affair with Eddie? Maybe they were just friends.

Eventually I climbed out of bed, showered, dressed and then sat in my kitchen with a short and incredibly sharp ristretto. The clock on the wall told me it was six o'clock and I pictured the house I'd seen Charlotte disappear into the night before. And then I grabbed my keys and another copy of *Children and Television* from off the shelf where I kept them and walked out to the car. Again, I reasoned that I couldn't exactly stand in the freezing cold waiting indefinitely to see if Charlotte reappeared, and instead drove over to Devonport Road in my black GTi and parked a little way down the street. 'Would she even be there?' I wondered as I sat staring out through the windscreen. She might have left later on last night (it was perfectly possible, perfectly reasonable) though it was unlikely, if she'd spent the night there, that she would have left before half-past six on a Monday morning . . . a light went on in an upstairs window. Then a figure appeared. A silhouette of a woman against the thin gauzy curtain. *It was her!* Or was it? I watched the house, a sweat building on my palms as my excitement gained momentum. After twenty minutes the light in the upstairs window was turned off but another appeared moments later downstairs. *Then the curtains were suddenly pulled back and I saw Charlotte standing there for a few seconds before turning away!* My heart pumped. I sat in the car gulping down my nervousness for ten minutes, picking at the dead skin around my fingernails. Then her front door swung open and she walked through it, turning to lock it before walking out on to the pavement. Where would she go? I watched her walk up the street towards me and was suddenly afraid that she'd spot me and recognise me from the day before. But she was too engrossed in getting her car keys out from her bag and I watched as she unlocked the door to a white Volkswagen Beetle. So she was driving somewhere . . . *where?* I started my engine and let it tick over while she pulled out into the street and then I followed her out on to the Uxbridge Road.

Again it seemed thrilling to be following her and I even laughed as I pursued her round Shepherd's Bush roundabout and up Holland Park Avenue. *It was so easy!* I must have seen a million films where one character tails another, a million cops and private eyes and spies following their quarry through traffic. But now *I* was doing it and it seemed that it was only as difficult as taking the decision to do it in the first place.

The lights on Holland Park Avenue were green all the way and I let two cars cut in between my Golf and her Beetle so that she wouldn't see me. Was she going to Notting Hill Gate again? Or was she doing nothing more sinister than simply going to work? This was more likely . . . *but I had to find out.* I didn't have to wait long. On Notting Hill Gate, she turned left down Pembridge Road and then parked her car on Kensington Park Road, ten yards away from the restaurant she'd sat in the afternoon before, and I pulled over a little way ahead before twisting in my seat to see what she was doing.

She wasn't doing anything. From where I was, I couldn't see if she had her notebook open, but she was staring through the window of her car with the same fixed expression that she had yesterday. 'What a dreamer!' I told myself, but also wondered more than ever before what it was she was up to. She certainly didn't seem to be going to work, though I realised that she could be waiting to give someone a lift. A colleague? A lover? Children? I watched her for almost an hour but learned nothing more. Charlotte just sat there, as she had done the day before, until almost eight o'clock when she switched on her engine and pulled back out into the road. I did the same and soon we were back on Holland Park Avenue but this time heading back down the hill. Was she going back to Shepherd's Bush? As it turned out, she did drive back that way, but then continued on down the Goldhawk Road to Chiswick where she seemed to be heading for the motorway. Suddenly I was faced with having to make a decision. What if she turned on to the motorway? Would I follow her? I trailed her car (we seemed to be in a procession of slow-moving traffic, a white van, a red Fiat Coupé and a grey Morris Minor between me and Charlotte, a red Audi, a 391 bus and a lumbering navy-blue Peugeot estate up ahead that drove impossibly slowly and seemed to be holding us all up), all the while not sure how far I was prepared to go. When she reached the Chiswick roundabout, I was sure that she was going to sail round it and up on to the on-ramp of the M4. But she took a left instead and drove over Kew Bridge before making a right and pulling over beside Kew Green and turning off her engine.

'Okay,' I thought to myself as I waited twenty yards away. 'What happens now?' All she seemed to be doing was staring out of the window again and suddenly I was starting to feel ridiculous. What was Charlotte up to? Was I wasting my time? It was then that I saw the most intriguing thing: instead of simply chain-smoking while she stared out of her window, I saw Charlotte burrow into her bag and take something out. A Walkman? A Dictaphone? She raised the object, whatever it was, to her face and it took a few moments for me to realise that she looking through a pair of mini-binoculars.

Curiouser and curiouser.

I strained my eyes to see what she was looking at and saw that she had the binoculars trained on something on the other side of Kew Green. I squinted across the grass too and saw a row of large expensive houses on the other side, a row of cars parked in front of them. Charlotte seemed to be scanning them and I looked again. What was so extraordinary about them? A blue Range Rover, a silver Mercedes, a black BMW, a red Audi . . . *a red Audi!* The same colour and model as the one that had drifted through the traffic in front of her earlier on. I sat back in my chair with astonishment: *was she following someone?* I couldn't believe it for a moment and searched for the rational explanation. She could be checking up on a potentially adulterous husband or lover. She could have just broken up with someone, was emotionally devastated and couldn't help but follow them for a while – that would certainly explain the contemplative expression that she seemed habitually to wear. Maybe she was a private eye? They existed . . . I didn't have time to think about this any further because she suddenly turned on her engine and drove away around the green. Quickly, and with only the shortest glance at the red Audi on the other side of the grass (yes . . . it *was* pulling away!), I turned the key in the ignition and followed.

The red Audi now headed back towards Central London through Chiswick, but couldn't get too far ahead of Charlotte and me because the traffic had slowed to a crawl at the roundabout and on the High Road. I guessed that the driver of the red Audi was driving to work, whoever *he* was, and it suddenly occurred to me that it was possible that *he* was Eddie, that Charlotte might have rung him up to say that she couldn't meet him and then followed him to see what he did when she wasn't around. Perhaps Eddie was her boyfriend and she had grown suspicious that he had a lover? As we all drove along King Street and through Hammersmith, I imagined the conversation Charlotte and I would have in bed after first sleeping with each other. She'd tell me, in a moment of intimate vulnerability, that she'd discovered that her ex had been two-timing her and

I'd wrap a reassuring arm around her even though I'd been watching from the sidelines all along (and of course I would have to engineer that 'harmless' meeting with her in the first place, perhaps ten days after she broke with Eddie so that I could swoop in and start applying some Tender Loving Care just as her anger started to turn to longing).

Soon we were on High Street Kensington, driving past the cinema and the Commonwealth Centre, past the shops and cafés, before Eddie's red Audi (I was sure it was him no matter how many times I reminded myself that it was only a *possibility*) signalled left and pulled over which meant that Charlotte pulled over and I pulled over. Charlotte again brought her binoculars up to her face and tracked Eddie as he dodged through the traffic and walked into a camera shop on the other side of the street. Was this where Eddie worked? No, it didn't seem to be. As I watched through the glass, Eddie browsed for a while (he looked like an arrogant little shit if the truth be told: one of those over-fed lawyer types in a brown suede blouson jacket and not the sort of man that Charlotte deserved at all) and then he talked to an assistant when she became free. This assistant then went into a backroom for a minute before coming out with a small black case which she gave to Eddie who then ran back across the road and got back in his car. *Where are we going now?* I muttered as he slotted himself in behind a black cab. I hadn't a clue, I realised. Was that why I was on this ridiculous adventure: because every second meant I was heading further into the great unknown?

Eddie continued along Kensington Gore, past the Albert Hall and on towards Knightsbridge before parking his car by the army barracks, getting out and disappearing up a narrow alleyway with an attaché case and the box from the camera shop. Charlotte followed him. I followed her. And as we all crossed the road and proceeded into Hyde Park, I couldn't help but worry. I was out of the car now and the park was still fairly empty. If Charlotte hadn't noticed me in her rearview mirror already, then all she had to do was turn around . . . I dropped back until I was almost fifty yards behind her, Eddie the same distance in front of her. Where was he going?

There was nothing more I could do but tag along. Up above us, the sky had brightened considerably and it was strange to be in the open air after having spent so much time indoors recently or stuck in the car. People passed by, joggers and dog-walkers, nannies with children, the odd park-keeper with his wheelie-bin and spade. Up ahead Eddie walked as far as the Serpentine and then turned right and walked round the edge before coming to a standstill. Trailing behind him, with her satchel slung over her shoulder, Charlotte quickly walked into the tea-room fifty yards away, all the time watching Eddie as he put down his attaché case and opened it up. Best keep my distance, I thought and sat down on a park bench on the far side of the water. Damn! I was too far away to see what was going on properly. I saw a telescope at the water's edge a couple of yards away from me – did I have ten pence? I scrabbled around in my pocket as I walked over to it and fished out the only coin I had in my pocket: a fifty-pence piece. But then I found that I needed a twenty-pence coin anyway and couldn't believe it: *when had these things started costing twenty pence?* It was daylight robbery. I looked around me – surely there was someone who might have some change? I saw two tourists and rushed over to them.

'Hi there? Do you have change for fifty pence? I need it for the telescope.'

'Excuse me?' They were German, I thought, or maybe Dutch, and I brandished my coin at them.

'Change? *Cambio? Weschel?*' I jabbered but they already seemed to understand me, the husband unzipping his belt-bag and pulling out two twenty-pence pieces and a ten-pence piece.

'Thanks. *Bedankt. Merci. Danke.*'

I ran back to the telescope and jammed in a coin. It took a little time to get a handle on how to focus the damned thing and I used up the first of the twenty-pence pieces working it out. Then I slotted in my second coin. *Okay*, I murmured, the ticking of the meter loud in my ears, *let's see what's going on.* For a second I was worried that neither of them would still be where they were earlier, but then I managed to fix the lens on the tea-room and zoomed in on Charlotte sitting there with a cup of coffee and the binoculars and her notebook. No change there then. What was Eddie doing? I swivelled the telescope. Eddie had unpacked a camera and attached a long zoom lens and was peering across the water. What was he looking at? Was he a photographer, taking shots of the park, the wandering ducks and the reflections of the sky and trees? I panned back to Charlotte – she was still sitting there – and then back to Eddie, the telescope still ticking in my ear. Eddie had his face jammed against his camera (he'd unpacked a small tripod and was crouched down on the ground on one knee) and ... I looked more closely. He couldn't be taking pictures of the ducks, not at that angle: *the lens was aimed too high.* Slowly, I carefully tried to follow his line of vision and panned along the waterline: nothing ... nothing ... nothing. Just trees and grass and railings and litter bins and a few stupid pigeons. I carried on turning the telescope, not moving it too fast so that the image didn't blur ... *suddenly there was a flash of colour, red and blue.* I looked up and across the water: there was someone standing about two hundred yards along the bank from Eddie, a woman with short dark hair in a long red coat and jeans. I dipped my head back to the eyepiece and scanned the space between them. *Yes!* Eddie was definitely looking at her, a woman, maybe thirty, and she had her back to both him and me, was staring at something in the distance on the grass over towards Bayswater . . . with a pair of binoculars.

The ticking stopped. Everything went black. I took my face away from the eyepiece and looked over my shoulder.

ENDGAME

Are you still harking back to where you came from or where you are? Well you can't have two homes.

Lord Tebbit

It's almost six o'clock on a broiling Wednesday evening.

'Dad! Dad!' the kids shout, already over-excited about the semi-final. Rajiv has his Alan Shearer shirt on, the one Mary and I got him for his last birthday, Pravin's wearing his Arsenal pyjamas, and they both run out of the lounge as soon as they hear me coming down the stairs and heading towards the front door for work.

'Dad! Dad! What lucky t-shirt are you wearing?' they ask.

'This one.'

I open my jacket, unbutton my work shirt and show them. 'OUR HEROES' it says, with a picture of the entire Italia '90 squad underneath: Waddle, Lineker, Gazza, Terry Butcher, Shilts, Paul Parker . . . the whole lot. *The Sun* sold them mail order after the last time England got to a semi-final and me and Pete got one each to remind us what a good time we'd had in Turin that summer.

'Dad?' Pravin tugs at the sleeve of my jacket.

'What is it?'

'Please stay and watch the football.'

Now Mary comes out of the kitchen, tells the boys to calm down for the hundredth time, and then turns to me, pushing a strand of hair from my forehead.

'Deepak,' she says, 'why don't you skip work and watch the game with them?'

I touch her hand, kiss her fingers and tell her that I'll take a night off at the weekend to watch England win the final.

I almost change my mind as I shut the front door behind me and walk down the path to the car. Part of me still can't believe that I'm going to miss the game! And do we really need the money? Two shifts into the week and I've already made as much as I'd expect to get in any normal week in June or July. *But you can't turn down work when there's money to be made!* Most summers, you can expect to sit on your arse in the control room for a couple of months, twiddling your thumbs and choking on everyone else's cigarette smoke while they win and lose a fortune at cards. The phones are dead. The radio's dead. All the punters are on holiday and in terms of work it might as well be January. But this year's been different, what with all the tourists in town for the Championships and everyone drunk every night and in high spirits. Talk about making hay while the sun shines.

I climb into the car, shut the door and turn on the radio. Lesley's on the box and there's the immediate commotion of jobs being dispatched and cleared, her voice cutting through the static and hiss.

'Alpha two-nine, two-nine . . . are you still P-O-B? If not then I've got a pickup for you at 14 Shandon Road, no buzzer, going to Albert Bridge Road. If you're quick, I've got you a pickup at Petworth Street straight after for quarter-past going up to the West End. It's a phone-out so call me when you get there, over. Alpha four-five? Aren't you clear yet? Get a fuckin' move on, darl'.'

I pull out on to Trinity Road and call in. 'Evening Lesley, One-One out and about.'

'Evenin' One-One. Didn't expect you to be out tonight, thought you'd be watching the match.'

'I'm a martyr to the cause, Lesley, a martyr to the cause. Busy tonight?'

'You know it, darl', mad rush, everyone trying to get home for the football. Where are you?'

I tell her and she gives me a pickup down Chestnut Grove on the other side of the Common.

'It's going up to Chelsea,' she says, 'and I've got a lot of work on the other side of the river so be as quick as you can.'

•

Why *Boston Cars?* Why, for that matter, *Olympic Cabs, Herald Radio Cars* or *Pegasus?* Pegasus won't send you a flying horse and our control room on Nine Elms Lane is a million miles from New England. Lesley tells me that Donnie, our guv'nor, has got this thing about the sitcom *Cheers!* But who really knows? One thing I'll say for *Boston Cars* though: of all the firms I've been with round here (and I've been at a few, bucket-shops like *Oasis Cabs* on Stockwell Road where my Carina has been the best car on the fleet, real fly-by-nighters like *Cavalier Cars* and *Privilege* over on Kennington Butts) they're probably one of the most professional. Reasonable circuit-fee, fair controllers like Lesley and Nadi who can't be 'fed' (too stoned to be dishonest if the truth be told), good account clients and no pickups from 'Pubs 'n' Estates' which means we get less than our fair share of runners, nutters and psychopaths. It may not be much but it's a lot better than some, if you know what I mean.

The Balham job's a group of northern lads going up to the Trafalgar Arms on the Kings Road to watch the match on the big screen there, the four of them already stinking of beer as they climb in and one of them asks if he can smoke almost immediately. I catch his eye in the mirror, say that I'd rather he didn't and expect an argument. But he's surprisingly polite about it (it's amazing how many get nasty about this more than anything else, especially after a few drinks) and he slides the cigarette back into its packet before all of them start on about Stuart Pearce's penalty against the Spanish the weekend before. It takes half an hour to get across the river and into Chelsea because of the traffic, and as I push the cab through the choked streets, I can see that all the black cabs and buses are full and that almost every pub is overflowing.

After them, I do another job coming back down the other way, taking a couple in their mid-twenties from a Fulham address down to Clapham Common South Side. She's smartly dressed, well spoken and with a confident rhythm to her voice (a Chelsea girl with a City job?) while he's scruffier, wearing jeans and a crumpled shirt and carrying a bottle of wine and a four-pack in a plastic bag. 'Are you okay?' the girl asks once he's opened the door for her and slammed it before getting in the other side.

'I can't believe Serena's going ahead with her dinner. I mean *tonight* of all nights!'

'It's her birthday.'

'Yeah? England are in the sodding semi-final of the European Championship . . . against the Germans. Do you even know what that *means?*'

'I'm sure they'll have a television there,' she replies as I make a left turn out on to the Chelsea Embankment. 'And I'm sure you won't be the only person coming tonight who'll want to watch it.' The boy grunts and looks out of the window.

•

The old cabbie cliché of having 'seen it all before' must almost be entirely true and especially for those of us driving the night shift. Maybe after five years I shouldn't be amazed at some of the conversations I overhear, the arguments to which I'm a silent witness, the backseat showdowns observed through the vibrating frame of my rearview mirror. For *them* it's dead time, a necessary interval between events spent in yet another anonymous car, the space between the important stuff, between work and home, between the party and bed (alone or otherwise), between locking the house up and catching the plane. No wonder people let things slip.

I know some drivers try and get into conversation with all their fares, say it helps the time go quicker, makes things more interesting. But I guess I'm more private, a speak-if-you're-spoken-to kind of guy. Perhaps this explains why people act as if I'm not there, why I see even more than my fair share. Sometimes I feel like a ghost, a transparent spectator, the ignored onlooker who gets a front-row seat for a million 'private' moments.

•

Lesley then sends me on a couple of local jobs, a group of girls going across Battersea and a pickup on Cringle Street who wants to get to Clapham Junction. By now the streets are like I've never seen. They're full, sure, more than they usually are at this time in the evening if the truth be told. But there's an extra urgency in the way the cars move off at the lights as the amber comes on below the red, an efficient, unfamiliar briskness as drivers let other drivers join the stream of traffic and concede right of way. There's a courteousness that you never expect to see on London's streets. Suddenly everyone has a similar purpose. For once everyone's moving in the same direction, as if everyone understands that everyone else has to be somewhere, *anywhere*, as long as they're in front of a television screen within the next half an hour.

Twenty minutes later, I clear another 'local' on Prince of Wales Drive. The two guys are in such a hurry to get inside before the start of the match that they give me a fiver and tell me to keep the change. And then everything goes quiet. The roads are suddenly empty except for the lone red bus rumbling towards Latchmere Road, the odd solitary figure walking a dog, beams of sunlight blinking through the trees in Battersea Park.

I pick up the radio, my mind thinking of Wembley, the players coming out of the tunnel and minutes away from kick-off.

'Lesley? One-One here — I've just cleared on Prince of Wales.'

'Thanks for the call, One-One. It's all gone dead for now — the game's about to start — but you're fourth on the plot so I'll let you know when a job comes up.'

I'm only a few blocks away from base so I decide to drive round the corner, park the Carina and walk up to the control room anyway. At least I can watch a bit of the game there while I wait. Inside, Leslie and Nadi are sitting watching the small television along with five of the other drivers.

'Alright there, Gus?' nods Preyesh. At work they've called me Gus ever since Lesley had a batch of pirate copies of Disney's *Cinderella* and someone thought I looked like one of the cartoon mice that trail around after her.

'Hi Preyesh.'

I say hello to the others, to Kojo and Clement, to Ben and to Hassan, and they all stop arguing for a moment to shake hands.

'Thought you'd be inside watching the game,' says Kojo.

I shrug my shoulders.

'No way are England going to win tonight,' says Clement, sipping from a mug of steaming red tea and dragging on a cigarette. 'Germany never lose. That Sammer in the defence — he *good*.'

The control room has been a hotbed of football debate for weeks, with Kojo and Clement usually at the heart of it. Of course, being Nigerian, they can't keep their opinions to themselves, and it was exactly the same during the World Cup two years ago, except that the drivers had the opportunity to support Cameroon, Nigeria, Saudi Arabia or Morocco back then

290

if they wanted. Now that's it's the European Championships, there's little else for them to do except argue.

'Anderton and McManaman are too weak,' adds Kojo. 'They are like little boys. You watch the Germans *crush* them.'

We're interrupted by the sight of the teams lining up. What team's Venables playing? Ince in, both Nevilles out. Three at the back with McManaman and Anderton playing as wing-backs. If Kojo's right, then it could all go horribly wrong. But if we're good enough? If we play like we did against the Dutch or that second half against Scotland? I'm almost too nervous to sit down, and part of me desperately wishes I was at home. *What happens if we lose?*

There are national anthems, the Wembley crowd predictably booing the Germans' and Barry Davies predictably remarking that it only serves to strengthen their resolve. And then the Germans get things started and suddenly our defence win the ball. Within a couple of minutes, England are surging forward, McManaman taking possession and probing down the left wing. Two German defenders jockey him towards the corner flag, forcing him to roll the ball back to Stuart Pearce who knocks in a deep looping cross only for it to get headed clear. But then the ball flies towards Paul Ince who deadens its trajectory with his chest before smashing it back towards the goal. Suddenly I'm on my feet. The ball's dipping in towards the German crossbar, travelling at high speed, and Köpke is forced to punch it over the bar for a corner.

'I don't believe it!' I shout, unable to stop myself. 'That was close.'

Clement remarks that Ince is a 'big strong black man' while Kojo suggests that it was a lucky strike, but then they're silenced as Gascoigne delivers a bending corner kick, Tony

Adams flicking it on at the near post into the path of Shearer who heads it through the flailing defenders . . .

GOAL!

I can't believe it. *We're one up within three minutes!* As Shearer peels away from the goal-line, right hand raised above his head in his trademark celebration, I think back to that balmy night in Turin. Andreas Brehme scored on the hour and the twenty minutes that England chased the game until Lineker equalised was the longest twenty minutes that I can think of, all of us in the terraces that night tearing our hair out under the watchful eye of the *carabinieri*.

But now? *Now it's the Germans' turn to chase the game!* Kojo says that the Germans will score straight away but for ten minutes he's proved wrong. England still dominate, Shearer leading the line, Gascoigne making a series of crunching tackles and managing to carry the ball through the Germans' reeling midfield on a couple of occasions.

'We're doing it,' I mutter. 'We're doing it!'

And then the Germans seem to change gear. Suddenly Reuter's carrying the ball infield, laying off a pass to his left. It's Helmer that receives it and he crosses as the rest of the German midfield swarms into the penalty box, Kuntz beating the offside trap and slotting the ball home.

'He fuckin' *walked* past Pearce,' says Preyesh.

'I told you so,' says Kojo, lighting another cigarette.

'That's typical,' I murmur. I can't believe it. For a moment, it looked as if England could consolidate their lead, as if they believed that the final was their destiny, that they refused to believe in the myth of the Germans' renowned efficiency. And then suddenly the Germans seemed to redress the balance by merely *willing* it.

Ten minutes later the Germans are still managing to dominate, their midfield finding a better shape than before and Sammer making more and more powerful runs into England territory, when the phone rings. Lesley picks up, takes down the details and then turns to Preyesh who's sharing a joint with Nadi.

'Preyesh, you're first up, mate. I've got Derek Langton on the phone and he wants to get to Borough High Street on account.'

Preyesh shakes his head. So do Kojo and Clement who're second and third on the plot, saying that they don't want to do any account work.

'Takes too long to get paid,' mutters Clement.

'What about you?' Leslie asks me. I stare at the screen as Shearer manages to get a shot in, the first England chance for maybe ten minutes, but then tell her that I'll do it.

•

Outside, the roads are still empty. I turn on the radio and hear the sound of the crowd chanting in the background.

Come on England. Come on England.

The commentators agree that England have now recovered from the equaliser and are starting to match the Germans again. Then one of the commentators' voices suddenly rises in pitch. It's an England corner, Anderton swinging the ball to Sheringham in a classic Spurs manoeuvre and Sheringham smacking the ball first time at the near post only to see it deflected by a defender's shin at the last moment. And then I'm outside Derek Langton's house on Edna Street. I ask Leslie to call him and after a minute he appears. He dips his head when he sees me and then climbs into the passenger seat.

'How are you, Deepak?'

'I'm good, thanks.'

'Anything happened in the last minute?'

Derek Langton knows I'm into football because he's a

Manchester United supporter, a real one (he's from up there originally), a season-ticket holder who travels up from London every Saturday when they're at Old Trafford. Once, when he'd missed his train, he called up and booked a car to take him the whole way to Manchester and I ended up taking the job for two hundred quid. United were home to West Ham that afternoon and a stag-night had meant that he'd slept through his alarm. Still, he couldn't face missing the game and we left his house at five-to-twelve, talking about football the whole way and pulling up outside Old Trafford a couple of minutes before kick-off.

'An England corner,' I tell him. 'Sheringham forced a save. Now it sounds pretty even again.'

'I couldn't believe it when we scored.'

'I couldn't believe it when they equalised.'

As we pull away, Derek tells me he didn't expect to see me working tonight. I tell him that there's too much work but that I've managed to watch most of the first half in the control room and that there's always the radio.

'What about you?' I ask.

'Would you believe that the alarms have gone off at work and I'm the fall guy who has to go and investigate?'

Now we're flying along the south bank of the river, along Nine Elms Lane and the Albert Embankment before cutting across along Lambeth Road towards Borough Road and Borough High Street. And all the time, we're listening to the radio, both teams now locked in a fierce stalemate. Finally we arrive at the car-park behind his offices just as the half-time whistle sounds.

'Can you do a wait-and-return?' Derek asks. 'I'll let you know if I'm going to be more than a couple of minutes.'

'Take as long as you like.'

He walks off and disappears for ten minutes and I sit there

listening to the half-time analysis. None of the commentators want to predict the result, though both are impressed by McManaman and Anderton. It's been frenetic they say, both teams playing at a breakneck pace. Is Gascoigne a liability, costing the team as much as he can give to it? Will the Germans continue to sit so deep? There are adverts and more discussion. And then Derek appears on the other side of the passenger window.

'Have you sorted it?' I ask him and he tells me that the engineers have arrived and reset the system.

'Let's get back to Battersea and not miss any more of this game than we have to,' he says climbing into the front seat. On the way back, we listen to more discussion. And soon we're back at Edna Street and I hand Derek the docket to sign only for him to pull out his wallet.

'Seeing as its you, Deepak, I'll do it for cash. I can claim it back out of petty cash tomorrow.'

'That's real good of you,' I say.

'No problem.' He pauses for a second. 'So, do you think we'll win tonight?'

I tell him that it's a bit too close to call right now and he tells me glumly that he agrees.

'After the last time I'm not taking anything for granted,' I say. 'You get so excited . . . and then you lose. It breaks my heart.'

'I know what you mean. Sometimes it's hard to imagine us winning,' he says, dipping a hand into his pocket for his front-door keys. 'Sometimes England are brilliant and sometimes they play as if they're the worst team on the planet. It's as if they don't know who they are, as if they don't know what kind of football they should be playing and all they're left with is passion and luck.'

'Well, let's hope passion and luck are enough and that we all go to bed happy,' I say and we shake hands before he gets out of the car and walks up to his front door.

•

I walk back into the control room to find Kojo, Clement, Hassan and Preyesh still sitting there.

'Paul Ince just had another long-range shot,' Hassan tells me.

'Yeah – I heard, on the radio.'

I sit down on the spare chair and focus on the screen. England have the ball and seem to have camped themselves on the edge of the German penalty box.

'It's been like this since half-time,' Preyesh tells me. 'Every time they get the ball either Adams or Ince wins it back. Other than that, we're outplaying them again.'

He's right. England have pinned most of the German players back behind the ball, Anderton and McManaman firing in crosses from the flanks or else making diagonal runs into the penalty box and forcing a string of tackles and clearances. On the hour, Gascoigne receives the ball on the edge of the box and teases it through the legs of three defenders before cutting it back from the byline only to see Dieter Eilts head it away from the waiting England strikers.

At that point Kojo and Clement put down their mugs and tell Lesley they're going home. Soon after, the phone rings and Nadi takes down the details.

'Alright guys, I've got a cash job going from outside the business village in Warriner Gardens out to Swanley in Kent. Preyesh?'

Preyesh looks up from the screen, taking his lips away from another joint.

'What?'

'I've quoted him thirty quid for a twenty-mile run.'

'If he doesn't want it, I'll do it,' I say.

Preyesh tells me to take it, that he can't be bothered right now and he's made enough money earlier in the day. So I get the pickup address from Nadi and walk back out to the car.

•

As I pull up in Warriner Gardens, the sky's turned a deep shade of indigo-blue. I give the horn a short tap and soon a man in his thirties comes walking out to the car.

'*Boston Cars*?' he asks. I nod and he gets in.

'Where are we going?' I ask.

'White Oak Hospital in Swanley. Do you know where that is?' he asks.

'I was going to do the A202 out to Lewisham and take it from there,' I tell him.

'That's great. My wife has just gone into labour, would you believe? Six weeks early!'

'That's amazing.'

'Probably. I just can't believe that it's happened tonight! I mean, *England* are playing.'

I tell him that sometimes one's responsibilities get in the way of football and he tells me that his responsibilities are *always* getting in the way of football. For a minute I think he's joking, but then I realise that he's being totally serious.

'Do you remember the last time we played the Germans, back in 1990?'

'I was there,' I say.

'What! In the *Stadio delle Alpi*?'

I nod. 'It was one of the most exciting nights of my life, right up until the point the Germans knocked us out on penalties anyway. At least I got to see Gazza cry.'

'I watched it in Germany.'

On the radio, the crowd is singing again.

Come on England. Come on England.

'You watched it in Germany!'

As we drive east, and then head south down Camberwell New Road, the man tells me how the company he works for sent him to visit a factory in Leverkusen on the day of the game.

'I used to work for this firm that imports German cooking equipment, not domestic stuff but the stuff that they use in kitchens in hotels and restaurants. Anyway, I was desperate for promotion so there was no way I could get out of it.'

He says that the inspection of the plant was scheduled for the afternoon of the semi-final and he thought he'd never get a chance to watch the match.

'As it turned out, me and the two guys I was sent with found out that they were screening the game in the plant canteen. So we asked the management if we could watch the game with the workers and they said that it was fine. So there we were, three of us and about a hundred Germans sitting in front of this giant television. You've never seen anything like it. By half-time the tension was unbelievable. Neither side had scored.'

I ask him what it was like, being with such a large number of opposition fans.

'It was weird. They sat in a massive group on one side of the canteen while we sat in a nervous huddle on the other. Nothing was said directly – but every time they came close to scoring, they'd all be on their feet, head in hands, some of them clapping.'

'What about when *we* came close?'

'To start off with, we were quite intimidated. I mean, there were a hundred of them. But as the game continued we couldn't stop ourselves getting more and more involved. And then Brehme scored.'

'The free-kick . . .'

'Paul Parker charging the kick down . . .'

'I couldn't believe it when the ball deflected off his shin and looped up over Shilton's head . . .'

'You should have seen us in the stadium, five thousand fans silenced . . .'

'You should have seen that canteen. A hundred Germans on their feet cheering.'

Again, I think back to that night in Turin, the twenty minutes of jangling nerves and heart palpitations as England pushed and probed.

'By the time Lineker equalised,' he says, 'we couldn't contain ourselves. The three of us were on our feet, screaming and cheering each replay of the goal. I swear I almost did a little jig right there on the canteen floor, in front of this massive crowd of German factory workers. And that was it. The gloves were off. For the last ten minutes of normal-time and the thirty minutes of extra-time it seemed to be as much about showing your support right then and there in the factory as it did about the football on the television screen. We would cheer every one of our near misses, and they'd cheer theirs. Every time the Germans pulled down one of our players, we'd be on our feet screaming at the referee. And every time we pulled down one of theirs, they'd do the same. You should have seen the uproar on both sides when Gazza got booked.

'And then there were the penalties,' he says, his voice dropping.

'These days I can't watch,' I say.

'Me neither,' he replies. 'But that night we watched them all. Lineker, Beardsley, Platt . . .'

'And then Pearce and Waddle.' I sigh.

'When Waddle shot his penalty over the crossbar, I remember sinking on to my knees. I couldn't understand how we'd lost, how after the games against Belgium and Cameroon – and then after that titanic hundred and twenty minutes against the Germans – we were going to come away with *nothing*.'

Both of us are silent for a second. And then I ask him how it was in the canteen, also thinking of how Pete wept openly beside me in the stands as we watched Bobby Robson walk from player to player, shaking their hands and putting a comforting arm round their shoulders. He says that he had his eyes shut for a while. Neither him, nor Doug nor Keith (the two guys he was with) said anything for minutes, and that all he could hear was the German factory workers cheering and laughing and hugging each other.

'Do you know what it makes me think of?' he asks.

I shake my head.

'It make me think of all those players sitting in the centre circle watching the last penalty. One moment, they're all sitting there together, the German team and the England team, all of them exhausted after two hours of football and ravaged with nerves. Suddenly, half of them are *devastated* while the other half are going wild with relief. Can you imagine what it's like to be Stuart Pearce at that point, surrounded by celebrating Germans wanting to shake your hand and swap shirts when all you want is for the ground to open up and swallow you? Well it was a bit like that for the three of us.'

'What did you do? What happened next?'

He pauses. 'It was amazing. The three of us looked at each other. I can't remember exactly, but I think Doug mumbled something like "Fuck this!" And then the three of us stood up and faced all the factory workers. We hadn't planned it, but we were about to give them a round of applause only to find most of them clapping us and some of them walking towards us to shake our hands.'

After that, he says that the three of them went out with twenty of the Germans and got 'blind drunk'.

By now we're driving through Peckham. The man tells me he's called Dave and I tell him to call me Deepak while the commentators on the radio observe that the Germans are about to make a substitution, Thomas Hässler for Mehmet Scholl. And then suddenly we're in the last ten minutes of the game. Dave wonders out loud if we'll manage to score before full-time but we agree that extra-time feels inevitable. Both teams seem to be cancelling each other out.

Then the whistle blows for the end of normal-time.

'I don't believe it. Not *again*,' Dave sighs, 'I'm not sure I can take it if this one goes to penalties.'

'It won't,' I say. 'We'll score.' But I know that I don't believe it. Then extra-time starts and within two minutes McManaman crosses the ball in from the right only for Anderton to smash it against the post and the ball to come rebounding back out and away from the German goal-line. Dave has his head in his hands and so would I if I didn't have to drive. A minute later, Helmer delivers a cross that flies through a crowd of bodies lurking on the English goal-line but thankfully rolls harmlessly on for a goal-kick. Dave and I are silent now, our minds only concentrating on the feverish voices of the commentators. They sound drained, tired.

'It's going to be penalties. I *know* it,' Dave says, suddenly cut short by the announcement that the Germans have counter-attacked and that Andreas Möller has forced a corner.

'Oh Christ!' he says. 'I've got a bad feeling about this one.'

On the radio, we hear that that the Germans have thrown everyone forward and I feel my stomach boil. Then the kick's taken and the commentator's voice starts up like a greyhound bolting out its trap . . .

It's a good one . . . it's swinging in . . . it's in! It's in . . . !
Kuntz has . . .

'Fuck!'

'I can't . . .'

But it's okay. The referee's disallowed the goal. There was some pushing in the box and England have a free-kick.

'I can't take much more of this. I really can't,' says Dave.

The second period of extra-time starts. A few minutes later, Sheringham plays a deep ball into Shearer who's drifted out wide to the right wing. He plays it in first time and Köpke leaps to grab it but misses. One of the commentators is screaming that Gascoigne's sliding in at the far post. *Will he get to it?*

He's inches away from scoring but again the ball rolls on harmlessly wide of the post for a goal-kick.

'That could have been . . . that could have been *beautiful*,' says Dave as I relax my grip on the steering wheel.

And then the whistle finally blows for the end of extra-time and Dave and I realise that it's penalties.

Penalties.

'Who do you think'll take them?' Dave asks.

'It'll be the same as in the Spain game last Saturday,' I say.

'Where are we?'

'Somewhere near Bexley.'

'We've got to watch this haven't we? I mean, there's got to be a pub somewhere nearby, hasn't there?'

The two of us stare out through the glass into the darkness – but neither of us can see any nearby buildings with a light on, let alone a pub we can run into to watch the end of the game.

'Let's pull over,' Dave says.

'What about your wife?' I ask.

'Well, I don't think ten minutes is going to make much difference,' Dave replies, and then smiles a nervous smile.

'And I'm not sure we should be on the road while all of this is going on.'

I nod and pull the car over. And then we're sitting there, in near darkness except for the lights on the dashboard and on the radio, neither of us saying anything. Shearer takes the first and neither of us believes that he'll miss. He doesn't, sending Köpke the wrong way, but then neither does Thomas Hässler straight afterwards. David Platt's next and he scores, but then so does Thomas Strunz.

'Pearce next,' I say. 'He'll want to get this one after missing in Turin.'

We listen as Pearce blasts his penalty-kick past the German keeper. Redemption. Then Stefan Reuter's next. Dave reckons that Seaman could save this one, his voice shaking, and he's not far wrong. On the radio, we hear that Seaman dives the right way, but also that the ball flies in even though he manages to get his fingertips to it.

'Fuck. Fuck. *Fuck!*'

'Gazza next,' I say. And sure enough, Gazza steps up to the spot and curves his just inside the right-hand post, the commentators describing him as he turns to the crowd and tries to rouse them. But Ziege gets his before Sheringham and Kuntz both convert their spot-kicks too.

And now we face sudden-death here at Wembley.

The commentators sound as breathless as Dave and me. I notice that Dave has his fists clenched.

'Who's going to take the sixth penalty?'

'I don't know. McManaman? Anderton? It's got to be one of the attacking players hasn't it?'

It's Gareth Southgate to take the sixth penalty for England . . .

'I can't believe it! Southgate . . . a *defender*.'

Now we're silent. On the radio, it sounds as if Wembley's

fallen into a deathly hush as well. One of the commentators describes Southgate placing the ball and then walking back a short distance before turning and running towards it . . .

'*Come on . . .*'

'*Come on . . .*'

Southgate hits it low and to his left. Köpke dives low and to his right and suddenly what neither of us have dared imagine comes into startling focus. England have to keep the next penalty out or that's it: months of anticipation and three weeks of manic support reduced to a moment. Dave mutters that Seaman will save it. 'What about Spain last week,' he says. 'What about the save against Scotland? What about Arsenal last year in the Cup Winners' Cup against Fiorentina? *He'll do it, he'll do it, he'll do it!*' Me? I cross my fingers, only for Andreas Möller to step up and roof his spot-kick past our flailing goalkeeper.

And then that's it. England are out.

Dave and I don't say anything for a while. We just sit there for a minute or so not saying anything. And then I start the engine and pull back on to the road and we drive away in near silence. It takes ten minutes to drive the rest of the way to the hospital and when we get there, Dave pays me and we both shake hands.

'Best of luck with your baby,' I say. 'I never asked: is it your first?'

He nods.

'I've got two,' I say.

'How is it? Being a father?'

'It's okay. It's better than okay.'

Dave smiles. 'It was nice to meet you, Deepak,' he says. 'And a pleasure to hear England lose in your cab.'

'What a night for it, eh?' I smile back. 'Let's hope we get it right in '98.'

•

On the way back, I turn off the radio and drive back towards London in silence. Foot's Cray. Sidcup. New Eltham. The road signs appear and disappear in a haze of sodium, the two hours of anticipation and excitement already in the past. Is that how I deal with it? Just put it in the past and immediately remember it as history?

Lesley's voice comes on over the handheld.

'One-One . . . One-One! You there, Gus?'

'Hi Lesley. Yeah, I've just cleared in Swanley and I'm on my way back into London.'

'S'a shame about the football. Anyway, I'm just calling to say that they've started rioting in Trafalgar Square.'

'Who has?'

'Skin'eads. Or something like that. Anyway, I'm not accepting any more fares to or from the West End at the moment and I don't suggest you lot go anywhere near there either. The place is overrun with *animals*.'

'I'll be sure to give it a miss.'

'Well, it's not like it's a problem is it, darl'? There's plenty of work south of the river so call me when you get to Lewisham and I'll tell you what I've got.'

A few minutes later, I'm in Eltham. At a junction, I bring the car to stop and stare up at the red light, half wondering what it would have felt like if Anderton's shot had gone in rather than hitting the post, or if Gascoigne had converted Shearer's cross . . . then the amber light comes on and I relax my foot on the clutch only to see a group of people still crossing . . . *damn!* I quickly apply the brake. But before I can curse myself for being so careless there's a massive bang on the bonnet. I look up to see two skinheads shouting at me through the glass, one of them in an England shirt, the other in a shellsuit slapping his hands down on the front of the car. I think about reversing, but another car's come to a rest behind me and I don't think the driver's seen what's going on. Suddenly there's the sound of the door being opened and I feel myself being hauled from my seat.

'Fuckin' Paki!'

'You almost hit my fuckin' girlfriend, you fuckin' *cunt*!' The skinhead in the England shirt spits while the other has his hands on my lapels and throws me against the railing surrounding the traffic island in the middle of the road.

'Look guys,' I start, not struggling, not starting anything. If I can just talk to them . . .

'Cunt!' he shouts. Somewhere in the background, I hear a girl's voice shrieking, another one saying, 'He's just a cab driver Vince, leave 'im.'

'L-l-look, I'm so . . .'

'*CUNT!*'

Now everything starts to blur. I get a glimpse of his yellow teeth (one missing, I notice, and one chipped and as black as an olive) and the gold stud through his earlobe and the dots tattooed across his knuckles as his knee hits me in the stomach. As I fall to the ground, I notice how much chewing gum has been squashed flat on to the tarmac. And then I can't feel anything for a moment before I find myself looking up at two snarling faces, spit dripping from their lips, every breath sending a shot of pain through my chest. A boot flies in, and another (and another).

'Want some more?'

'Fucking cunt!'

They kick me again, but somehow all I feel or see or understand now are their faces, the jaundiced whites of their eyes and their pale white faces battered with acne. Do they know that the haircut makes their ears stick out? How stupid to be thinking about their ears. Somewhere, I hear another shriek, one of the girls screaming for them 'not to do it'.

'Don't do it,' she screams. 'Don't do it!'

But they do.

Acknowledgements

I would especially like to thank the following at this time. Jeff Hargreaves for his continual support and generosity; Damian Peel and the Peel family for theirs; Joanna Johnston for her inspirational contributions to 'Higher Society' and 'Ink'; Charles Lambert for his key contribution to 'The Project'. I would also like to take this opportunity to thank Angus Graham–Campbell, Mark Moore, Ian Crocombe (Mr Knox.com), Stephanie Cabot, Dan Franklin and everyone at Random House.

Finally, I would like to acknowledge the tremendous support of Hannah Griffiths and Paddy Grey.